THE RISING GULL

THE iniquity of a debtor's prison early last century forces three innocent men to seek freedom regardless of risk. Their haunt amid wild Welsh uplands is unexpectedly invaded by a gently nurtured girl fleeing from a callous father who insists on her marrying an aristocratic rake.

She is chivalrously protected by a man whose life she saves and a new happiness is dawning when her pursuers discover her and drag her back to misery. The manner in which her rescue is plotted and achieved provides a series of dramatic situations and thrilling episodes. Gipsies and smugglers pit their wits against a former Bow Street Runner.

Much of the action takes place amid the rugged moorlands and crags forming the approach to the renowned Nant Ffrancon Pass, the description being given by one familiar with the terrain. The difficulties confronting the surveyors engaged on the gigantic London to Holyhead road scheme are depicted and the Great Telford is introduced to play a pleasing subsidiary part in the plot.

NORMAN TUCKER

The
Rising Gull

Norman Tucker

JOHN LONG LIMITED

LONDON * NEW YORK * MELBOURNE
SYDNEY * CAPE TOWN

First Published 1952

Made and Printed in Great Britain by
GREYCAINES
(Taylor Garnett Evans & Co. Ltd.)
Watford ,Herts.

PROLOGUE

THE Fleet Prison early in the nineteenth century. A debtor's prison! Noisome haunt of depravity and vice! Sordidness and stench and squalor! A babel of riotous noise, raucous laughter, ribald jokes, curses! Drunken shrieks from women gambling at cards mingled with the wails of children forced to suffer for their parents' depravity. Blending with the noxious odours was the heavy sickening stench of stale spirits. There was a public-house in every gaol. Prisoners drank in the hope of forgetting their misery. When liquor failed to supply the necessary opiate they drank again. And again! The money which might have brought them release found its way into the gaoler's capacious pocket.

A paucity of light and air filtered through the window grills. Through the bars were thrust emaciated arms which rattled collecting-boxes before pedestrians passing down Farringdon Road.

"Pity the poor prisoners!" "Pity the poor debtors!" The whine rose persistently above the clamour.

In a remote corner, in sullen silence, a young man sat on the soiled straw and stared at the wall with unseeing eyes. His coat, stained and rent, was of fine texture. His features were refined. His was the jaw of a man of action. The deep-set eyes were inflexible; steeled with the bitterness of disillusionment. Prisoners had learned that the morose man wished to be left alone. He had a tongue which cut like the lash of a whip, and a fist even more efficacious. Only two men ventured near him. It was as though these three realized intuitively that they differed from the common herd. They were men of character. Life to them had been unkind. Unjust!

The second man was a bearded giant. With flexible fingers he whittled from a piece of wood the graceful hull of a schooner. A Welshman—Heilyn by name—he had no knife but laboured to fashion his little ship with the aid of a fragment of bottle glass, scraping until the hull was as smooth as if he had used sandpaper. As he worked he sang softly to himself, and his voice was rich and pleasing.

The third man was puny. His bowed legs were still clad in riding-breeches. These he had endeavoured to keep clean with the fastidiousness of one whose life is spent in polishing leather and burnishing brass. At times he would raise his head to listen when the clip-clop of a horse's hoofs sounded in the roadway outside. It was music to the ears of little Jem Dance.

Neither spoke to the irascible scholar. They seemed content, these two, to be privileged to sit on the straw beside him. They alone had not been driven away by a sudden ebullition of suppressed temper which at times sent him berserk among the disorderly horde.

Jonathan Gale had drunk the bitter dregs of disillusionment. It was sufficiently humiliating that he, who prided himself on his integrity, should be cast into prison. It was cruel enough that he, who had been bred in an atmosphere of culture, should have every susceptibility lacerated. It was galling that he to whom the open air was the breath of life, should be incarcerated in this sink of iniquity. But the deepest stab of all was that his misfortune emanated from people he had trusted. He had thought so highly of Charlotte. But for her extravagant ways he would never have incurred the debt for which the bailiffs had haled him to prison. And when he had written, telling her of his dilemma, she had not replied. And Ned Baxterley, the man he thought was his best friend, had borrowed from him. Borrowed, not because he had met with disaster, but because he had played for too high stakes. Though a hurried appeal had been sent to Baxterley there had been no help forthcoming, only a message which savoured of indifference, if not insolence. Jonathan Gale's mouth tightened as he endeavoured to control the fierce surge of resentment which shook him. He could picture Ned at the Club chuckling over the incident; treating it with levity. He could catch the echo of Ned's mocking voice—"Heard the latest about Jonathan Gale? Poor devil—he's been clapped in the Fleet for debt!"

Baxterley had played him false, failed him in his hour of need. So, for that matter, had Charlotte. The two might well have conspired to bring about his undoing. Perhaps they wanted him out of the way!

He started so suddenly at this possibility that the two men

beside him glanced up anxiously, wondering what fresh thought demon tormented him.

Perhaps, thought Gale, it was a conspiracy! He was not fashionable enough for a high-flyer like Charlotte! That was it! It *had* been a conspiracy. What a blind fool he had been! Nothing, he mused bitterly, was easier than to deceive a person who trusted.

He clenched his fist. "If ever I get out of this damned hole——!" he burst out.

The big sailor patted his knee. "I know, lad. That's just how I feel. I'd like to knock hell out of somebody, but I don't know who! I want to smash the life out of somebody and I don't know who to hit! It was a trick that got me here. Debt? I'm a man who owns his own ship! Falsely sworn I was! But I don't know who did it."

"I," said Jonathan in his sardonic voice, "have the advantage of you! I KNOW! and I'll tell you this! You shall be my witnesses. Once free, I go straight to Ned Baxterley's house and I'll strip it of every valuable he possesses."

"Easy now, Mister!" It was the little man who spoke. "Don't go touching property. Thrash 'im—half murder 'im if you must—(no one cares for 'uman suffering) but don't touch property. Property is sacred. There's two 'undred crimes they can 'ang a man for, so I'm told."

"I'd sooner hang than endure this degradation," said Jonathan.

"Ay, it's gall and bitterness. But it's 'ard on us, too, Mister. I can tell as you're a gentleman from your fine speech. In me 'umble way I'm an 'onest, self-respecting man. And married to a fine, upstanding woman, too. Wouldn't never have been 'ere if me master 'adn't died owing me six months' wages. Second groom to Lord Cheshunt I were, and followed 'is lordship to London. But 'e lost 'eavy at cards and shot out 'is brains."

"So you, too, have been betrayed!" Jonathan's tone was sympathetic.

"It's the 'orses as I miss most," said Jem Dance sombrely.

"Ay. And I miss the sea and the ships," said Heilyn. "Never thought I'd come to this. Strange thing about life. Something's always happening you never expected to happen to you. To others, maybe, but never to you! There's beauty in a ship under full sail or the swoop of the gulls. Many's the time I've watched them in the Menai Straits." His eyes were wistful.

"There goes the Warden. Our damned jailer! See, 'e's letting somebody in to pry at our misery!" Jem pointed to a burly, coarse-featured fellow who came thrusting his way through the disorderly throng. "Damn him! My missus saved enough to pay me debt and free me. And what did that swine do? Pinched it for 'imself. Says it was due 'im for me lodging."

"Once you get in the Fleet Prison the chances of getting out are slim," said Heilyn reflectively. "Specially if you're a small debtor. If you've any money at all the Warden gets it out of you. He takes your money so that you can't pay, and then keeps you here for not paying! Clever, isn't he? That's how he makes an honest living."

"That, and selling spirits!" added Jem Dance. "I don't mind a pint of ale after a thirsty day, but look at them drunken sots! And it's all 'is doing. 'E takes what money they scrounge and plies 'em with drink until they're sodden. Well, I ain't sunk that deep yet. Mates"—he looked about him—"let's make a bargain. Whoever gets out of this 'ell-'ole first shall try to get the others out?"

"Here's my hand," said the Welsh sailor, putting down his ship model.

"I agree." Jonathan smiled sardonically. "It will be pleasant to think about. That's as far as it will get."

Heilyn pointed to the grated window. "See," he said, "an omen! There's a gull rising. See how it spreads its broad wings and seeks the open seas. It is *free*. That's a sign for us, my lads! We, too, shall be free!"

"Your chaste symbol of hope has probably been scavenging in the filth of the prison yard!" Jonathan Gale was bitter.

The jeering, jostling crowd swayed back, making way for a man in uniform.

Amid so much squalor he glittered like a star in the firmament. But it was no grandee, no prince of romance, who advanced—just a hard-riding sergeant of hussars, his cheeks browned by Spanish sun, home from fighting the French. Not a tall man, he carried himself with a swagger which gave him height. His spurred, polished boots picked their way daintily among the filth. His sword scabbard, gripped in his left hand, glittered like silver. His tight trousers were of sky-blue, his tunic of navy blue, frogged with gold. His shako was gay with a red panache and gold cord.

"See! He comes our way," said Jem Dance. His tone was awed.

"Well, my lads," said the sergeant, halting before the men who sat with their backs to the wall. "I'm sorry to see you down on your luck."

"Thank you, sergeant." Jem Dance spoke respectfully, his eyes fixed greedily on the gleaming spurs. Heilyn nodded acknowledgment with his massive head, but went on smoothing the schooner's hull. Jonathan Gale stared straight ahead, ignoring the soldier's presence.

"I've come here specially to make you lads a proposition! Why come straight to you? Because I know a man when I see one, and you are fine upstanding fellows, the kind the army likes. It's a mortal shame to see you cooped up here like rats in a cage when your King and Country have need of you. We've got the French on the run in the Peninsula. Make no mistake about that. We're going to teach Boney a lesson. Look at me! Fit as a fiddle. Now, I'm not beating about the bush. I'm recruiting. What about enlisting in Sir John Moore's cavalry? You, lad, are a horseman. You've got it written all over you!" The sergeant of hussars glanced appraisingly at Jem Dance.

"Second groom to Lord Cheshunt, I was. Been with 'orses all my life," replied the little man. "But what's the use of talking to us? We're 'ere, and 'ere we stay."

"Not a bit of it, my lad. Say the word and I'll have you out of this death trap in a twinkling. Two debtors died this week! Get out while you can. All I ask is that you join the Army."

"Honest?" Jem looked up incredulously. "Well now, you're talking! I'd sooner be shot under the open sky than die 'ere of fever."

"That's the spirit. You'll like the Army. New countries to see. A good horse to ride. Plenty of plunder—if you know your way about, see? And as for dark-eyed senhoritas!" The hussar blew a kiss to an imaginary charmer.

"I'll enlist, though I don't want none of your gay senhoritas, Sergeant. I've got a good wife. I know as she'd sooner see me fighting like an 'onest man than dying like a criminal."

"What about you?" demanded the hussar, turning to Jonathan. "You know anything about horses?"

"Anything about horses?" Gale repeated the words softly. They brought back memories, pleasant memories. Ever since he had stretched chubby legs across the broad back of the vicarage pony, horses had been his ruling passion.

The sergeant of hussars knew his man. He spoke no persuasive words to Jonathan Gale, but waited: waited while the man with the tense face fought an issue in his mind.

Jonathan rose slowly to his feet. "I'm with you," he said. "But I shall want the best horse you can get me."

"You shall have it. I'll see to it. I like men who are eager."

He looked at Heilyn doubtfully. "And what about you, my bearded brother?"

"Nay, I'm no horseman, Sergeant," said Heilyn. "You'd make nothing of me." Heilyn regarded his schooner with thoughtful eyes. "Seems as if this is where we part, messmates." He, too, heaved himself to his feet.

"There's a press-gang ashore, recruiting for the frigates," the sergeant informed him briskly. "I had a drink with the man in charge only yesterday. Shall I tell him to drop in and see you?"

"Thank you, Sergeant. I've no fancy to remain here without my shipmates. I'd sooner be with the fleet than in the Fleet, and that's a fact."

"Adieu, Heilyn," said Jonathan Gale, holding out his hand. "Good luck to you, if we never meet again."

"That rising gull has brought us luck," said Heilyn. "I've a notion we'll meet again."

He watched his two companions depart. They looked unkempt as they picked their way through the filthy straw in the wake of the dapper sergeant of hussars.

CHAPTER ONE

As the darkness increased the weather grew worse. Hail, carried by fierce gusts, rattled on the stage wagon's canvas tilt, making the heavy structure sway so that when one of the great wheels slid into a rut, the whole vehicle lurched as though it would capsize. Celia Upton, frail and fair, turned eyes which were large with apprehension, towards the swaying hood. She wondered how much longer it would shelter them from the fierceness of the storm. Though she was wretchedly unhappy her spirit was such that adversity would wring from her no murmur of complaint. She had chosen her bed and must lie on it, though why, *why* (she asked herself) had she ever resolved to make that bed in a stage-wagon! Never had she been inside one before. She came of a class which did not condescend to so plebeian a mode of travel, but the great vehicle had looked so cosy and comfortable as it stood in the sunlight outside the inn yard at Shrewsbury, while an ostler carried a wooden pail with pump water to refresh the eight draught horses which were harnessed to this ship of the countryside. The wagon master, Wiggins by name, ruddy faced from the elements, had buried his nose in a pewter tankard. He must refresh himself for the next lap of the journey which was to carry the wagon out of the placid plain of Shropshire into the Welsh mountains which already began to show their blue crests along the sky. Wiggins seemed so friendly that Celia resolved to join his company.

The very sharpness of the outlines of the hills betokened approaching rain to the weather-wise! At the outset there had been planks placed across the fore-part of the wagon in lieu of seats, but the luckless passengers had long ago abandoned these. The wagon floor afforded greater security if less elegance. Strange company, thought Celia, looking about her. The swaying lanthorn cast weird shadows within the rounded canopy of the stage wagon. Amid the medley of goods she could make out the living members of the company—human and otherwise. Opposite her was a buxom young mother of two children. The smaller nuzzled against her warm breast, asleep now, despite the lurching of the vehicle. The other child, a boy of three, found warmth if not comfort, against the woman's side. Next to her, with her broad back propped against a corded trunk, was a middle-aged woman, bonnet awry, whose coarse face and bleary eyes betokened her fondness for gin. There was a countryman (a shepherd, perhaps, or small farmer) who wore a dirty smock and patched corduroys, and braced his hobnailed, manure-stained boots against a sack of potatoes, while he sucked morosely at an empty cherry-wood pipe. Between him and Celia was his mongrel, part sheep-dog, part lurcher, whose wet coat gave forth a warm canine smell. He looked sly, and Celia noticed that his white fangs kept nibbling gently at the rind of a great round cheese, several of which were stacked in the wagon's capacious interior. Live fowls and ducks, legs tied, huddled in a wicker hamper which had a netting across the top. Occasionally a stifled squawk drew attention to their hapless plight. The rocking wagon awakened the baby who was sick and started to wail. Celia put an inadequate handkerchief to her dainty nose. Never before had she encountered such a conglomeration of obnoxious odours. The countryman smelt of tobacco, manure and socks, the middle-aged woman smelt of gin, the baby smelt like sour milk, the cheese smelt, the hens smelt! When a gust of wind tugged back the canvas flap there was the pungent smell of sweating horses.

Celia shivered and drew her collar closer about her ears. Would the journey never end? Unsteadily she crawled to the opening of the canvas and peered forth. Her pretence was that she wondered if she could see anything ahead, but in truth she felt that unless she filled her lungs with pure air she would faint. The cold rain beat savagely against her hot cheeks. She could see the broad heaving haunches of the sodden wheelers, and could hear the clink of chain, and the suction of thirty-two broad hooves irregularly squelching through the mire which courtesy termed a road. Dimly, by the light of the wagon lamps, she could see the outline of Wiggins on his miry cob, methodically lashing horse after horse and exhorting them to—"Pull, y' devils! Pull!"

Need highways be like this? Must travellers be subjected to so much suffering? She sighed. There was nothing ahead but blackness—a blackness which could almost be felt. Celia shuddered and crept back to her place in the swaying stage-wagon. The dog, she noticed, had taken advantage of her absence to bite into the cheese. She was too indifferent to chide him. The creature looked starved. She touched him with a sympathetic hand for she loved animals, and was rewarded with a startled snarl. The countryman awakened from his doze and cursed the dog. "Are we there?" he demanded. "There?" the gin woman cackled. "No, we ain't there, we're 'ere! 'Ere, wherever that is! I'll tell you what it is, we're lost."

"Lost nothing. Wiggins knows the way."

"There ain't no way! No road, no 'edge, no nothin'. Stick your 'ead out, and have a look-see."

The man tried to struggle to his knees, but as he did so one of the great sixteen-inch broad wheels struck a boulder, heaving up the corner of the wagon to an angle which sent the man rolling to the other side. He landed in the lap of the young mother and had his ears boxed as both her offspring set up a frightened squealing. The wagon flaps burst loose and flapped noisily in the gale. "The light!" cried Celia.

The lantern, dislodged from its hook, crashed on to the merchandise and flared ominously. The girl grabbed its wire handle and flung it recklessly through the opening in the flaps. It struck a gorse bush and blazed in the darkness. Wiggins brought his weary team to a halt and turned his cob back to find out what had gone amiss.

"Hey!" he yelled angrily. "What kind of a joke d'yer call this? I ain't got no lanterns to spare. Chucking 'em away like that."

"Shut up, Wiggins," growled the countryman. "If this little lady 'adn't 'eaved it out, yer'd 'ave lost yer wagon, 'n everything."

Celia was wrapping her kerchief about a hand which had been scorched by the flame.

She looked up suddenly. "Hush!" she commanded. "What's that?"

The talking ceased. All turned their faces to the driving rain.

"Wot's wot?" demanded Wiggins.

"I thought I heard a cry."

" 'Tain't likely, Miss. Not on a night like this."

"Ssh! There it is again."

From out of the murk came an unmistakable shout.

"*Help! For God's sake, help!*"

The two men looked at each other.

"Aren't you going?" demanded the girl. The rain-soaked horseman on the muddy cob stared at the countryman. Both men shook their heads shrewdly.

"Ain't no concern of mine," quoth the farmer.

"Most like to be some blamed footpad," agreed Wiggins.

"Shame on you!" cried the girl. "If you are afraid to go, I will. Someone is in trouble."

Catching up her skirt she struggled over the tail-board and leaped.

For a few seconds she floundered in the mud ruts until she recovered her balance. Wiping her muddy hands she laughed, a little ruefully. The distance had been greater than she imagined.

"Yer see!" called the countryman, a little maliciously. "Serves yer right for being so blam' foolish."

The girl threw him a scornful look and turned to brave the storm. Head down, her skirts whipping and billowing, she ran into the night. "Come back," yelled Wiggins. "He may be a footpad."

"I don't care!" she shouted back, "you can't desert a man on such a night as this."

Once she paused in order to regain her breath. She could see the rounded hood of the stage-wagon glowing ghostly in the gloom, and the side lanterns flinging faint beams on to the glistening hides of the motionless horses. Then she battled with the storm again.

"Help!" The voice—a man's voice—sounded nearer now. A little to her right. She had almost overshot the mark.

"Coming!" she panted.

Then she saw a face gleam white. A man lay stretched on the mud, propped up on his elbows, his sodden hair plastered across his streaming face. He was caked with mire.

"My horse—fell—on—me," he gasped as she crouched beside him.

"Are you badly hurt?" she asked anxiously.

"My left leg—numb. Can't move it. I seem to have crawled miles . . . saw a light. . . ."

"It is the stage-wagon," she explained. Then she leaped to her feet. "Come here," she shouted. "Come, you cowards! Wiggins, there's an injured man here. Help me if you have any compassion in you."

Sufficient of her words were carried down breeze to shame both men, who came ploughing towards her. Wiggins, who had experienced road-side mishaps before, carried one of the broad planks which served as seats. On this they laid the injured man. By their united efforts he was borne, with much slithering and slipping, to the rear of the wagon and hoisted on board.

The two women in the wagon cleared a space on the floor. A rough bed of sacks had been arranged by the young mother. The older woman proceeded to make her contribution.

Gazing down on the young man who was shaking with cold, and pale with pain, she brought forth a bottle of colourless liquid and drew the cork as ceremoniously as one performing a formal ritual.

"Take a swig of this, lad," she said, not unkindly. "Puts new life into you."

He drank a little, then feebly pushed the bottle away.

"I shall be all right," he muttered. "Let me alone. I'm spent." He turned stiffly and pillowed his face against his sodden sleeve.

Celia took off her cloak and spread it over him.

"Poor fellow," she said softly. To her watching eyes, the man seemed already asleep—the sleep of exhaustion. His hand was bleeding. Celia wiped away the mud and blood and bound it with her kerchief.

"Wonder who he might be?" surmised the young mother, returning to her children.

"Who might 'e be?" repeated the owner of the gin bottle. "Why, comes to that, 'e might be a gentleman of the road. Like as not 'e is. But 'e's in a sorry plight, whosoever 'e is, poor devil. If 'e ain't broke 'is leg, 'e is most like to catch 'is death of cold."

She turned her head to Celia.

" 'E owes 'is life to you, dearie," she said. " 'Ere, have a drink. You're blue with cold, and soaked to your blessed skin."

"No, thank you," said Celia, and sat down. She was trembling now, experiencing reaction. The wagon lurched forward. Her cheeks were flushed. Her wet clothing clung to her and she shivered. The dog snuggled against her leg and she was glad of his warmth. Her head ached. Well, she had saved a man's life— or so they said. It was worth enduring some discomfort, even suffering. But would a village never be reached?

CHAPTER TWO

IT was not surprising that Celia was ill. She could remember, as though a dream, the arrival at some village the name of which was still unknown to her; the babel of voices, the bark of a dog, the flashing of lanterns, strange faces, kindly hands. She was carried into a kitchen where a fire of split logs roared in the wide grate. Over the flames hung a huge kettle, suspended from a sooty chain. She gloried in the blaze. For a moment she stopped shivering as she stretched her numb hands to the heat. A plump and kindly woman dragged off the sodden clothing, and then drove, with harsh words, her menfolk from the room ere she peeled off the stockings, tipped steaming water from the kettle into a tin bath, and made Celia put her feet into the hot water, to which mustard was added. A thick grey shawl was wrapped about her shoulders. Then she found herself sipping a basin of gruel which almost scalded her throat. For a brief while she was comfortable and content. Then she felt suffocated and threw off the shawl. It was not long before she was trembling with cold. The woman touched the flushed cheek with a work-coarsened finger.

"It is feverish you are, *cariad*," she said, with concern in her tones. "Bed for you. The best room with the feather bed, yes?" Then calling to the rear of the house: "Mair, take the hot brick from the oven and wrap it in flannel. Put it in the bed, it will warm her cold feet."

They were kind, these good folk, in their rough way, and she was grateful, but had not the words to tell them so. All she desired was a pillow on which to rest her aching head. She wanted to sleep; to forget about the jolting of the stage-wagon and its smells, and the cold, and the fearsome night. She shuddered—less from the fever than from the thought of what she had endured. . . .

The bedroom was cold. Obedient as a sick child she let her underclothing fall to the floor as she struggled into a night-gown of heavy Welsh flannel. It was far too big for her, and the coarse material chafed her tender flesh; but, once it grew warm to her burning body, its rough caress was strangely comforting. She buried her face in the pillow.

"You are very good to me," she whispered, "very good to me."

"You get better, my dear. This terrible night. That you are still alive is a wonder. Now sleep, and tomorrow we shall have the doctor if we can get a message to him."

The doctor's visit, too, was vaguely remembered, and the poultices of burning linseed on flannel which followed, and the hot bricks at her feet, renewed as they grew lukewarm. But for the most part she felt too ill, too racked with a cough, too aware of a stabbing pain in her back, to note much of anything.

And then she began to get better. One morning she opened her eyes and seemed to enter a new world. The fever had left her and though she was almost too weak to move her head, she was conscious of a great calm. Something told her that she had walked in the valley of the shadow, but she had turned back and was once more in the familiar world to which she belonged.

The room was not very large. Two small dormer windows pierced the low roof, the angle rafters of which cut awkwardly from the corners so that a tall man must duck his head when he passed that way.

On one side was a tallboy, the work of a local craftsman, and beside it a small chair with a rounded back and horsehair seat. Under one of the windows, both of which were crossed by frilled curtains of light chintz, stood a dressing-table, also draped in chintz, and on it an oval mirror. With a thrill of pleasure as if one encountered an old friend, she saw her valise on the floor close beside it. Her hair brush had been taken out and placed ready for use. Outside the window there trailed a few green tendrils from some creeper, and beyond them were sunlight and blue sky. It seemed strange. After that dark, dark night, Celia had formed the impression that she would never see sunshine again.

The examination of the room wearied her. She closed her eyes and slept. A voice wakened her.

"You are better, *cariad*." It was her good-hearted hostess. "You look better. The flush has gone. Glad I am to see you so. My name is Mrs. Parry if you would know."

She had brought her a glass of warm milk with a fresh egg beaten in it and a dash of spirit. Celia drank and felt revived.

"Some day I will repay you," she said softly, and touched the woman's hand which rested on the coverlet.

"You get well fast! That shall be my payment. Though, indeed, yesterday I was given two golden guineas. Not that I wanted them."

"I am glad, Mrs. Parry. You must be paid for the expense to which you have been put. For your kindness which has saved my life I can never repay you."

"There's pretty you talk, my dear. But from what I hear you saved a life too, so that's as it should be."

"Ah!" said Celia, remembering. "The man! The man who was hurt. How is he?"

"Better, my dear, though he has a bit of a limp, and a bruise like a thundercloud, so black it is. We all thought his leg was broke when he came dragging it, but there was no break, only something the doctor called it which I misremember."

"I am glad his leg is not broken."

"Each night he comes to ask after you."

"He is well enough to go out then?"

"Ay! And it's restless he is. I bid him stay until his leg was mended, but he must be off as soon as he could put foot to the floor. Queer, that's what men are, my dear. I have bin married this twenty years come Michaelmas, but I don't understand men any better than I did at the start."

Celia closed her eyes.

"There, I weary you with my chatter. Go you to sleep. You will be better when you wake."

Twilight had fallen when Celia awakened. Each sleep replenished her strength. The latch clicked; the door opened slowly. Mrs. Parry pushed it with her carpet-slippered foot and entered with a brass candlestick in each hand. These she placed either side of the oval mirror and drew the chintz curtains with a rattle of small brass rings.

"There is somebody to see you, Miss," said she.

The girl's eyes instantly grew wide with surprise—or was it apprehension?

"A gentleman," added the woman.

"I don't wish to see anyone," said Celia hastily. "I am too ill, indeed I am. I wish to rest."

"You will see me," said a firm voice. The door swung back to admit a stranger, a tall man who bent instinctively because of the rafters. He paused, looking down upon the flushed girl in the bed. Mrs. Parry retired, pulling the door behind her.

"Who are you?" demanded Celia, shrinking into her pillow. "What is it you want?"

Her eyes took stock of the stranger. Lean-faced and pallid, he had thick unruly hair. His eyes were deep-set and piercing. He wore a bottle green coat of fine broadcloth, but in marked contrast to its texture, his shirt was of plain grey flannel, open at the neck. His riding breeches were of white buckskin, tailor-shaped, but showing a neatly mended rent at the left knee. His feet were hidden from sight but she assumed he wore riding boots.

"What is it I want?" He repeated her question slowly, and his voice was low. "I have come to tell you how grateful I am to you for saving my life. It would seem you jeopardized your own in so doing."

Seeing the bewilderment in Celia's eyes, a smile leaped into his, making the stern face momentarily tender. "I perceive you do not recognize the forlorn creature you dragged from the mire on the night of the storm. I do not wonder. I must have looked a ghastly spectacle. It has meant hard work making myself presentable again."

Her eyes searched his face, seriously, deliberately. "Yes, I can see some resemblance," she said. "There's the scar on your chin, like the mark of an old wound."

He frowned slightly. "I wonder you could see my features. I was covered with mud," he observed lightly. "I was spent when you reached me. My leg was numb as a log of wood."

"What had happened?"

"My horse put its foot in a hole some fool had digged in the roadway. He stumbled and fell on me, crushing my foot. I came near to drowning in a puddle—the ignominious death of a cock sparrow! He began to drag me but I managed to kick free of the stirrups, and so lay in the mud wondering whether I was really alive. I set out to crawl to higher ground, trailing my game leg, but I was exhausted when I saw a sudden flare."

"It was the lantern!" she explained. "It upset, so I flung it out of the wagon."

"Where it flamed like a friendly beacon. My benison on you.

I was at the end of my tether when the light gave me fresh hope. What a blessing a gleam of light amid darkness can be."

Celia sighed. "I see none," she said, as though soliloquizing. She pulled herself together. "I am glad I was able to assist you. Tell me, what happened to your poor horse?"

"Your compassion for the luckless animal is a reproach to me. I have spent my time cursing him for my plight."

"Which was surely unreasonable?"

"Men can be confoundedly unreasonable, at times, especially when inconvenienced. The brute had a change of linen in the saddle-bags. Thus you see me, robbed of my shirt!"

"Better to lose your shirt than your life."

She lay back and closed her eyes. A look of concern crossed his face. "I weary you," he said. "I was forgetful. As we have just agreed, men can be inconsiderate."

"I still feel weak," she confessed.

"You must lack nothing," he said hurriedly. "I have instructed the good woman here to care for you."

She heard the clink of coin and opened her eyes quickly.

"No," she said, as though anticipating his intention. "You are not to."

His smile was mocking. "Never take money from a stranger! How admirably you have been brought up, my dear lady. Your scruples do you credit. All the same, I insist. I have an account to settle, though, try as I may, I shall never be free of the debt."

The candle sparkled on guineas; golden guineas!

She remained obdurate. The man smiled and looked about him. "The good woman below," he explained, "will tell you that she keeps her hoard of wealth in a stocking. At least, that is what many country folk do. They have, quite properly, an aversion to banks."

He picked up a slender stocking of white silk with clocks embroidered in pale blue at the ankles.

"Oh!" exclaimed the girl, flushing, "you are hateful, to embarrass me thus while I am helpless."

He opened his palm and let a golden cascade tinkle into the hose. Then, with a smile, he tossed it on the bed.

"You will be glad of the money," he said. "Money is always useful to a girl who runs away."

Celia's eyes grew wide with fright.

"How do you know?" she demanded.

"A guess, only. My occupation teaches me to be observant. Why should a lady, gently nurtured, endure the discomfort, and the uncongenial company of a stage-wagon when she is accustomed to her own carriage? Why does she travel towards the Welsh hills in a storm? And I have—this! Let me return it with my thanks. It is un-ironed but I have made some attempt to wash away the blood stains."

He held out a dainty kerchief. "You tied my injured hand with this," he said, "and it tests my honesty to return it. I would keep it as a souvenir. There is a crest in one corner. It is daintily worked but I would suggest that you occupy your time in unpicking it if you wish to preserve your anonymity."

She almost snatched the kerchief he proffered.

"Do not distress yourself," he said. "I am not seeking to pry into your affairs. Heaven knows I would render you service rather than embarrass you. I am not curious; I do not ask your name. I do not desire to know anything about what you do, but let me say this: If you are in difficulty and need my aid you have but to command me."

"I do not know you." She regarded him suspiciously. "You say that I am in flight. You might be in flight for all I know."

"Then we are birds of a feather," he retorted lightly, "so must needs stick together. Call me, if you will, Jack."

"Is that your name?"

"It will suffice. And you shall be 'Jill'. We'll climb this troublesome hill of difficulty together, if not in company at least in spirit. Now I must go. My presence might bring harm where I desire only good. Listen." He sat on the side of the bed for a moment. His voice was low. "To prove my trust in you I will let you into a secret. As you travel the roads, should you come to an inn, study the sign. If it has a splash of white paint, as though by accident, on the outmost corner, you may confide in the landlord. If you have a message to send me—mark it only 'The Rising Gull'—it will reach its destination. If you want my name, you may call me Jack Tempest."

He lifted one tiny hand to his lips. "*Adieu,* fair rescuer. Remember, Jill, unpick the family crest!"

CHAPTER THREE

SPRING was on the way. With the resurgence of life the colour returned to Celia's cheeks and a more animated expression to her tired eyes. When the weather was mild she sat, wrapped in rugs, inside the porch in a high-backed chair which Mrs. Parry carried out for her so that she might take advantage of the sunlight which streamed in at noonday. The village children paused to stare at her for a while but the novelty of the pretty stranger's presence soon palled, and they returned to their skipping, tip-cat, hop-scotch, or other juvenile devices for bringing trade to the cobbler. It was a small enough village, little more than a hamlet. A brook meandered through a hollow, crossed by a low stone bridge. Originally there had been a ford, but now the stage coaches had begun to pass that way a bridge was necessary. The road sloped down from the east and climbed towards the west, with a bend at the top so that once travellers had ascended the hill they vanished from sight. The cottages, some thatched, some with roofs of thick purple slate, were all lime-washed. They showed white, the variety of the shade being determined by the fastidiousness of the occupiers. Most dwellings had front gardens, with small wicket gates, green painted for the most part, let into the low white-washed walls which shut them off from the highway and gave them an appearance of cosy seclusion. Snowdrops were brown and faded. Primroses were beginning to peep in their curly green nests, and lesser celandines glinted like yellow enamel. One cottage, which kept its half-door open during the hours of daylight, served as the village shop. The parish church amid its solemn tombstones crowned the hill to the west. It was a small affair, twin-aisled, with a bell-cote in place of a tower. The Methodists had built a rival tabernacle, mostly by voluntary labour, at the top of the eastern slope. Half-way between, by way of compromise, the tiny Wheatsheaf Inn waited comfortably on the west bank of the brook, its barns and stables straggling away from the road, and a crude water-trough reposing near the bridge for the refreshment of passing horses.

Celia never stayed long in the porch. Whenever the tooting of the coach-horn—considerately blown a couple of hundred yards away—heralded the approach of the stage, she would gather her rugs about her and hasten to the seclusion of the front parlour, peeping from behind the curtains to scrutinize the passengers on the coach top. Sometimes there was a pause at the bridge for the horses to quench their thirst—particularly if guard and driver also wished to satisfy theirs—and then the animals would walk straining at their collars, up the slope which led to the lych-gate. Celia knew the procedure. They were given a moment's breathing space, the guard who had puffed up the hill behind the coach would swing up into his seat. The sunlight would flash on the bright copper of the coach-horn, there would be a farewell blast, the jingle of harness and the clatter of hoofs, and the coach would go trotting on its way to the coast, to the ancient city of Bangor beside the green and placid Menai Straits.

Celia grew to know the designations of the coaches which seemed as familiar as ships' names. The 'Harkaway' was red and black, the 'Tally-ho' all red, the 'Duke of York' black and yellow. The coaches seemed a link with a far-off civilization, or with a mode of life which had become a thing of the past. One day the guard of the 'Venture' dropped off at the gate and placed a parcel on the wall. Mrs. Parry walked down the flagged path to the gate and brought it back, staring curiously at the writing.

"You must read it yourself, dearie," she said. "My eddication only lets me read printed words."

Celia took the parcel. It bore, in a flourishing calligraphy, the superscription:

"To the Lady Jill from her humble Jack."

Celia flushed, walked inside, and undid the knots.

Her fingers touched the furred collar of a coat of finest workmanship. She unwrapped it and held it up. It was just suited to her height. There was no word inside.

"I can't take it," she told herself, flushing. "I really cannot. But it is lovely." She stroked it, then tried it on. It fitted her to perfection. She sighed. "What is a girl to do under circumstances like these? Perhaps I—I might just borrow it and return it, or repay the giver when conditions are more propitious."

On another occasion she found that a basket containing oranges and apples had been left during the night, and with them a brace of pheasants.

"I don't know what to do," she exclaimed, distressed.

"Why, eat them, *cariad*," replied the practical Mrs. Parry. "That's what they were sent for, to be sure."

The next day came a note. It was brief and its contents were less welcome.

"*Gentleman—of a sort—down the Shrewsbury road, making enquiries about lady answering to your description.—Jack.*"

Celia walked to the fire, thrust the note into the blaze, and held her hands to the warmth as though the unwelcome news had chilled her physically.

"Oh, dear," she claimed, "I must go."

"Go? And where might you be going?" asked Mrs. Parry, pausing in the midst of slicing a quartern loaf.

"I know not. But I must go somewhere."

"The letter bore bad news?"

"Yes, indeed it bore bad news. Someone I am afraid of is searching for me."

"It is running away you are, my dear?" asked Mrs. Parry shrewdly.

Celia looked distressed. "I may as well confess it. I am running away. But do believe me, I have done no wrong."

"Bless your innocent face, of course I believe you. Bad luck to them who have worried you so."

"I must go, I am nervous."

"But you can't go nowhere. And you only just getting well again after being at death's door. You are afraid because our house is so near the road, isn't it? I will tell you what I will do. You shall go to my sister's house, which lies but a mile up the lane. A small farm it is. She will have a spare room I'm thinking. It is safe you will be there, with Mrs. Evans."

"You are good to me," cried Celia, holding out both hands. "I do thank you. I will pack my valise this moment."

She climbed the narrow stairs to the bedchamber above and

with trembling hands thrust her few possessions into her travelling case. Several times she paused to listen as though she feared some pursuer might be riding down the road.

"My son Tom will carry your bag," called Mrs. Perry from below. "You must not overdo your strength."

Celia realized that this was only too true. It would test her stamina to walk a mile to the farm. As the twelve-year-old son of her hostess went up the stairs two at a time to fetch the valise, Celia drew out her purse and began to untie the cord.

"You owe me nothing, *cariad*," said Mrs. Parry, putting up a restraining hand. "It would have been nothing but my Christian duty to tend you, ill as you were, but I have been paid by the gentleman whose life you saved."

"What can I say? Please let me give you something. You have been so kind."

"Some day you shall, perhaps when you come back again, but not now. There, go to Annie's. She will look after you—or I will give her a piece of my mind. Tom will take you the shortest way." She picked up the new coat and held it open. "Wear it," she said.

"No, I can't take it."

"He will be hurt if you don't," said Mrs. Parry simply.

Celia made a sudden resolve. "Then I will wear it," she said, throwing off her torn and soiled garment. "You speak the truth. He would be hurt if I scorned his kindly gesture." She fastened the coat about her and followed the boy into the garden.

As she made her way up the lane, Celia was strangely silent. This was a disappointment to the boy who longed to chatter. He jumped a stile and pointed to some new lambs in one of the meadows. Then he indicated a mossy stump where a wren was preparing her nest. He did not know much English but he endeavoured to be as entertaining as he could. At times he would glance shyly into the face of the lady when he knew he was unobserved. Never before had he seen such beauty so close at hand. Celia walked slowly, for the muscles in her legs were still weak. At each rise she paused to recover her breath and to admire the view. The twig tips were tufted with green. Celia regarded fondly the swinging hazel catkins which quivered in a light breeze. How like the tails of the lambs in the fields, she thought.

In the grassy banks beneath the hedgerows wild flowers were beginning to peep, cautiously, as though unsure of their welcome. The grass appeared greener.

A dog barked and ran into the lane, stared suspiciously, and then wagged his tail vigorously as Tom called his name. A woman came to the farm door, hurried to welcome her guest, and offered her well-moulded arm to the girl who was beginning to totter with weariness.

Celia was soon at ease in the farm kitchen. The woman pulled off the girl's muddy shoes and let her wriggle her toes in the warmth of the hearth, to the disapprobation of a ginger cat which had hitherto had undisputed possession of the rag mat. The bed, so Celia was assured, had been aired, and all was ready for her when she chose to go upstairs.

It took the girl a few days to accustom herself to her new environment. There was kindness everywhere. A strange, contradictory world, she mused. Strange, indeed. Strange that she should be forced to flee from her own kindred because of their hardness of heart, and yet received consideration from people who did not even know her name.

It was a strange existence, too, for a young girl, hitherto healthy and happy, to be continually apprehensive, like a creature of the wild, always listening and watching. If the dog growled, or a milk-pail clattered, or a horse in the stable drew its head-chain against the manger, she held her breath awhile as she strained her hearing. She felt herself becoming nerve-tense, and wondered how much longer it would last. When would it end? And how?

Two evenings later, when night had fallen, she heard the sound of hoofs. There could be no mistake. And they gave forth the sharp, clean-cut clatter of a saddle animal, not the ponderous plodding of a farm horse. She had been seated by the fire, alone in the kitchen, for the good woman was in the dairy when the ominous sound struck her ear. She leaped to her feet, heart palpitating, hands to her mouth as if to stifle a scream. Steps sounded on the slate flags outside the door. The heavy latch clicked. She turned as if to flee, she knew not whither. Then she heard a voice; a reassuring voice. It was repeating a silly nursery ditty which was sweet to her ears. . . .

"Jack and Jill went up the hill. . . ."

The door swung open. A cheery voice sounded.

"No need for alarm, fair lady. May I enter?"

Her visitor did not await a reply but moved easily into the kitchen, dodging the swinging hams which hung from the rafters as he swept off his hat.

He was better dressed now, a caped riding-coat, still of the shade of green he appeared to favour, a high stock, gloves and a riding-crop which he tossed on to the kitchen table. His spurred boots, though mud-splashed, retained a fastidious polish.

"Sit down, your legs are trembling."

"They are not. In any case, how could you tell?"

"You are trembling all over. There is no reason to suppose your knees are immune!"

"I wish you were not so observant."

"You should be thankful I am. I see undesirable folk sometimes. You had my note, I take it, or you would not run away."

"Did you have difficulty in finding me?"

"Of course not. Mrs. Parry told me where you had gone. I knew the note had reached you. I don't know why I made that inane remark. Something to say, I suppose. Tell me, do you feel recovered?"

"Much better in health, only . . . this continual suspense . . . begins to tell. I jump if a sparrow chirps."

"I know. We must see what remedy we can devise."

"There is none. Tell me about this—this man you saw. Where was he?"

"Questioning an ostler outside the Raven when I was in Shrewsbury."

"A corpulent man, going bald, florid features?"

"Your father?" He raised his eyebrows, but she did not answer.

"No," he resumed. "This man was tall, black moustache, muddy complexion. Foul of talk. . . ."

"Oh, no, not that man!" she exclaimed piteously. "Not him!"

"He was asking the servants, and, indeed even passers-by,

if they had seen a lady whose description resembled your charming self."

"Oh dear!" Her distress was pitiful.

"I volunteered information."

"You did?" There was surprise in her eyes. "YOU?"

"Even I! Told him I had seen one who seemed like the lady he sought. I even told him where I thought he might find you."

"Oh, how could you? How could you?"

He appeared unmoved. "Even so. I said I had seen you dining in the Feathers at Ludlow the evening before." The grim expression relaxed as he gave a mischievous chuckle. "He set off post haste along the Ludlow road. He should be there long before this."

"Oh!" She looked relieved. "I thought——"

"Come, my dear. You don't think, surely, that I would harm one I am so anxious to protect—one to whom I owe so much."

She stared into the fire. "Forgive me for misjudging you."

"I should not have plagued you. You must forgive me."

She forgave him with a glance. "But what am I to do? He will discover the hoax and will be furious."

"With me? I trust so. I anticipate his displeasure with pleasure."

She was still staring into the blaze, thoughtfully.

He leaned forward and touched her hand.

"You trust me?"

"Yes."

"Implicitly?"

"I don't know why I should when I have seen so little of you, but I do."

"Don't you think that I could serve you better if you told me your story?"

She sighed. "Perhaps."

"Not perhaps!"

"It is not that I am unwilling to unburden my heart to you —indeed I think it would be a relief, but, somehow, the mere contemplation fills me with a sense of shame."

"Then I shall guess. Is it a forced marriage?"

She shuddered. There was a silence broken only by the fall of some ashes into the hearth. Then she said: "Yes".

"And this fellow I headed off along the Ludlow road is the bridegroom-to-be?" She did not answer. "You have my sympathy. Faith, I took an instinctive dislike to the fellow. Has he pestered you?"

"Scarcely that. It is a family arrangement. My father is a landed proprietor in Shropshire. The—the man you saw is our neighbour. His lands and ours adjoin. He suggested to my father that it would be a mutually profitable move to unite the two properties."

"And your father consented?"

"My father is ambitious. The man you saw happens to be a baronet. The match would be regarded as a good one."

"Your wishes were not consulted?"

"Nothing was mentioned to me until the contract between the two had been signed and the date of the marriage fixed. I could not face it!" She shuddered. "I will not wed him. He is a drunken brute, the father of several children in the village as everyone knows, a gambler, a libertine. And I have heard something even more horrible about him. I will not give myself to him, not even to please my father."

"And this," said the man, "is Christian England! I am no paragon. I am a man who lives by his wits, but I'd not soil my hands by anything as foul as that. Come, cheer up. You shall not wed where you do not love. I'll save you from that creature if I have to hang for it."

"You are not to run any risks on my account."

He laughed. "My dear. I love to run risks. It is the spice of an otherwise insipid existence. Risk stimulates the mind and the heart, develops the body, and makes living infinitely worth while. Many a time have I incurred risk without rhyme or reason. Now I risk for the honour of a fair lady. I am to be envied."

"I have forgotten my story," she interrupted. "The wedding was to be next week. The banns were called and no man had courage to uplift his voice in protest, such was the awe of my father. It was a good match, I tell you!" Her tone was heavy with bitterness.

"I could not trust my maid, for he had bribed her. I got together what money I could. I smuggled out of the house clothes I might require, concealing them under a haystack in the Home Farm every time I went for a walk with the dogs. I gathered what jewels and trinkets I valued. Then one night, when my father and the man of his choice were drinking themselves under the table, I stole out through the french windows of the drawing-room and across the park. My pony was in the field. I dared not clap a saddle on her but I put the bridle on and rode her across the fields until I could gather my valise. It was my intention to ride on all night—I know not where—but the little fool bolted while I groped for the valise in the darkness. She was off like a flash. It may be for the best, for if they followed her hoof marks they would have been led off on a false scent. I walked until I prevailed upon a farmer on his way to the market at Shrewsbury to give me a lift. He looked suspicious enough, but I gave him half a sovereign and told him I was sweethearting. After breakfast in Shrewsbury I was wondering what next move I could make when I saw the stage-wagon waiting for its passengers and merchandise. They told me it was going into Wales. It sounded a safe place, somehow. Here amid the mountains, I might be able to hide. And—that's all I know, save that the terrible storm broke, and I feared that it was a judgment on me for being so disobedient to my parent."

"Rubbish and nonsense. I admire you for your pluck. Now listen to me. I sympathize with you. I will stand by you, help you, fight for you if necessary. And rather than let that creature have you I'd shoot him on the steps of the church."

CHAPTER FOUR

CELIA sat silent. She wanted to ask the man about himself. He was an enigma. A dozen questions trembled on her tongue but some sense of delicacy held them back. Was it fair to question him? If he wished her to know he would tell her. Surely he could depend on her discretion. If he did not want her to know, was it her place to embarrass him—him to whom she owed so much? The kitchen table was set for the evening meal. Jack, as his eyes lit on the food, cut himself cheese and bread and began to eat without ceremony.

"My manners," he assured her gravely, "are not of the best. It is strange how uncouth one gets living away from what we term civilization. The veneer wears off. The essentials only remain. Hunger is a primitive instinct like fighting, or killing one's enemy. The freshness of the bread means more to me than a damask tablecloth, or whatever it is such things are made of. I doubt if I shall eat again tonight, so I'll take food while I may."

He poured himself a tumbler of buttermilk and tossed a florin on to the board by way of payment.

"I must depart," said he, pulling a watch from his fob-pocket. "Now, harken. If you move from this place, leave a message to say where I may find you. You cannot keep in touch with me, but you must make it possible for me to keep in touch with you. Moreover, I advise you to conceal your valuables; hide them in various places so that if one hoard is lost, others will remain. We have to pit our wits against that rogue who wants you. Tell me his name." He spoke peremptorily.

"Sir Guy Goadby," she said quietly. "He is a man of consequence, wealthy, a Justice of the Peace, a Deputy-Lieutenant. You cannot defy him. You must leave me to my fate." She spoke wearily.

"Never." He sliced at the cheese viciously as though it were Sir Guy he had beneath the knife blade. "This Goadby may be a grand fellow in his own eyes, but I have served among men who set little store on titles. I could take you to places where a

Deputy-Lieutenant is unknown, or introduce you to rascals who consider a Justice of the Peace an object of derision. In truth, my dear, I consider I am no fit person for you to associate with." He turned and regarded her impudently with his bold eyes. "It is you who had better leave *me* to my fate."

Celia smiled. "I shall repeat what you said—never!"

He took one of her hands in his. "We are friends, gracious lady?"

"For ever, I trust."

"There are not many things I set store on in this world where disillusionment is rife. But one thing is to me above rubies. That is—loyalty. You will find me loyal, Jill. I pledge thee my troth."

"And you will find me loyal, Jack."

"I know it. Listen. If you must travel, avoid the popular routes. Ask for the Drovers' Road."

"The Drovers' Road? I have not heard of it."

"It is not a road as folks use the expression. It runs across the mountains to the English border, and it has been trampled by the passing hoofs of a million black cattle through the centuries as the drovers take them from the Caernarvonshire and Anglesey meadows to the markets of Barnet or Smithfield."

He stood up, wound a dark muffler round his throat, and buttoned his cape coat.

"Oh!" exclaimed Celia. "I had forgotten. How could I forget?"

"What have you forgotten?"

"To thank you for my new coat. It is beautiful."

"It is merely to take the place of the one you ruined in coming to my aid. It was not a gift, Jill, merely a replacement."

"I shall consider it a gift."

"Then I am glad it pleases you." He bent over her hand. "Bless you, Jill," he said. "You give me a new interest in life."

She heard him cross to the stables; heard the clatter of hoofs as he led his horse on to the farmyard cobbles. The girl caught up a shawl and wrapped it about her head and shoulders. It was a moonlight night. The horse he rode was black, and in his dark green coat the rider was almost invisible in the shadows

C

of the byre. Only his face gleamed white. She saw him raise his riding-crop in a farewell gesture, then his mount's hoofs were muffled by the roadside grass.

"God keep you," called Celia softly, and returned to the lighted doorway. The room was empty; it felt not merely empty but deserted; desolate.

Though Celia was cared for at the farm as assiduously as she had been in the village, she did not feel so much at ease. A restlessness took hold of her; possibly a mental condition rather than a physical. March, despite its winds, proved reasonably fine. As her strength increased she began to walk across the farm fields and up the bleak sides of the neighbouring hills, following sheep tracks among the whin. It was new country to her eyes, the like of which she had never seen before. The rounded and wooded hills of Shropshire with their green and pleasant valleys had nothing in common with this bold and rugged land where outcroppings of limestone thrust through the sparse grass, and the whole country heaved and undulated as though its primeval formation had never wholly forsaken it but remained to defy the mellowing influences of civilization. Though there were hedgerows in the lower parts, the hillsides were crossed by walls of dry stones into which, in places, were woven pens for the mountain sheep. Their woolly forms added a softening touch to the landscape, and their complaints, mellowed by distance, were borne pleasingly down the wind.

At times Celia would come across in a hollow the *bwthyn* of some cottager, a low, white-washed cot of stark simplicity— a door and two small windows which gave it a human appearance of nose and eyes. A curl of smoke might ascend from the squat chimney at one end of the slated roof. Celia wondered what manner of life was lived by the people who dwelt so humbly in the heart of nature's solitude. She spoke to one man, but he could not understand her nor she him, so she accorded him the universal language of a smile and passed on her way blithely, leaving the peasant staring after her as one who had entertained an angel unawares.

And then, rounding a spur of the hill, she came across a track which merited not the designation of a road and suddenly all her lightness of heart departed for she saw a group of men ahead. Like a nervous creature of the wild the girl stopped in her tracks, and then cautiously retreated around the bend.

From the cover of a clump of gorse she took stock of the intruders. It was a drab March day with a whipping wind, and the men ahead looked chill as they stood holding on to their hats, their coat tails fluttering. With them were several waiting horses with tails streaming in the breeze.

Only hardy men, she felt, would venture so far from home on so bleak a day. Four men stood in the lee of a small cart, the wheels of which had sunk into the sodden turf until they appeared to have been sliced off at the bottom. The horse, a rough-coated bay, stood with drooping head patiently awaiting the desires of his masters.

Several saddle-horses, tails turned to the wind, were tethered behind the cart while their riders watched, as staff officers might await the pleasure of their general, a man who sat his horse several yards in advance, staring intently at the valley into which the trackway descended. But for his civilian attire he might well have been a military commander. He turned in his saddle and held out his right hand. Immediately one of the young men hurried forward and handed him a small telescope. Then once again the figures became inanimate as the leader resumed his scrutiny. The sight of the glass filled Celia with dread. Quickly she crept behind the slope of the hill and hurried back to the farm. Surely they must be seeking her!

Once the farm was reached, Celia (having cast many a backward glance) hastened inside and closed the door as though the dropping of the latch afforded her a sense of security. Walking to the window she stared into the yard. It was as quiet—and as dirty—as usual. A muddy sheep-dog scratched itself near the open door of the shippon; several bedraggled hens pecked for fallen seeds among the cobbles outside the stables. The only sound came from the ecstatic quacking of a concourse of ducks, indulging in their ablutions in a pond near the farmyard gate. Slowly she slipped off her coat, the old, rent coat, not the beautiful furred garment which had been given to her. Then she walked to the great fire-place, and stood, toe on fender, staring meditatively at the sooty kettle as a clairvoyant might consult a magic crystal. Who were these men on the hillside? Why did the leader scan the countryside with a glass? Were they searching for her? All the unrest and suspicion which had tormented her mind for days came surging back. Whither could she fly? She went quietly to her bed-chamber and began to pack her valise. As she handled her jewel-case, Jack's warning recurred to her. She would not carry them with her. She would hide them. But where? She prised up a floor-board and inserted the case between the rafters, casting a glance or two over her shoulder to make sure the door had not opened while she was thus engaged. Some of her money she tied in a handkerchief. Walking casually to the barn, she made sure it was deserted. With a mattock she scooped a cavity in the hard earth floor beneath the cobweb-covered window, thrust her wealth from sight, and stamped the earth as hard as her tiny shoe would permit. The two eyes which watched her belonged to the muddy sheep-dog. She patted his shaggy head.

"Did you think I buried a bone?" she whispered. "You shall have a bone if you promise you won't tell what I have hidden."

CHAPTER FIVE

BACK in the empty kitchen she stood and pondered. It seemed cruel, discourteous, graceless, to slip away like a thief in the night without so much as a word of appreciation for kindness shown.

"Mrs. Evans," she called, "where are you?" But there was no answer. Just a soughing of the March wind in the trees, and the singing of the great kettle as it swung from its chain. The fire, she noticed idly, required attention, and she thrust several more billets of wood into the embers. It must be getting time for the midday meal. The woman's instinct in Celia took charge. She saw that there were potatoes, ready peeled, in a pan. She put in a pinch of salt and stood them on the fireplace. Suddenly she paused. Her ears caught a sound in the farmyard: a clatter of hoofs, the rumble of wheels, the murmur of voices. It could not be Mrs. Evans returning. She caught her breath. Footsteps approached the door; a firm, male tread. There was a sharp rap.

"Is anyone at home?"

Celia moistened her lips. She could not have spoken.

The latch clicked and the door was flung wide, letting a shaft of light into the gloomy room.

"What chance of a meal for some hungry men?" demanded a cheerful voice. A young man, whose muddy attire contrasted with his cultured voice, peered towards the fire-place. His was a frank, cheery, open countenance. He seemed to be in his early twenties. When he saw Celia, a little of his boisterous assurance left him.

He brought his heels together and bowed. "Your pardon, madam. I had expected to find the good wife here, not so fair a guest."

"Mrs. Evans is not at home." It called for an effort to utter the remark calmly. Having done so it occurred to Celia that the observation was inane. Obviously Mrs. Evans was not present. The new-comer did not appear to find anything ridiculous in her remark.

"I am sorry," he said courteously. "I must not trouble you further." She could see he was regarding her curiously.

"I—I am staying here awhile," she explained hurriedly. "For my health."

"It is bracing enough, of a surety," said he. "From the colour of your complexion I would say that your health has been restored."

"Oh, yes, thank you. I feel much better."

"Admirable. And now, I suppose I ought to go."

She did not contradict him, yet he seemed surprisingly loath to put his words into effect. His eyes never left her face and before the scrutiny Celia found herself colouring. She turned her attention to the potatoes on the hob.

So did the young man. "Here, let me help you. You must not burn those dainty fingers."

"I am quite all right," she assured him, and disproved her words by nearly dropping the pan when the hot handle burnt her fingers.

The man's firm hand rescued it in the nick of time. "You see how invaluable I am!" he said. "I have a most practical nature. That is why I was sent ahead to supervise the commissariat. You see in us, madam, a collection of hungry men. I am tempted to say starving, so keen set is our appetite. Might I ask IS there any chance of our obtaining a meal for which, let me add, we are prepared to pay? Not lavishly, perchance, but as adequately as impecunious surveyors may aspire to!"

"Surveyors!" Celia sounded relieved. "Surveyors. I have never seen surveyors before."

"Look well at me, madam. A typical specimen. A noble fellow I assure you, who braves the elements for the comfort and well-being of posterity. A pioneer who gets little recognition for the service he renders humanity. I trail my chain over muddy tracks, I set up my Jacob-staff on windy heights, I plough through mud, I shiver, I freeze, I sweat, I starve, and now"— he sighed, "now when I find a shelter from the stormy blast, a store of goodly food for famished wayfarers, I am all but turned from the doorstep by one whose hardness of heart is belied by her graciousness of feature."

Celia could not repress a smile, the first smile that had sprung to her weary eyes for many a day.

"I would not be hard of heart, Mr. Surveyor," she explained, "but this is not my house. However, I am sure that Mrs. Evans, who is a hospitable soul, would not have you perish of starvation."

"Excellent," he cried cordially. "I will summon the rest of the party."

"There is bacon in the larder," said Celia as though in soliloquy, "and cheese and bread and farm butter and eggs. . . ."

"Enough, enough," he said. "Fetch forth the fry-pan and let me exhibit my culinary powers."

He walked to the door and at his beckoning several men who had been engaged in rearranging instruments in the cart walked in his direction leaving their two attendants to see to the unharnessing and feeding of the animals.

"There is an inn in the village not a mile away——" began Celia.

"Hush! Not a word. This is where we dine."

"But why?"

"Your counterpart will not be found at the inn."

"But you do not contemplate eating me, I trust!"

"I feast my eyes on you," he replied, unabashed.

"Oh hush, you must not say such things."

"Are you annoyed?"

"Terribly."

"You would be far more annoyed if I said you were so ugly I could not bear to look at you."

Celia bit her lip to repress another smile. "Possibly, but need I be the subject of discussion at all? I thought you were more interested in bacon and eggs."

He heaved a sigh. "One of life's problems is to be both romantic and practical at the same time."

"Then be practical. Here come your companions, and I am sure they will favour the practical aspect."

"I hope so," he agreed, breaking an egg on the edge of the fry-pan and watching it sizzle in the bacon fat. "I feel I have a proprietory right of you. I saw you first."

The tramping of muddy feet across the flags put an end to further conversation. The doorway was darkened by the muffled figures of several men, who pushed eagerly towards the glowing fire, only to pause, in some astonishment, when they saw how fair a person stood beside the hearth.

"How d'ye do, Ma'am!" said the leader. Celia, looking at him curiously, saw a clean-shaven man in his early fifties with dark hair, slightly greying, curling over a noble brow. His mouth was sensitive; his eyes penetrating but kindly. He spoke with a suggestion of Scotland in his voice. "We began to wonder why it was that we luckless mortals had to stand freezing in the yard while this graceless rogue who was sent to arrange for our comfort, basked in the warmth. No longer do I wonder why he dallied."

"You are welcome to a meal, sir," said Celia politely. "It will be rough fare, I fear, but I know that Mrs. Evans, to whom the farm belongs, would not have me send you away starving."

"Then we will lend a hand to set the table," said he. "I am an old campaigner, Ma'am, and have learnt to shift for myself in some queer places, from the Highlands of my native land to the mountains of Cambria. I am knocked about by life like a tennis-ball, but I can't truthfully say that it displeases me. And I have found this—that to a sharp-set man, the smell of bacon is just as appetizing no matter in which country it is fried."

The party were seated about the broad, well-scrubbed table, eating with the lack of ceremony which characterises those whose appetites have been whetted by exposure, when Mrs. Evans returned, profuse in apologies for the lateness of her arrival.

The men had concluded their meal, but she insisted on unlocking the tea-caddy and brewing them a pot of tea.

There were many expressions of goodwill when the surveyors departed, though the leader and Mrs. Evans almost shattered the harmony by the heated argument they had over the cost of the meal, Mrs. Evans insisting that she was over-paid.

"A Scotsman never over-pays, Ma'am. It is an insult to my race. We have had good value for our money. And we shall be returning, I'm warning you, when next we pass this way."

"I am sure you will be welcome, sir."

The young man who had first arrived contrived to cross to Celia's side.

"You heard what he said? We shall be back. At any rate I shall."

"I may not be here."

His self-assurance ebbed. "Then where shall I find you? Heavens, I'm not letting you disappear after the Fates arranged this encounter. It is not to be thought of. My name's Harry Standish—I have almost completed my indentures, so soon I shall set up for myself as a qualified surveyor. What is your name?"

"Celia."

"Celia what?"

"Just plain Celia for the present."

"Plain! Plain! Perish the thought. All right, sir, I'll be there. Confound it, we are on the move again. We have another six furlongs to survey on today's stretch. Don't forget. Expect me shortly."

He smiled and waved so ardently that he collided with the door-frame, and her last impression of the ebullient Harry was a rueful smile as he rubbed his head.

Once the party had left the farm-yard Celia turned to the stairs.

"A nice gentleman," commented Mrs. Evans.

"Yes," said Celia abstractedly, thinking not of the leader but of young Mr. Standish. "I hope," she added hastily, "that I did not do wrong in providing a meal for them. They seemed so hungry and cold I hadn't the heart to turn them away."

"Wrong? Of course not. This is a Christian country, isn't it? No man shall be turned hungry from our door while we have food to spare. Besides, they paid for what they ate. Paid handsomely. I did not like taking so much."

"They would not have given so much if they had not wanted to," was Celia's retort. She made her way to her bedchamber.

Her first act was to cross to the mirror. Young Standish was completely enamoured; she had enough sense to realize that. A nice boy, too, fresh and wholesome as though the cleanly breeze had purified mind and body. The frame of a man and the impetuosity of a school-boy. Celia touched a curl which had strayed.

"I must have looked a fright with my hair all blown

about," she told her reflection, but she did not believe all she said.

The episode, brief though it was, had done her good. It made her feel how foolish, how utterly needless, her fears had been. She had feared discovery, yet the intrusion she dreaded had given her happiness and a fresh interest. For an hour at least she had ceased to think of herself and her woes, and the respite had eased her mind and uplifted her spirit.

After she had rested for an hour, as was her custom, she donned her warm clothing and sallied forth, calling Bob, the sheep-dog to follow her. Normally he was not a sociable creature, but something about the girl appealed to him and he was always willing to follow her to the hillside. "You know my secret," she whispered to him. "You know what is hidden in the barn. You will not betray me?" The wag of his tail was reassuring. The day was milder and the frolicking of the lambs spoke of spring. The countryside looked greener already. She felt care-free and well content. It was only after night had fallen, when the door was shut and the curtains drawn that the old feeling of dread began to reassert itself. The cosy room seemed a thing apart. An owl hooting in the woods behind the village sounded an eerie note. It suggested that many things might be happening in the darkness of the outer world unknown to her.

It was Mrs. Evans who answered the door when an unexpected knock caused Celia's heart to palpitate afresh. She was more reassured than annoyed by the voice which she heard. "Good evening. This is Harry Standish calling upon you. Sorry to disturb you, but I believe I dropped my pencil when I was here this morning."

"Come inside," said Mrs. Evans, succinctly, and withdrew tactfully to the scullery and closed the door.

Harry obeyed with alacrity. "Good evening," he greeted Celia affably. "Fortunate to find you at home."

"Did you imagine I should be out?"

"Well no, come to think of it, I did not. Anyhow, I am pleased you are not out."

"And the reason for your visit?"

"Did you not hear? I dropped my pencil this morning. I think I must have dropped it here."

"I have not seen one. Is it important?"

"Tremendously so. You have no idea how important a pencil is to a surveyor."

"But you have others?"

"Certainly we have. But one can't afford to go on losing pencils in this wild country where shops are few. And this was a particular favourite of mine. It must be somewhere."

"A profound truth. Perhaps it has rolled into a corner. I have not set eyes on it."

"It may have done—I will search." He dropped on all fours to peer beneath the table. There was a slight tinkle and a pencil rolled on the slabs.

"That looks like your pencil," observed Celia helpfully.

"It does. How strange. It must have dropped from somewhere."

"From your coat pocket."

"You saw?"

"Yes, I saw it fall. How thoughtless of you not to search your pocket before setting forth on a long walk. How did it not occur to you? You really should have looked in your pocket first."

"But I should have found it, and then I should not have had an excuse to come here again to see you."

"Did you need an excuse?"

"You mean, I could have come to see you without an excuse?"

"I mean nothing of the kind. What I meant was that it was unnecessary for you to call to see me."

"You must not say such things. You have no idea how necessary it was. We are spending the night in the inn at the village and I could not remain so close at hand without calling. You must be reasonable, you know."

"Am I unreasonable?"

"Perhaps I should not have said that. But you have no idea after a fellow has been in the wilds for days and days with no one to talk to but the fellows he works with, or an occasional shepherd, how marvellous it is to come across a really charming girl. In a lonely farm too."

"You must not take advantage of my loneliness. Suppose you tell me about your work now you are here."

"Just now we are trying to find a new route across the moors here so as to eliminate an awkward bend in the turnpike. We have almost finished the survey. Tomorrow we shall join up with the turnpike again, and then we shall go—on and on, I suppose, until we find another dangerous bend. I will say this, there are plenty of dangerous bends. They'll keep us near here for weeks—thank goodness."

"That sounds as if you were indifferent to human safety."

"I did not mean to be. What I thought was that the more we have to survey the longer we shall stay in these parts. Yesterday I hated the place. Now I find it full of interest."

"Have you been long at the work?"

"Weeks and weeks. All winter. He says that an idiot can find his way about in fine weather. What we need is a road which will withstand the elements. A road that will be undamaged by snow or flood or storm. So we have to be out in all weathers, sampling conditions at their worst. Two of our men have gone down with a congestion of the lungs, but he's as tough as Scottish granite."

"He is? Who is he?"

"Mr. Telford, of course. We are engaged in the great survey for the Government. We are to bring the highway from London across the Welsh mountains and the Menai Straits to Holyhead, and so shorten the dispatch route to Dublin."

Her eyes gleamed. "What a huge undertaking. But you mentioned Mr. Telford. You mean the celebrated Mr. Telford? How I should love to see him."

"See him? You have seen him. He was here this morning."

"What! And I talked to him and did not know to whom I was speaking? How exciting."

"And now," said Harry complacently, "perhaps you are glad I called."

"Yes. You are forgiven."

"I have a suggestion to make."

"I must be cautious about your suggestions. You do not contemplate losing your pencil again, I hope?"

"Now, just you listen. This is serious. We will be working on the bend a mile or so to the west."

"Which is west? I never can remember."

"Over there. Where the sun sets, or thereabouts."

"Of course. But what then?"

"If the morning is fine—heavens, I hope it is fine—you must walk that way. You can, if you wish, be quite surprised to encounter us. Then we will start chatting——"

"I would not interrupt your labours."

"I shan't mind a little rest—a 'spell *bach*' is what one of our labourers calls it—and you may take it from me Mr. Telford won't allow any slackness. Well, if you were there, I could introduce you to Mr. Telford, then you can say you have properly met him."

"And I shall say nothing about having improperly met you."

"Now that's quite unfair. My behaviour has been exemplary. I hope. But if I am to introduce you I must know your name, Celia. By the way, is your name really Celia?"

"Sir, do you insinuate I do not speak the truth?"

"Heaven forbid, but Celia is so appropriate. It suggests the sky. And skies are blue, and your eyes are blue."

"Then I am glad the name is appropriate. A name should be."

"Mine isn't. They christened me Henry before I was old enough to protest. Now, do I look like a Henry?"

"I have no idea what Henry is supposed to look like."

"Something horrible, I believe. You may call me Hal if you like."

"Not just yet."

"You haven't told me your surname. Why are you reticent?" A look of concern disturbed his urbanity. "You are not married?" he asked quickly.

"Married!" The frightened, pursued look returned to her face. "No, of course not. Married! How absurd to suggest such a thing. I—I am not of age yet. Now you really must go. Mrs. Evans will think you are an unconscionable time in finding your pencil."

Harry sighed and rose dutifully. "Very well, I will depart. And you won't tell me your name?"

"Some day, perhaps. Do not press me. For the present Celia will be enough."

"It should be enough, goodness knows. Well, good night—Celia."

"Good night—Mr. Hal."

CHAPTER SIX

No mariner ever scrutinized the sky with a more searching gaze than did Harry the following morning. The thrushes were still singing in the early morning when he leaped from his bed in the inn, striking his head on a rafter in his eagerness to peer out of the tiny dormer window. He saw a graceful outline of deciduous trees against the clear morning sky, noticed that the sun was kindly, and decided that the day would be fine. It would, at least, be fine for him if it enticed Celia to walk the survey road.

The party engaged in the survey were early astir. The two-wheel cart which carried their instruments was dragged into the yard and the patient bay backed into the shafts. Into the cart, which had a canvas hood, went a hamper of food and a demijohn in a wicker case, for Thomas Telford was too old a campaigner to run the risk of being short of provisions in some outlandish place where neither inn nor farm could cater for their needs. Then the saddle horses were led out, sturdy, shaggy nags, devoid of breeding but serviceable. The party mounted and rode up the road past the parish church and vanished around the bend. Some miles farther down they halted at the roadside, picketed their horses on the grass, took their instruments from the cart, and set about another day's work.

Mr. Telford indicated the direction he meant to take. The chain-men plodded ahead measuring the way, while others set up Jacob's staff or cross-staff, and plotted the proposed route. Harry kept scanning the landscape despite the early hour. He dropped one of the staffs. Then he tangled one of the chains in a wayside furze bush. His agitation reached its peak when he miscalculated. Mr. Telford raised his eyes from the pad and regarded his junior assistant with some asperity.

"If it depends on your calculations, Mr. Standish, the Government's new highway will arrive in Machynllech instead of Holyhead, I'm thinking. And what might this figure signify."

"I'm sorry, sir."

"If you would apply your scatter-brain mind to the task

before you, instead of dreaming of yon blue-eyed lassie at the farm, there'd be more hope of your becoming a surveyor some day."

"Yes, sir. I confess, sir, that—er—my mind is a little distracted this morning."

"A mild way of putting it. Very mild."

"Well, sir, you saw her yourself. Now, could you blame me?"

"If I were your age, my lad, instead of being what I am, I have no doubt I should be every bit as big a fool, but Government Commissioners are unreasonable and they are not likely to take into consideration a young man's tender susceptibilities when they find our calculations are out."

"I will try not to go wool-gathering again, sir. I promise I will try to dismiss the lady from my thoughts and to concentrate. By Jove, sir. Look! There she comes."

"You're clean daft, lad. Go and have word with her. I can see I'll get no work out of you today. Heaven send that the lassie returns home soon or else I shall have to shift you to the eastern section of the road, or maroon you in Anglesey."

"Thank you, sir." Harry hurried to the mountain path along which Celia was walking. She was wearing her new coat. The wind had whipped colour to her cheeks. Harry, hat in hand, fell into step with her. He assured her that Mr. Telford was aware of her coming.

"He could have seen me without the aid of his glass, of that I am certain."

"You must come to him now and let me present you. He is in a good mood. I have made a great fool of myself and he has overlooked it."

"What have you done?"

"As a matter of fact I've made some silly errors this morning."

"But why?"

"Because I was day-dreaming. About you, Miss Celia! But here we are."

"Mr. Telford, sir. This is Miss Celia——" He paused.

Celia gave her hand calmly. "Miss Celia Upton, Mr. Telford, of Upton Magnus."

"Well, young lady. I presume you came this way purely by
chance and were surprised to find us at work—or rather, not
at work?"

"No, sir. I came of deliberation."

"Come now, that is candid of you. And might I ask why you
came, or is it not permissible?"

"Certainly it is permissible, sir. I came to meet formally the
great Mr. Telford."

"Ah!" said the great man. "A moment since I commended
your candour. I can see I shall have to walk warily or I shall be
as far out in my reckonings as this young man here whose
foolish head you appear to have turned."

"I was unaware of the identity of our distinguished guest
yesterday, Mr. Telford."

"The meal was none the less appetizing on that account.
I take it you are not from these parts?"

"No, Mr. Telford, I am from Shropshire. My father is Squire
Upton of Upton Hall."

"Don't know him, I fear. His land does not border my
highway. I find myself classifying people in two categories, young
lady. Those connected with the turnpike trusts, or who have
land across which I must arrange way-leaves, and people who
don't matter."

"I see. Then my father happens to be one who doesn't
matter."

"I speak professionally, of course. I have had no dealings
with him about his estate."

Harry, watching the girl's face, saw the animation fade. At
the mention of the estate she became *distrait*.

"I interfere with your work, Mr. Telford. I must not interrupt.
It is a great work."

"Yes," he said quietly, "it is a great work to open up the
country. To make a way where no way existed. To make rough
places smooth and crooked places straight. In less than twenty
years I shall have passed my three score years and ten if I survive
so long. It pleases me to think that men and women who never
knew me will use the highway I have constructed. It is known
as the London to Holyhead Road. Some may term it Telford's
Road. And I ask no other memorial or monument."

He shook her hand, raised his hat. His formal bow testified that the interview was at an end.

"Now, lad, back to work. We have had enough dallying for one day. We are on the King's business!"

Faintly Celia heard the firm words as she retraced her steps.

As she walked she saw in the green path she followed a new significance. It bent and twisted, yet every bend and twist means that a stone or a bush had been avoided, or a swampy spot circumvented. How had the path been worn? By feet. By countless feet. The men who fashioned it thought only of their own affairs yet they were shaping a route for posterity. A path became a track. A track became a lane. A lane became a road. A road became a highway. It seemed an epitome of man's sojourn on earth.

Hitherto she had taken roads for what they were worth—and many of them were worthless. If roads were made smooth, if they could be used in winter as well as summer, traffic would increase, travel would increase, trade would increase. Distant places would be made accessible. There seemed limitless possibilities. And the pioneers were these men with their measuring chains, their cross-staff, and their compass, unobtrusively labouring in remote places, the advance guard of a great host which would follow the trail they blazed.

Unless one were of venturous temperament one must follow a road which led to a destination. Celia sighed. She was on a road, but where it led she knew not. To perilous places, or to a desired haven?

. . . . . .

As though to make amends for his aberration that morning Harry Standish put his mind on his work and laboured with such zeal that even the critical eye of Mr. Telford could discern nothing worthy of blame. He sighted and he measured. He prepared his triangulation. He calculated. And all the while he was intent. It was as though he would repay Mr. Telford for his forbearance. Or perhaps it meant that he felt anew the dignity of his chosen profession. If Celia was proud of Mr. Telford,

Harry meant to see that she was proud of one, at least, of Mr. Telford's helpers.

Presently he paused. "Mr. Telford. I know you must have a reason, but why do you bear Eastward here when yonder way is the more direct to the turnpike?"

"Because I mistrust yonder foundation. Go, if you wish, and test it for yourself. It is not firm enough for heavy traffic. Listen, boy, and pay heed. The Romans knew how to build roads. No people have ever built roads to equal theirs. They went to infinite trouble. Why have their roads endured? Because they had solid foundations. There's your secret of roadmaking, lad. Get good foundations. Small stones will bed into soil. I could hurry this work through, I have no doubt. But I want my work to last as long as roads are in use. The time may come when mankind no longer has use for roads, but it would take a wiser man than I to prophesy when that will come to pass. It is beyond my ken. Mankind needs roads, and the more he uses them, the better the roads must be. See that your foundations are solid. Dig deep. Lay them well and truly, never mind the time or the labour or the cost. Build on solid foundations."

He stared at the rocky pass ahead. "And the same applies to life as well as roads, my lad."

The distant note of a horn came down the air. All men stopped work and shaded their eyes. Over a low hedgerow they could see the course of the turnpike which they would shortly rejoin.

The stage-coach was passing by. Men consulted their watches. They saw four horses approach at a trot: the coachman deftly handling the ribbons. Five passengers were outside, and some packages close beside the guard's hand on the rear seat.

"The good old 'Duke of York'," exclaimed Harry. "I can tell it by its yellow wheels."

They always stopped to watch the coach pass by. It was a recognized custom. All felt that it was a visible connection between towns, between people. The coming and the going of the coach seemed to carry an assurance that all was well. Men went back to their labours more contented once the gay coloured conveyance had gone by.

That afternoon the surveying party rejoined the turnpike. They had their noon-day meal beside a roadside fire.

Then they pressed on with their task. The turnpike had to be surveyed as part of the general scheme into which it must be incorporated.

Harry had lingered behind the rest of the party. Intent on his work he was taken by surprise when the sound of hoofs came to his ears. He glanced up from his calculating.

A post-chaise drawn by two horses was approaching at a walk. It was a well-appointed turn-out. The horses were sleek, though lathered, muddied, and lean as if they had been well worked of late.

A peremptory voice commanded "Stop!" and the postillion reigned up and sat motionless.

A window was let down and a man with a rubicund face leaned forth. "You, sir, a word with you!" Harry laid aside the board on which he was drawing and approached the chaise. The man was richly dressed, a man getting on in years by his whitening hair; one whose features betokened good living and hard drinking.

"I require information." The man looked at Harry keenly as though assessing his station. "I am sorry to interrupt your occupation. You are?" His tone was pompous.

"A surveyor, sir. Engaged on the proposed new road from London to Holyhead for His Majesty's government."

"Yes. I might have known. I have heard much of it, but did not expect to find your work so far advanced. I am a Justice of the Peace in my own county, and as such I naturally take an interest in the maintenance of highways."

"That is understandable, sir," replied Harry politely.

"You have been here long?"

"On this particular stretch of road only an hour, but in this vicinity, well, eight or ten days."

"Indeed. You have not seen a young lady on horseback?"

"I have not, sir. Apart from a market-woman riding pillion behind her good man, I have not seen a woman on horseback for fourteen days at least."

"Walking, perhaps, along the road? A young lady, fair, pleasing to look at. She would surely have caught your eye."

The description seemed to coincide so closely with someone who was not far from Harry's thoughts that he found himself colouring.

"No, sir. I have seen no such lady walking the road." The man regarded him keenly. "Come, come. Let there be no misunderstanding. I notice you are blushing. You—I don't mean it unkindly—are not being evasive, I trust?"

"No, sir. I speak the truth. But yesterday, by chance, I did meet in a farmhouse a young lady. And your words brought her to my mind."

"You interest me, my dear sir. In a farmhouse, you say? And a young lady? Fair of hair, blue eyes?"

"Yes, that would describe her."

"Good. This is a fortunate encounter. Very fortunate. Let me be more explicit. I would not have you think I am wasting your time out of idle curiosity. Did the young lady explain how she came to be at the farmhouse. Your tone implies that she was not the farmer's daughter."

"Oh, no. She was a lady of quality. She was there, I understood, for her health."

"For her health," exclaimed the man. "Precisely. Let me take you into my confidence. The young lady I seek is my daughter. My only child."

"Indeed, sir. I shall be happy to be of any assistance I can," exclaimed Harry eagerly.

"She—er—came to the hills for her health but when I called at the house where I expected to find her, I was told that she went out a couple of days ago for a walk and had not returned. You can imagine my concern."

"Indeed I can, sir."

"She might have met with an accident. She might have been lost in these hills. Or something worse might have befallen her. But let me show you her picture and then we will be certain it is the same person we are talking about."

With hands which trembled the man unfastened his travelling coat, fumbled in his capacious waistcoat which Harry saw was of red silk sprigged with gold, and then produced a small miniature in a gold case.

The artist had done full justice to the flesh tints. Harry

found himself looking into the face which he regarded as the fairest in the world.

"It is, sir. There is no doubt about it."

"Where is she?" The words were shot out vehemently. Harry, in his excitement at meeting Celia's father, found nothing in them but natural parental anxiety.

"You go to the village cross-roads. Turn right. A mile up the lane. The first farm. I hope you find your daughter well, sir."

"Drive on!"

CHAPTER SEVEN

THE house in which Squire Upton dwelt had been built in the reign of Queen Anne when the artistic possibilities of brick in architecture were gaining merited recognition. Passing years had mellowed the fabric. The well-ordered flower garden with its broad gravelled walks and clipped trees, furnished a restful setting. Tall windows and an ornamental portico contributed still more to the appearance of opulence which was dear to the heart of the owner. If the squire was proud of his ancestors it was only in proportion to their contribution to his personal pride. So stately a habitation might well have held beneath its roof comfort and culture. But the squire regarded his home merely as a background to his own dignity. He was interested in himself and all that pertained to him. Among the ancestral portraits which graced his walls was a full length picture of a lady. It was from the brush of Lawrence who had accentuated the richness of her robes and a sweet charm in her delicate features. The squire invariably referred to the picture as "my late, lamented wife", but if reports were true, the decline which carried her to her grave before she had attained her fortieth year, was not unconnected with a broken heart. Celia had inherited something of her mother's beauty of feature and disposition, stiffened, perhaps, by a touch of her father's pride. The squire was proud of his daughter. He would have vowed, possibly with some justification, that he loved her, but love which found expression in tenderness and devotion was a sentiment unknown to his cold and calculating disposition. He loved his daughter as he loved his hounds, his favourite hunter, his broad acres or his ancestors. He loved her because she was his property and her beauty enhanced his worth in the eyes of the world. He could exhibit her without shame, as a connoisseur might gloat over a rare specimen the possession of which was calculated to arouse envy in the breasts of less fortunate collectors.

His wrath when she ran away was the anger of a man who had been robbed of a precious jewel. Now that the treasure was recovered the choler had somewhat abated. But precautions must be taken to guard against recurrence.

In response to his pull of the bell-cord, a butler swung open the tall door of the room and mutely awaited instructions.

"Is Miss Celia in her room, Bates?"

"She is, sir."

"The door locked, according to my instructions?"

"The door is locked, sir. Here is the key."

"You are not to let it out of your possession unless I tell you. Should Miss Celia require food, or the ministrations of the house-keeper, or her waiting-maid, you are to unlock the door and remain in the corridor until they leave. Then you, personally, will lock the door again."

The butler bowed.

"And, Bates, tell Miss Celia that she may come downstairs to take tea with me today."

The butler withdrew. Five minutes later he tapped at the door.

"Miss Celia, sir, sends the message that she does not wish any tea."

"Wish! I was too polite to the disobedient minx. Go to her, Bates, and tell her I order her to join me at tea. Whether she eats is a matter of indifference to me. She is to sit at the table. And Bates, see that all the outer doors are bolted and the windows fastened while she is loose—er, while Miss Celia is not in her bedroom."

The girl entered the room reluctantly. Her pallor was not pronounced, but there was a listlessness about her movements which, for the moment, made her father lift his eyes to Lawrence's portrait of his 'late, lamented wife'.

"Your holiday in the hills does not seem to have benefited your health. You have no appetite, I hear from Bates."

"No, Papa, I do not desire food."

"Fasting by way of penance, I suppose!" The squire's wit was as ponderous as his frame.

"Folly!" he burst out. "This comes of your acting like an irresponsible hot-headed young fool. The story I heard was that you were in the country for your health. Is that right, eh?"

"It is true I was ill. Very ill."

"I should, I suppose, observe that I was sorry. Instead I can only say—serve you right."

"That at least, would be typical."

"Typical? You mean I have no sympathy for you? Neither have I sympathy nor patience for your silly whims. A nice dance you have led us with your stupid tantrums. So you really were ill."

"Yes."

"No wonder, trapesing in winter weather without proper protective clothing. You must take more care of your health. You might have inherited some of your dear mother's tendencies. I can't have you incurring risks."

He spoke roughly, but his voice was not devoid of concern— the concern he would have felt if a pedigree animal was out of condition.

"Now, sit down. Pour me some tea."

The girl sat down and picked up a solid silver tea-pot of Georgian design. It bore the family crest—the mailed hand holding an arrow—the same crest which she had unpicked from the corner of her kerchiefs. Instinctively she glanced at the one in her lap. It was one she had acquired since her return and the crest was in evidence. There was no need to remove it now!

"What are you day-dreaming about?" demanded the squire, noticing her pensive look.

"Nothing." She raised her eyes a little defiantly. "After all, there is nothing to think about, is there?"

"Nothing to think about? There is your wedding dress."

"Father! You do not intend to force me into this odious marriage!" The flush coloured her cheek.

"What! That's no way for a maid to talk. It is an excellent match. You are a lucky girl. Your husband will be a baronet with a pedigree as long as our own.

"That, I suppose, is something which really matters." Her tone was heavy with irony.

"Matters? Of course it matters. Breeding always counts in blood stock."

"Surely you are not elevating me to the level of your blood stock?"

"Now! Now! That's not the way to talk. I have been a lenient father to you, Celia. Given you a sound education. Allowed you to travel. Bought you everything a girl could want. Now I arrange for you an excellent match. And you are ungrateful!"

"It is ungracious of me not to fling myself into the arms of a man who has made love to all the wantons in the village."

"You ought to know better than to listen to gossip. Some folk are always ready to spread scandal. Revel in it! I have no doubt that your future husband is a man of the world, but he is probably all the better for that. Reformed rakes, you know, make the best husbands!"

"And what if the rake hasn't reformed?"

"That does not come under consideration. I have had long talks with Guy, and he has assured me he means to make you a good husband." Mr. Upton leaned forward and touched her hand with a thick finger. "Believe me, my child, your interests are my first consideration. What I do is for your good."

She looked at him with surprise in her eyes. "Do you know," she said, "I really believe you believe that. How little you know about women."

"I know enough to pick a good husband for my girl. Now, listen to me, Celia. I mean to have no more of this foolishness. You are shy. That's what it is. Quite right too. So would any nice young maid be when confronted with such a drastic change in her mode of living. But you'll be surprised how quickly you'll grow accustomed to married life. You'll very quickly bed down."

The Squire laughed.

"Demme, that's not bad. I must tell Guy that! A good joke, upon my oath!"

Celia sat flushed, but otherwise unmoved. "Might I pour you another cup of tea, Papa?"

"No, one's enough, by gad. I can't grow accustomed to these female drinks. Must leave some room for port after dinner. By the way, Guy's coming to dine tonight. Return of the prodigal to be celebrated in style. Bring out the fatted calf, eh?" Again he laughed at his own wit.

Then he sobered. "I shall expect you to wear your newest gown." He spoke as though issuing orders. "Put a bit of colour into your cheeks, one way or another. And for heaven's sake look less like a cat that's had its kittens drowned. You'll take to Guy when you grow used to him. Now, get back to your room. Bates will escort you."

"You don't mean to run risks," said Celia with scorn.

"True, very true. I have learned my lesson. I'm glad to see you appreciate the seriousness of the situation. We're not having the bride disappearing on the eve of her wedding."

Head held high Celia followed Bates from her father's presence.

At the door of her room Celia paused and regarded Bates who stood respectfully a yard behind her, key in hand.

"What did my father mean, Bates?" she asked. "The eve of my wedding."

"You are to be married, Miss Celia."

"I know that is contemplated, but what does 'eve' signify?"

"A special licence has been obtained, Miss Celia. The date is fixed for Friday."

"What! So soon?" She stared at the butler, wide-eyed, biting her lips, fighting for self-control. Then she said in an even voice: "I notice you do not wish me happiness, Bates."

"No, Miss Celia."

"Your reticence is significant."

"Yet I do pray that you will be happy, Miss."

"Thank you, Bates. Now, play the turnkey. Secure your prisoner!"

"It pains me to have to carry out my instructions, I assure you, Miss Celia."

She caught his sleeve. "Don't let him take me away, Bates. I pray you. Don't let me get into the clutches of that lecherous brute . . . I beg your pardon, Bates, that was unworthy of me. No, I'm quite all right. And quite capable of looking after myself. Now lock me in, and don't look so melancholy about it. I know it goes against the grain."

"Indeed it does, Miss Celia."

The lock clicked softly, slowly, as if a reluctant hand turned the key.

When Sir Guy Goadby dismounted from his hack at the front door of Upton Hall that evening, the groom who walked forward to take the animal's rein noticed that the baronet was dressed with fastidious care. Sir Guy walked with dignity up the steps and handed his hat and gloves to Allen, the footman, who stood respectfully holding open the door.

"Good evening, Sir Guy," said Bates, moving noiselessly

forward, "Mr. Upton is expecting you, sir. In the small dining-room, this evening."

Large candelabra illuminated a tablecloth which gleamed with silver and cut glass. Candle-light twinkled on the decanters which glowed with the warm hues of brown sherry and ruby port. Sir Guy's eyes took in the preparations at a glance. Places were set for three.

"Come in, Guy," called Mr. Upton from the hearth-rug. "Delighted to see you."

" 'Evening, Upton. How's Celia? Come to her senses yet? It's about time you brought her back! Had you been unsuccessful this trip it was in my mind to put Black Tom on her trail."

"Bloodhound?" inquired Upton.

Goadby permitted himself a sarcastic smile. "I've called him that more than once! No, he's a former Bow Street Runner I employ at times. Useful man. Possesses the tenacity of a bulldog. However, as you've been lucky I can save my money. And he's expensive—but I must say I've never known him to fail. So I suppose he earns his price."

"Celia seems well enough in health though what her mood is I can't make out," remarked the squire. "The filly seems to have the bit between her teeth."

"Well, apply the snaffle."

"I have, in a manner. She's locked in her room. Bates holds the key."

"He's trustworthy? She couldn't wheedle him?"

"Oh no. Bates knows which side his bread is buttered—though I'm not so certain of Allen. I'm not risking her taking fright and bolting again. Can't make out what possessed the girl. She's never defied me before."

"Oh, it's common enough, with these inexperienced chits. The fear of the unknown. She won't find marriage so bad once she's broken to double harness."

"Well, I hope she takes to it. Her attitude is a revelation to me, Guy, and a disappointment, I confess. A damned good match, I call it. Two old families, neighbours for a couple of centuries at least. Chance of uniting. Seems ideal to me. Then the silly child starts her tantrums. I've no patience with these whims. Anyhow, I've told her she must come down to dine tonight."

"I confess I am curious to see her again. Has her adventure changed her?"

"Ay. But how, I can't just say. You had best see for yourself." He touched the bell.

"Bates, tell Miss Celia that we are waiting for her presence."

Guy walked to the fire-place, bit the end off a cigar, and stood with it unlit but poised, waiting. It was apparent that Celia was not hurrying. The Squire had caught the bell-pull to send a servant to hasten her, when the door was flung open and Celia stood in the opening. She was arrayed in her best gown, which she had arranged to hang so low that it almost slipped from her shoulders. Her hair was piled high, her cheeks rouged until they resembled a painted doll.

"Good evening, gentlemen," she said, dropping an elaborate curtsy. "The filly has come to be put through her paces."

"Come in, girl," said her father. "Shut the door and don't act the fool."

"But I am your dutiful daughter, Papa! And I imagined it was your desire that I should play the fool."

"Well, you're succeeding. Aren't you going to speak to Guy? I consider he has been demned decent about this silly escapade of yours. There are not many men who would have been so tolerant."

"Does not my appearance speak for itself? Do I not appeal to Sir Guy? Lud, I have spent hours trying to make myself appear like a harlot so that he might feel more at home. You must excuse me, Sir Guy, if I am not to your liking, but I confess in my innocence and ignorance I have little knowledge how such creatures appear, let alone how they behave!"

"Celia!" cried her father sharply. "You're mad."

"I try to rise to the occasion. We must make Sir Guy feel at home. Is it two or three of his offspring Sal Summerfield has weaned in the village? Only two? There, I felt you were maligned, sir. But let us drink their good health."

She slopped some port into a glass and held it high.

"To Guy and all the Guys! And, I forgot, my good parent says you have come for the fatted calf. I trust I don't disappoint you, Sir Guy!" With a whirl of petticoat she placed a red-slippered foot on the table. "The calf is scarcely fatted, lord and master, but I have no doubt I shall grow plump with the passing years. But drink! drink! Great heavens, I was told you were both three bottle men. Why trifle with glasses. Your healths, kind gentlemen, who are so desirous of my happiness."

She seized a decanter and gulped at the red wine, spilling some over her slender white shoulders.

"Stop her!" cried her father.

"Oh, the room goes round already. Round and round! Now for a health to the blushing bride!"

Her father swore and flung wide the door. Bates stood there, amazement on his face, and behind him the footman and the housekeeper and two maids.

"Damnation!" roared the Squire. "What are you staring there for. Here. Take her to her room. She's hysterical. She's mad. Lock her in. We must have the physician to her."

Celia, still laughing, was led with unsteady steps towards the stairs.

"Stop it!" ordered the Squire furiously. "D'ye want all the servants to hear? Shut your damned row you little fool. Stop it, I say!" he raised his hand.

"Don't you dare touch me!" cried Celia, sobering.

"Dare! You dare me!"

He brought his hand a resounding slap across her face.

"Oh, you beast!" cried the girl with spirit.

"What! You speak to your father thus. I'll teach you a lesson!" Again he struck her across her mouth with such force that the blood came. Celia stepped back, mechanically wiping her lips, and stared at her father as if he were a stranger.

"You struck me," she repeated, and this time there was a subdued fierceness in her tone. "You struck me! I'll not forget. Never. You struck me—bully."

Guy watched with a cynical smile, finding diversion in the scene. In the background the faces of several servants showed white in a dark doorway. They looked distressed and dismayed, but too subservient to think of challenging any act of the Squire who was their uncrowned king.

Celia's eyes fell on the saturnine Guy. "And you do nothing! You stand like a coward watching a woman struck. I suppose you are taking lessons so that you will know how to treat me when I am your wife. You think I'll be your wife. Fool. I'll drown myself first."

She lowered her head in shame and ran nimbly up the stairs to her room.

"Bates!" bellowed the Squire. "Where are you man? After her quick. Lock the door. See that she gets no chance of freedom."

He turned back into the room. Guy was smiling sardonically.

"Well, it has been an illuminating lesson in the joys of parenthood," he said, reaching for the decanter.

"Why couldn't I have had a boy?" said the Squire bitterly.

"Demme, Guy, you're going to have your hands full with that vixen. Do you still want her, or do you cry off!"

Guy gave an ominous grin. "I want her," he said. "I was never more anxious to wed. It'll amuse me to undertake the taming of the shrew."

CHAPTER EIGHT

It was only when the black horse moved a hoof that attention was attracted to the figure of the dark-coated horseman waiting close to an ivy-covered wall of the farm in the gathering night. His gaze was on the lonely farmhouse in the windows of which the yellow glow of candle-light was making its appearance as Mrs. Evans prepared the evening meal. When the white-washed walls had softened to an indistinct glow, the horseman shook the reins and walked his mount over the turf until he was able to tether the black horse to a ring in the stable wall where the shadow lay deepest. Caution seemed to fit his shoulders as closely as his coat.

He walked quietly across the farm-yard and rapped on the back door. A dog barked. The door swung open and the glow of firelight and candle-light fell on the keen features of Jack Tempest.

It was the farmer's wife who stood looking out into the night. It might have been surprise, or disappointment which quietened his tongue. Tempest uttered no word. It was the woman who spoke. Intuitively she understood the reason of his presence.

"She is not here," she said.

"Not here? Is she out, or do you mean she has left you?"

"She has left us. And she was not too happy to go, if I am any judge." She held the door wide. "Come inside. We can talk better than on the doorstep."

A grim look settled on the dark features of the horseman as he moved into the farm kitchen, where he stood, a somewhat incongruous figure with his long green coat of broadcloth and his spurred boots.

"What has gone wrong?" he demanded, and though his voice was low it was tense. "Where has she gone? Back to the village?"

Mrs. Evans shook her head. "I doubt if we shall see her pretty face again. She has gone home. Her father called for her."

"Her father! Now, how the devil could he have known she was here? Someone must have told him. Did she go willingly?"

"She looked broken, poor child. There was a fine carriage outside in the lane. Two horses and a rider. It was left just out of sight of the door. We heard a step on the stones and a knock, and she jumped up all quick and bright. It was you she was expecting, if I can read her mind. Then she opened the door and who should stand there but a man, not so tall, but with a red face, and a fair round belly on him as if he didn't go short of victuals. 'Well, my girl,' says he. 'Get your things. You're coming home with me.' And she shrinks back as if she had been struck. 'Your health is restored, I can see,' said he, and I felt as if he was gloating over her surprise. 'Go, get your bonnet on. And bring your things. It's time we were back home. A pretty chase about I've had trying to find ye.'"

"She looked about her, a bit wild, and then she drooped her head. 'Yes, papa,' she said, and she looked as if her heart was broken. Then she went upstairs and came down with her little bag and off they went to the carriage in the lane. 'Goodbye, Mrs. Evans,' she says to me, 'thank you for being so kind. And tell——' Then she stopped, and I says 'Tell who?' but she shook her head. 'It doesn't matter,' she says, 'nothing matters now.' The door shuts with a bang and off goes the horses. I watched until they was out of sight. And that's all I know."

He stared before him into the embers, pondering. "Mrs. Evans, if you had a daughter, would you force her to marry a man she loathed?"

"I would not. Is that what the trouble is?"

"I believe so."

"Poor lamb. Well, I'm sorry, but 'tis no affair of mine."

"It's no affair of mine, either, but, by heaven, I mean to make it so."

"What can you do?"

"I cannot say yet, but I shall do something. I owe my life to her kind heart. But how on earth did the man find her? I thought she would be secure here. Somebody must have talked."

The woman nodded her head wisely. "That young man who is measuring for the new road as like as not. He is a great talker, and none too wise for all his education."

"What young man?"

"There's a big engineer man called Mr. Telford. Some of his men are measuring to bring a fine new road from London."

"I know," he said impatiently. "I have seen them at their work. How does she know this young fellow you speak about?"

"They all came here one day for a meal and this lad was fair struck with her loveliness. Back he came that evening on an excuse so as to see her again."

"And then what?"

"She went out the next morning, over the hills, to meet them again and came back all smiles."

"You think she'd been to see him?"

"Sure of it. She said as much, not knowing, like."

"Then?"

"It was later in the day her father called. So putting two and two together——"

"I see!" He frowned and moved impatiently as though his thoughts were restless.

"This fellow's name—did you hear it?"

"Oh, yes, I know that much. Harry Standish I heard him say it was. He's a nice young fellow," she added, for Jack Tempest's brow was black. "Nice enough—but a bit addle-headed."

"Thanks," he said shortly. "I'll have a word with him." Abruptly he strode from the door, towards his horse.

The following morning, as Harry Standish was busy with his cross-staff, he noticed a well-dressed horseman walking his mount along the short-cropped grass which flanked the mountain lane. It was a fair, fresh morning, and Harry was engrossed in his task, though his mind not infrequently went straying to the girl with blue eyes. He became conscious of the horseman fixing an intent gaze on him. There was nothing unusual in this. Harry had become accustomed to being watched by curious eyes as he performed his daily work. Then a shadow fell across him and he heard a slight clink of a bit-ring. The horseman had moved quietly across the grass and had pulled up beside him.

"Your name?" demanded the horseman.

Harry flushed. "Why should I tell you?"

"I merely wish to ensure I am not addressing the wrong person. The one I am looking for is Standish. Harry Standish."

E

"That is my name." Harry straightened his back and waited.

"You have made the acquaintance of a young lady who stayed at a farm a few miles back."

A defiant look cross Harry's face as he flushed. "By what right do you interfere in my affairs?"

"The right of one who has the welfare of the lady at heart."

"I bid you good morning," said Harry, and picking up his chain he gave his attention to his work. A moment later it was wrenched from his grasp with a force which tore his fingers.

"Damn you!" shouted Harry with a sudden fierceness which was foreign to his normal cheery disposition. "Get out of this!"

The man at the far end of the chain laid down his portion and began to saunter to the covered cart. Standish watched him out of the corner of his eye. "I don't know who you are," he said, carefully modulating his voice, "and I can't say I greatly care, but let me tell you I don't allow people to conduct themselves as you do. Dismount and pick up that chain."

"If I dismount it will be to thrash you."

"The task will not prove as easy as you think."

"Stop talking and listen to what I have to say. Have you told anyone where that lady was staying?"

"It is no concern of yours."

"It's very much my concern. If you do not answer my questions I'll force you to." He tossed back a folded cloak which lay across the saddle-bow and Standish saw that the cape concealed holster pistols. "Answer my questions or I'll put a pistol to your head."

"You see that cart?" retorted Standish. "My colleague has just crossed to it. We carry a rifle just in case we are molested by foot-pads or gentlemen of the road. I have an idea that Stephens has just gone to see if it is loaded. He is a good shot and you are within range."

The horseman apparently had not heard. "I wished to know whether you gave information about the place in which she stayed. I need not press you, for your conduct has given me the answer I require. Have no fear. I would not even soil my boot toe on a creature who betrays a helpless and innocent woman who has never done him harm, into the hands of enemies."

"Betray?" shouted Harry indignantly. "Enemies! Why you

fool, it was her father who inquired. It was only proper I should tell him when he was seeking his daughter."

Tempest turned his horse about. "Most generous and gracious of you. She is now being dragged back to be forced into marriage with a debauched reprobate and will have a life of hell—thanks to you."

Tempest shook his rein, and the black began to move smoothly across the sward.

"Stop! Stop!" shouted Standish, running after the animal. "Is what you say true?"

"True?" demanded Tempest reining up and looking with scorn at the young surveyor. "And does your feeble intellect suggest to you that I have ridden thus far with a cock and bull story? It is only too true! I hope the remembrance of the evil you have done will haunt you to your dying day."

"What are you going to do?" demanded Harry.

"Do? I cannot say. My first task is to find out where she lives."

"You don't know?"

"No."

"Then I might help you."

"When I have to resort to assistance from you I shall be in dire need."

"I could tell you her name and where she lives."

"What. You know that? Tell me."

"At a price."

"Name it."

"That you let me assist you."

Tempest laughed. "Not likely!"

"Very well," said Harry calmly. "I will manage my own affairs. I have the advantage of you. I know where she is to be found—you—whoever you might be—do not! Evidently you don't know the lady as well as you would have me believe. I shall certainly manage my own affairs, and I shall stop at nothing to remedy the wrong I have unconsciously done. To think that you, or any other fool, would ever imagine I would harm a hair of her head."

"Tell me her name," said Tempest ominously, dropping his hand to his pistol-butt.

"I will not. Threaten me if you will but you'll not make me talk. You go your way, and I'll go mine. Why should I tell you? Who are you? For all I know you may have some devilish scheme to harm her. I'm not taking risks. I'll not help you."

Tempest laughed. "Good for you. You've more spirit than I thought. I'll take you at your word, Mr. Harry Standish. I am half a mind to listen to your appeal and join forces, but your challenge appeals to me. I relish pitting my wits against another's. I bet you five guineas that, though you have the advantage inasmuch as you know her name and place of abode, I will have rendered the lady practical help while you are still wondering what to do next."

With a touch of the spur, Jack Tempest cantered in the direction of the Shropshire border.

CHAPTER NINE

FOR a while Harry stood motionless, staring with the fixed gaze of one who does not see the thing at which he looks. He did not notice Stevens get out of the cart and begin to walk towards him. He did not notice the horseman take the road and rapidly vanish from sight. In his mind he saw a picture of a girl with blue eyes; and the eyes were troubled.

Stevens' step on a patch of stone brought him out of his reverie.

"Who was that fellow?" demanded Stevens. "When he snatched the chain from you I thought there was going to be trouble. I wondered if he might be a night rider, and so I slipped back for the rifle. I had him covered while you were talking."

"Thank you, Steve. I have no idea who the fellow is. He is well dressed and well spoken, yet I have a feeling you might be right in your surmise."

"What did he want of you?"

Harry coloured. "I may as well out with it," he said. "You remember the girl at the farm?"

"The one you lost your heart to? I'm not likely to forget her."

"Yesterday a man in a post-chaise stopped me. He said he was her father and asked if I had seen her. I told him—like a fool!"

"Wasn't he her father?"

"Oh! Yes."

"Then what's the bother about?"

"Why, you see, she had run away. How was I to know? The old sinner is trying to force her to wed some man she hates—a good match, I suppose."

"Where does our green-coated lad on the horse come into the picture? Does he know her?"

"He's interested in her mightily, if I'm any judge—yet he can't be a friend for he does not know her name. He was furious because I had revealed her hiding-place, but how the deuce was

I to know the manner of man her father was, or what he was up to?" Harry looked aggrieved. "At all events I know something that inquisitive devil doesn't know. I know her name and her home. I offered to exchange with him."

"Exchange? For what?"

"To join forces with him."

"Join forces. To do what? Hold up the coach?"

"Don't be facetious, Steve. I don't feel in the mood. No, I have a fancy that he is going to try to do something to help her. Lord, if he can, I can."

"What could you do?"

"I haven't an idea, Steve, but I must do something. To think I was the one who brought about her undoing—I, who would do anything to serve her."

"My advice is—put her out of your mind, and get on with the job. You'll only make a fool of yourself if you thrust in where you are not wanted, besides, the bridegroom may not be as bad as you suppose."

Harry appeared sceptical. "I mean to find her, if I can. If I can't be of any assistance at least I can tell her I am sorry."

"Don't be a fool," said his companion sharply, but Harry was resolved on being a fool, and walked away.

His rough-coated nag was tethered near the cart, cropping the grass. Harry slipped the bit in its mouth and swung into the saddle, mentally thinking how different his animal was from the sleek and swift creature which had but lately departed.

He urged the cob forward, seeking Mr. Telford whom he knew he would find far in advance, studying the route. They had reached even wilder country now. In places the road was little better than a horse-track.

It was a land of lichen-coated rocks and great boulders, some tufted with heather which had taken root where soil had collected in crevices. The grass was sere—a carpet of yellow and brown, broken by occasional dark pools around which the slender spikes of rushes thrust. Rocks were strewn on every side like pebbles scattered by a giant's hand. High and gaunt and grey rose the craggy sides of the mountains, ascending until their tops were lost in wisps of mist. Streaks and seams of frozen snow still lingered in the highest hollows. On the lower pastures sheep grazed contentedly, oblivious of the majesty by which they were surrounded. Some stunted oaks grew, mossy and gnarled, but there was little verdure. It was a bleak and inhospitable region through which the great mail-coach road must pass on its way to the sea. In the valleys, streams in spate foamed and cascaded like white ribbons, and little runlets traced their way down the rockface like veins in marble. The whole scene was a study in grey and green and white. Alongside a small, dark tarn which reflected the crags in its still surface, Telford was seated on a roadside boulder studying the formation of a low arched bridge which crossed a small ravine.

"See yon bridge?" said he. "The Romans made it. To touch it would be sacrilege when it has thus far resisted the assaults of the elements and time's destructive hand. I will fling another bridge across alongside it. Where the Romans went it is usually wise to follow."

"Yes." Harry felt in a monosyllabic mood.

Telford raised his eyes. "You're not interested in Roman bridges, I gather!" he observed succintly.

"Sir," burst out Harry, "I am come to ask for permission to commence my vacation."

"Indeed! It is vacation which appeals to you more than vocation! And is it the hard work which is not to your liking, or maybe the inclement weather?"

"It is neither, sir. I trust you will not think me ungrateful, Mr. Telford, for all the information you have imparted from your store of vast wisdom, but I must get away awhile."

"Ah!" said Telford drily. "It is the lassie, maybe."

"Sir," said Harry earnestly. "She is in distress."

"And you would go to her rescue, I have no doubt. If you take the advice of a man old enough to be your father, you will refrain from thrusting your nose into other folks' affairs. It only leads to trouble."

"No, sir. I must go. And at once."

"And jeopardize the result of your examination; mar your career? Harry Standish, you are a fool."

"I care not. I must have leave, and, begging your pardon, Mr. Telford, and not intending to offend you, go I must—with your leave or without it."

Telford pursed his lips and returned to the study of the Roman arch. "What was the secret of the mortar which could weather centuries in an exposed spot like this?" he mused. "I cannot tell! And you are never likely to find out, Standish, if you go on gallivanting when you should be attending to your work. But get you off. I'll not deny you. It might be better for you if I did. Now, if I grant you leave of absence it is not to be interpreted that I approve of what you do. Nor that I am weakening. Understand that? I am not the sort of man you can twist around your little finger, Master Standish. I am letting you go because I realize full well that I shall never get any worth-while work out of you while you're in this daft mood. Pray that it will soon pass. You'll be adding the height of Snowdon into your calculations before the week is out, and a man who is not to be relied on is not the man for Thomas Telford."

"Thank you, sir, thank you." Harry was profuse in his protestations of gratitude, but Telford turned his shoulder on the young man who interpreted the gesture to indicate the interview was at an end. He was at liberty to depart.

He had, he felt, sacrificed some of his master's respect, but he was reckless. Hurrying to the waiting nag he eagerly fumbled for the stirrup, clambered into the saddle, and urged the shaggy creature into some semblance of a trot. He paused at the cart for a cloak and some food. Then he set off down the turnpike which led towards the Shropshire border, a lonely figure on a lonely road. No knight errant ever looked less romantic, but despite his appearance Harry Standish was resolved chivalrously to render some service or die in the attempt.

The horses allotted to Mr. Telford's helpers were chosen for their hardihood. The question of speed never entered into the calculations. Harry found his mount exasperatingly slow. He appeared to be continually kicking his spur-less heels into its stout ribs in an endeavour to induce the animal to hasten. It was some time before he came to a hedgerow. When he did so he searched carefully for a hazel stick of sufficient size to warrant his cutting it. Having trimmed the twigs, he remounted with this as a whip, and by diligent belabouring he induced his nag to mend its pace. The road seemed to stretch on and on interminably. He was reassured for a while when he descended into the valley where grey houses clustered cosily among the trees at Bettws-y-Coed. But after crossing the river, he ascended a long hill only to find himself again confronted by miles of dreary moorland. The horse, lacking the stimulus of romance, showed waning enthusiasm, and it became plain to Harry that if he wished to reach the Shropshire border he must curb his impatience and give the animal its rest. So he spent the night in the warmth and comfort of a roadside post-house which also provided bedding and fodder for his over-tired steed.

When the next day drew to its close, Harry was still in Wales but considerably nearer the border, with prospects of reaching his destination the following day. For the first time in his life Harry envied men who could afford swift horses, or who could hire relays of post chaises to speed them on their way. Though not fashioned in heroic mould, Harry possessed a modicum of British tenacity which stood him in good stead when the going was hard. By the close of the second day his impatience had changed to stubbornness. He was prepared to journey not merely to Shropshire but to Scotland if needs be, and if the nag died under him he would get another. At first when he made inquiries, no one he spoke to had heard of Squire Upton of Upton Hall, but once over the Shropshire border, Harry was cheered to find that people recognized the name. Finally he came across a man who actually knew where the hall was situated. Harry cast off his lethargy. He was, he trusted, nearing his journey's end. In the village of Upton Magnus, which he reached towards the close of day, he proceeded with more caution. Impatient though he was, he took pains to conceal it. He made some purchases in the village store, removed the stains of travel, and endeavoured to make his appearance as presentable as possible. It was almost dark when he made his way, on foot, to the lodge gates and rang for the gate-keeper. He controlled his voice to speak with assurance and, so he imagined, a touch of authority. Had Mr. Upton returned with Miss Upton?

He was relieved to find that both had returned. Was it far
to the hall? He had left his horse at the inn as it was almost
foundered after a long journey from Caernarvonshire. The
porter assured him that the distance was not far, that the Squire
was at home, and that he entertained Sir Guy. Harry thanked
him curtly and set off for the hall, resolved to do—he knew
not what.

CHAPTER TEN

It called for courage on Harry's part to venture thus into strange surroundings, uncertain of his welcome, not knowing what he meant to say or do, but resolved in his heart that he would, if it lay in his power, remedy the ill he had unwittingly caused.

The bell pealed—unnecessarily loudly it seemed to his strained nerves. He confronted the footman and ascertained that the Squire was at home and was dining.

He sent in his name. The footman, Allen, returned with the curt message that the squire had never heard of him.

"Tell him," said Harry, "that it is the young man who gave him the valuable information on the roadside in the Welsh hills."

Back came the footman. "Would the young man send a message. The Squire was concluding his meal and did not want to be disturbed."

"Then I will wait until his meal is finished," said Harry with composure, and walked forward with assumed hauteur. "The message I have is for his ears alone and I do not intend to have it relayed and so reach him second-hand."

He was left cooling his heels in the gun-room. The low murmur of voices sounded through the closed door. The Squire was not impatient, seemingly, to satisfy his curiosity about the message or the messenger.

Harry had become so accustomed to waiting stoically that when the door was flung open he was taken by surprise.

"Well, young man?" said the Squire brusquely. "I have no idea why you have called, but if you expect a reward——"

"Nothing was further from my thought," exclaimed Harry hastily.

The Squire appeared relieved.

"Then what brings you here? Explain yourself."

"I scarcely know how to explain——"

"Damnation!" the Squire was irascible. "You force an entrance to my house, you interrupt my meal, and then you calmly assert that you know of no cause for your remarkable behaviour."

"I have called about your daughter, sir."

"Not, I presume, to request her hand in marriage?" The tone held an irony which Harry chose to ignore.

"It is—certainly—about her marriage!" said Harry boldly. "When I told you where she was hiding—I use the word advisedly, sir—I was quite unaware that she was being forced into a wedding which was obnoxious to her."

"Proceed, sir. I may as well hear all you have to say before I order my servant to throw you out."

"I wish, sir, first to acquaint the young lady with the fact that if I have caused her suffering it was the result of ignorance on my part for which I would make amends. My second request, sir, is to appeal to your better nature as a father not to ruin your daughter's life by a marriage which, I am convinced, will break her heart."

"And how long have you been acquainted with my daughter?"

"Two days, sir, but it does not take two minutes to realize that she is a young lady of exceptional nobility of character and one of tender susceptibilities."

The Squire threw wide the door. "Guy," he called, "do join us, I beg you. Here's a young spark moralizing, and you are missing the choicest selections of the homily." The steps which came down the passage-way were deliberate, even slightly unsteady. There was no introduction. Harry found himself staring at a man who neared middle-age, dressed in the height of fashion. The baronet held a half-emptied glass in his right hand. Gross feeding and heavy drinking had left their mark, and even though there was something aristocratic about his high-bridged nose, his mouth was sensual and his eyes cruel. Harry studied him, deciding that he had never beheld a coarser face. And this was the man to whom the delicate Celia was being sacrificed to satisfy a father's pride.

"What's this fellah want?" demanded the baronet in a thick voice.

Harry took his fence without a falter. "I have come, sir," said he carefully modulating his voice, "to appeal to your better nature."

"My what?" He found himself scrutinized by haughty eyes which narrowed ominously.

"Perhaps I should have said, to appeal to your honour."

"What the devil is he raving about?" Sir Guy turned, with simulated bewilderment to Mr. Upton.

"It's about Celia," said Mr. Upton. "The young man feels compelled to intercede on her behalf."

"Intercede? About what?"

"He shall tell you himself," said Mr. Upton grimly, as though enjoying the situation.

"Well, speak out!" The baronet came closer.

"The lady, sir, does not wish to get married." Harry felt that his words lacked conviction.

Sir Guy laughed.

"Are you her advocate? Did she send you to plead her cause? Gad, I was unaware of the cause of your visit when I entered."

"She does not know I am here. But I feel that as I have done her a wrong, I ought to rectify it."

"Done her a wrong?" Sir Guy's voice became metallic. "You had better be more explicit."

"I revealed, unwittingly, to her father, where she was hiding."

A laugh followed. "That wasn't wronging her, my lad. You've got hold of the wrong idea. That was rendering her a service."

"Then you won't release her, sir? It would redound to your credit if you did."

"My credit! I've never been able to get credit for years, demme if I have!" Sir Guy's voice was mocking.

"I appeal to you, sir."

"No." The tone was curt and final. "And let me add, that it is only the fact that I am under a roof which is not my own that constrains me from answering with greater vigour."

He turned away.

"Damned impudence," he muttered. "Get rid of the fool, Upton, and bid him mind his own affairs and not interfere with those of his betters."

"Sir," exclaimed Harry, holding out a restraining hand to the Squire, "let me entreat you to convey my regrets to your daughter and say I implore her forgiveness for the injury I have done her."

Mr. Upton gave a grim smile. "You shall convey your apologies yourself," he said. "This evening was becoming stale but, by gad, you've added spice to it. Lord, to think of you appealing to Sir Guy's better nature. There'll be a laugh at the Club when I tell the tale."

He picked up a riding-crop and rapped loudly on the top of an oak chest. "Bates! Bates!" he bawled. "Where the devil are you?"

"Here, sir," quietly replied the imperturbable butler, appearing from behind a door so rapidly that it might have been assumed that he had been listening to the conversation.

"To Miss Celia's room. Lead the way. You have the key?"

"It is here, sir. It never leaves my possession."

"Unlock the door. Bid her step on to the landing. Say that a friend—I can't say an old acquaintance—would have word with her. Now, young man, follow the butler. Guy, are you coming?"

"Demme if I am," retorted the baronet, walking back to the room to replenish his glass.

"Then I'll accompany the delegation," said the Squire. "I am curious to know how you will conduct yourself in the presence of my daughter, sir."

Bates walked ahead with a stoical expression. Then came Harry, trembling slightly with emotion rather than excitement. The Squire, sardonic, brought up the rear. Bates inserted the key. There was a click. He turned the handle. The door did not open. He tried again. The door did not budge.

"I am afraid Miss Celia has bolted the door on the inside, sir," said Bates respectfully.

"By heavens, if she has dared!" shouted the Squire. He hammered on the panels. "Open this door!" Utter silence followed as the three men stood listening. "Open!" cried Mr. Upton again. "D'y' hear? Open this damned door at once." He rattled and hammered.

"It's bolted, sir," expostulated the butler as the Squire paused to rub his smarting hands, for he had struck harder then he intended.

A look of surprise crossed his face. "Bolted? How the devil could it be bolted, Bates? There's no bolt on the inside."

"Of course not, sir. I forgot."

The Squire went to the banisters. "Guy!" he yelled. "Here man, quick. There's something wrong."

The baronet came up the stairs two at a time, his face red with anger.

"What is it? She hasn't done herself in?"

The colour ebbed from the Squire's face. "I—never—thought —of that," he muttered. "The door's wedged—with furniture, likely. Come, all together, let's burst it in!"

Three men hurled their weight against the door, but it was stout, and though it trembled it did not give way.

"Bates! Go and fetch a crow-bar," ordered the Squire.

"And an axe," added Sir Guy.

It was some minutes before Bates returned. He ran up the stairs with a speed not usually associated with his dignity.

"Where's the axe, fool?" demanded Sir Guy.

"I could not find one, sir. But as I passed the shrubbery on the way to the wood-shed I tripped over something."

"Well, you haven't broken your silly neck."

"It was a ladder, sir."

"What about it?"

"I looked up and Miss Celia's window was open, sir, and the curtains blowing out!"

Guy swore viciously. The Squire swore. Harry was thrust against the wall as they clattered down the stairs. The butler followed, and after the butler ran Harry. He found the men standing on a lawn staring up at the side of the silent house as though they expected the open window to speak. Indeed, in its silent way, it spoke loudly enough. Celia had fled. But how? Who put up the ladder?

Sir Guy turned furiously on Harry. "By gad," he snarled, "if this is your doing, I'll break you."

The amazement on Harry's face proclaimed his innocence more eloquently than words.

"The stables! Quick!" shouted the Squire.

All three men hurried across towards the stable yard where they were joined by the head groom.

"The horses, quick, Ted!" ordered the Squire, catching up a lantern the groom carried. Across the cobbles they clattered.

The groom fumbled with a key and undid the padlock, while the Squire fumed. "Quick, man, hurry!"

The half-doors were swung open. The Squire held the lantern which flung its yellow beams on the glossy coats of several horses in their stalls. The animals turned curious glances on the intruders. The groom picked up a saddle and flung it across the back of the first horse, Sir Guy snatched a bridle from its peg. Even the butler joined in the scramble for harness. Soon the horsemen would be on the trail of the fugitive girl.

Harry stood miserably outside the open door watching the turmoil within. His eyes lit, as if by chance, on the padlock and key which the groom had thrust into the unfastened hasp. Harry never knew what impulse prompted him to act as he did.

Softly he closed the lower half of the door and bolted it. Then he pulled shut the upper half.

"Hi! what's going on?" It was the Squire's querulous voice. Harry's trembling fingers thrust the hasp over the hook. He was only just in time for fingers were fumbling and scratching at the inside of the door. He clicked the padlock home and turned the key.

Muffled shouts, and curses, and hammerings sounded in his ears. He tossed the key into a watery ditch and darted into the shrubbery.

Then he made for the village and dragged forth his weary nag which, willy-nilly, had to take the road again.

As Harry felt the horse break into a reluctant trot, something assured him that his venture, though not glorious, had not been wholly in vain.

CHAPTER ELEVEN

JACK TEMPEST was unruffled as he rode his fine black steed down the road to the east. His face looked calm but resolute. It was the face of a man whose mind was made up, who knew what he intended to do and how he intended to do it. Once he was well out of sight of the party engaged on the road survey, he drew his horse into a gully and led the animal out of sight. Tempest scrambled up the slope until he was able to obtain a view of the roadway he had vacated. Peering around the side of a boulder so that his head was not silhouetted against the skyline, he kept the distant figures under observation. Taking a small telescope from his pocket he extended it and focussed the glass on the group. He saw Harry Standish turn away from Telford and mount his nag. Tempest shut the glass with a snap.

Once he was sure that Harry was returning along the road, he descended the slope and stood at his horse's head until the sound of hoofs indicated that Harry had jogged past. Then Tempest led his horse to the road. It was not his intention to travel on the heels of his quarry. Instead he rode inland over a scarcely perceptible track and once clear of the village, shook his horse into a canter. For several miles he went at this sharp pace, slackening only when he had to deviate for a patch of scree or bogland. Finally he came to an outlying farm, built of white-washed boulders, with a low slate roof. Its squat chimneys and tiny windows under the eaves showed that the building was several centuries old, though the barns which adjoined were modern and spacious. A dog barked. Tempest whistled, at which the animal emerged and after a discerning glance wagged a greeting. A man of small stature came to the doorway, pipe in mouth. He was in his shirt sleeves, bow-legged, short and slim as a jockey.

"Anything amiss, Cap'n?" he asked.

"Nothing to disturb you, Jem. Is your lad Tim about?"

"I'll get 'im."

At his shout a youth of some thirteen years who had

already over-topped his father, came quickly forward, looking up at the horseman with a gaze which revealed hero-
worship.

"Get your pony out, Tim. There's a young man riding eastward astride a rough-coated bay nag. You'll not mistake him.
Take some food in your wallet. Keep him in sight and report
to me when I overtake you."

"Yes, Cap'n. But hadn't I better have a horse——"

"Do what you're told. He'll not out-pace your pony.
And keep well back. I don't want him to think he is
followed."

The boy darted off to the stable eager to undertake the
enterprise.

The business-like manner in which the boy rode from the
farm-yard indicated that he was trustworthy. Tempest dismounted and made his way into the low-beamed kitchen.

He helped himself to some bread and cheese which he found
on the table.

"Go to the stables, Jem, and saddle the two best animals.
Put a woman's saddle on Jess—she's the best tempered. Make a
roll of horse-cloths and oilskins and pack some saddle-bags
with food. We may be gone several days."

"Ay!" said Jem quickly, as though scenting adventure. "I'm
to come along with you, Cap'n?"

"Yes, I shall want you. See to my horse. We must be away
in fifteen minutes."

"I'll tell the missus," called Jem as he vanished.

Tempest seated himself and stretched his booted legs towards
the hearth. He seemed at ease, but it was the calm of a man who
keep his emotions under control.

When the clatter of hoofs sounded, he rose quietly and
walked with unhurried step to the yard. Three horses stood
awaiting him, all sleek steeds, of a quality which one would
not expect to encounter in so remote a setting. In addition to
Tempest's black, there was a dark brown on which Jem was
sitting holding the reins of a led horse. This was Jess, a slender
dark chestnut, obviously a thoroughbred, and on her side-
saddle were strapped the rugs and the food.

Tempest mounted. Without speaking the two men rode

forth on to the broad hillside. From the farm doorway a well-built, dark-eyed woman watched them anxiously. Then she went in and shut the door.

An hour later, Tempest took the led horse and Jem rode ahead to have a word with his boy. Thus they proceeded along the road to the east. First in the procession went the unsuspecting Harry Standish, intent only on coaxing speed out of his reluctant nag, next, unobtrusively, a youth on an insignificant pony who kept almost out of sight, behind him a small man on a restless horse which resented the leisurely pace, and finally, well to the rear, Jack Tempest with the led horse. When Harry sought shelter for the night, the shadowing party did likewise, taking it in turn to stay on watch so that the pursued did not depart without their knowledge. The following day's procedure was a repetition. When they neared the English border Tempest summoned the boy back to him.

"You have done well, Tim," he said, and handed him a gold coin.

"I don't need no payment, sir," said Tim. "It was good fun. Mayn't I come further?"

"Tim!"

"Yes, Cap'n?"

"Would I have told you to go back if I had wanted you to stay?"

The lad hung his head, and turned slowly away. "Tell your good mother to have a bed aired and a good meal waiting—the best she can prepare. We hope to entertain a lady of quality. From now on you will be more hindrance than help. You have done your job and done it well. As it is we three may have to ride for it—hell for leather."

Tim mounted his pony and jerked its head towards the west.

"Tim, what's that coin made of?"

"Why, gold of course, Cap'n."

"What else is golden?"

The boy looked puzzled. He was keen eyed, and experience had taught him to be alert when he talked with Tempest. What else was golden? Nothing obvious, of course.

"Silence is golden, Tim," Tempest reminded him.

The boy grinned and nodded his head. His pony broke into a trot.

Night was nigh when Tempest and the man Jem approached the village of Upton Magnus. They rode slowly and cautiously, surveying the landscape with critical eyes. Harry was close ahead. They saw him abandon his horse and walk to the lodge gates.

"We must avoid the turnpike, Jem; there's probably a toll-gate," said Tempest. "Our first task is to find a spot where we can leave the nags without their being seen."

"That 'ollow's a likely place."

"Too shut in. Don't forget, we may be pursued. No, open yonder gate. We'll take 'em in that field as if to pasture. Like as not they'll not attract attention in the darkness, for there are cattle already there."

Jem undid the gate, listening to see whether anybody approached. The riders dismounted and led the animals well into the centre of the broad meadow where, in the gloom of night, they mingled with the grazing cattle. Tempest gave the reins into Jem's hands.

"Now I must trust to my wits, Jem."

"What are you going to do?"

"I must get into the park but not, as our young friend has done, through the orthodox gates."

"And then?"

"I must have word with the lady."

" 'Ow?"

"Well—I have two proved keys. This first." He patted a pocket which clinked with gold. "If that fails—this." He drew a small pistol of choice workmanship, and carefully looked to the priming. "If both these fail, Jem, we are in for a merry time, but it won't be the first occasion you and I have had to fight our way out."

"And it won't be the last, Cap'n. Good luck to you."

Tempest removed his spurs and thrust them into his holsters. Next he tossed his great coat over the back of his horse. Light of foot he crossed the dewy grass and vanished from Jem's watching eyes.

Leaping a low white paling he found himself in the shrubbery which flanked the drive to the hall. From the cover of some laurels he saw Harry crunch to the door and heard the clang of the bell.

Every word of what followed was clear to his ear.

Hardly had the door closed than he hurried to the side of the house and crept cautiously on to the porch. He turned the front-door knob—it opened. The footman, Allen, standing in the back of the hallway, looked up curiously. He saw in the doorway a well-dressed man, bare-headed, who smiled and beckoned.

"A word with you," said Tempest in his compelling way. "I have business to transact which will reap a rich harvest for you."

Allen regarded him doubtfully. "May I ask, sir, who you are?"

"I am a friend of your mistress. Do you care for her welfare?"

The look in the footman's eyes reassured Tempest. It became sympathetic—friendly.

"Care? Of course I do—but——"

"Then listen. She is to be married against her will——"

"Don't we know it! Every servant in the place is up in arms, but what can we do?"

"Take this," said Tempest holding a handful of guineas. "No, man, don't hesitate. I'll not beat about the bush. I'm here to save your mistress. I'll not let you run any risks. Put that in your pocket. All I ask is that you show me her room, and tell me where a ladder is to be found."

"You swear you will not harm her?"

"Go to her room if you will and tell her that Jack has come to rescue her. See how she responds!"

"Swear you'll not harm her! I'd not do her harm for all the gold in England."

"I swear. I feel as you do. I'm risking much to save her from hell."

"Ay, you are right. Well, that's her room. There's a ladder against the side of the fruit garden wall, hanging on staples. I think it is long enough but I'm not sure. I'll go to the back and quieten the dogs. I daren't do more."

"I'll not betray you," said Tempest. Allen, looking somewhat scared at his own temerity, hurried inside. One hand was
in his pocket clutching more money than he had ever handled
in his life before. He passed silently through the house and into
the yard, where he fed the two dogs with some meat hurriedly
snatched from the larder. He paused more than once to watch
the ladder being noiselessly raised against the side of the house.
To give the man his due he was resolved, had Miss Celia called
for help, to raise the alarm. Her silence reassured him.

CHAPTER TWELVE

ONCE she was locked within her bedchamber, Celia's bravado forsook her. Great waves of desolation engulfed her so that she felt she would be submerged by the floods of her grief. She flung herself on to her bed and wept until the pillow was wet. Then the sobs ceased to shake her frame and she became calm. It was an ominous calm, for it savoured of despair. Only once was the utter silence of the room broken. She heard a soft step outside and a discreet tap on the door. The footman's voice said respectfully: "Would Miss Celia take a cup of tea?"

"No, Allen. Take it away."

"Thank you, Miss."

"Thank you, Allen; thank you for being so thoughtful."

"I wish I could do more, Miss Celia."

She returned to the world of her mind. It was a dreary world with no bird song, no scent of flowers, no gleam of sunshine on the horizon. It was a world which was bleak and drear and chill; a world devoid of hope.

She moved slightly and noticed there were spots of blood on the pillow. Tenderly she felt her mouth. Her father had struck her! She repeated the thought as though it were incomprehensible: the product of her imagination. Yet her swollen, bleeding lip testified to the blow. He had never been kind to her, resenting her having been born a girl when he had desired a son to perpetuate the family name, yet never before had he offered physical violence.

She had, in the past, accorded him obedience and respect. These, she felt, were due from a child to her parent. It was in that belief that she had been nurtured. She would, had he encouraged it, have given him love; in fact, as a child she had offered it spontaneously, for such was her nature, but having met with repeated rebuffs had grown chary of even permitting herself any show of affection.

"He struck me!" She repeated the words out loud as though to convince herself of the unlovely truth. For the first time since reaching her room she moved. Lowering her feet slowly from the bedside, she walked, a little shakily, to the looking-glass. There was a time when she took pride in her apartment. It had an Adam's fireplace, exquisite in its delicate embellishments. Her furniture, too, was of Adam's design, possessed of a graceful, dignified formality which somehow seemed in keeping with its fastidious owner.

She tilted the oval mirror and examined her face. Her eyes were swollen from weeping and her upper lip from the blow. A thin smear of blood had traced its way down her dainty chin. She tried to rub it off with a handkerchief which, with a child-like gesture, she moistened with spit. When that failed she crossed to the ewer and tenderly bathed her face.

"He struck me!" Again she repeated the words in a dull, faltering tone. A flood of colour brought life to her pale cheeks and a sparkle of anger to her eyes.

"I hate him!" she said softly but fiercely. "Hate him. Hate him! He is no longer any parent of mine. I disown him. I would sooner walk the streets than be beholden to him. He struck me as if I were a bitch from his kennels that had leaped with miry paws upon a new coat. And he would sell me to that beast of a neighbour with as little compunction as he would dispose of a hound."

She shuddered. "I'll kill myself before I'll endure that man's vile touch!"

It was growing dusk. Again there was a tap on the door, Allen's voice said: "Your candles, Ma'am."

"I—I do not want them, Allen, thank you. Leave me alone with my misery."

"Oh, Miss Celia. I am sorry. We are all, if you permit the liberty. I—I would serve you if I could, Miss Celia."

"You can't, Allen. Nothing can be done. Leave me to my fate."

"Miss Celia. I—I shall leave Mr. Upton's service if—if——"

"Now don't upset yourself. Just go about your duties as if nothing had happened. I—I shall be all right." She tried to speak bravely. "And please go, Allen." Her voice broke. "Yes, Miss Celia." The soft footsteps departed. She was touched—touched and humiliated. Even the servants knew that her father was treating her as he would a dog. Worse than a dog!

She lay down again on the bed and drew the coverlet over her, for she was shivering. Emotion seemed to have sapped her vitality. One of the dogs barked—Ruby—she knew the tone. The front bell clanged. She wondered vaguely who the caller might be. In the gathering gloom she lay, a prey to disquietude which verged on despair.

Again the door-bell rang. Curiosity got the better of her and she tiptoed to the window, pulled back the curtains and raised the sash. But she had been too slow and the caller had entered.

Celia returned to her bed and lay, face hidden in the warm comforting softness of the pillow. She wanted to cry again but the reservoir of her tears appeared to have become empty. It was as she lay there in the darkness, aching with misery, that a soft thud, thud, sounded on the wall. She sat up, wide-eyed, wondering what it could be. She could hear no further sound, but some sixth sense, some intuition, told her that something unusual was taking place. Quietly though she moved, the bed gave a tiny creak. It sounded unnaturally loud in the stillness. Hardly had her feet touched the carpet when she heard her name called so softly that it seemed only the product of her disturbed imagination.

"Jill!" The voice came from the window which she had left slightly raised. "Jill, are you there? Come to the window. Quick. It is Jack."

"Jack!" Hope leaped, setting her heart beating furiously.

She ran to the window and flung it up. The white features of Jack Tempest seemed quite unreal—the produce of her fevered imagination perhaps.

"How did you get here?" she demanded.

"Never mind. Is it correct you are being forced into this marriage?"

"Yes. On Friday."

"You must escape. I have the horses concealed in the field. Quick. Get your warmest cloak."

"But, Jack——"

"Get it, I say," he commanded.

As she obeyed he scrambled over the window-sill into the room. She handed him the cloak and he flung it into the darkness.

"Now your stoutest boots. There's no time for anything else."
He caught her arm and dragged her to the window. As she looked
into the night and saw the slender ladder descending into space
her nerve failed her.

"Oh, no, I cannot! I should fall. I am dizzy at the thought."

"You prefer to be wed?"

"Oh, no, no," she whispered.

"Then get on to the ladder. Every minute counts. I'll make
you," he added savagely. His arm was about her waist and he
picked her up in his arms. Celia gave a little cry of anguish and
despair. "Cling to my neck," he said. She obeyed him so literally
that he found difficulty in breathing.

"I'm only going to lower your feet to the top rung. Once
you feel the ladder beneath you it will be easy."

Unexpectedly he gave a mischievous chuckle. "Did you think
I was going to throw you out of the window, Jill?" he asked.
The laugh restored her as nothing else would have done.

"It would have been quicker," she said. Her little hands
gripped his shoulders fiercely until she felt the ladder beneath
her feet. Cautiously she took a downward step while Tempest's
firm fingers about her arms gave her assurance. She went a
rung lower, and then lower still. One more pace and she groped
for the ladder with one hand while the other still clung to Tempest.

"I'm all right now," she breathed. "Let go."

"Good girl. Take your time. It isn't far."

Tempest darted back into the room. Snatching the fire irons
he wedged them beneath the door. He put a chair-back beneath
the door handle, and dragged a tall-boy against the door itself.
Picking up the heavy boots, he thrust them into the breast of
his coat and swung a confident leg over the window-sill. Before
he stepped, he glanced down and saw dimly the white anxious
face of Celia upturned. Quickly he lowered himself and descended
the ladder. He thrust the boots and cloak into her hands and
pointed to the way through the shrubbery. "Wait beside the
white fence," he whispered. "I must hide the ladder."

She obeyed, pausing to cast a quick glance over her shoulder
to note the neat manner in which Tempest lowered the ladder
rung by rung until it was deposited silently on the lawn. She saw
him run to the shrubbery with it.

He was beside her. His strong arms lifted her over the fence. The dew of the meadows struck cold and wet through her light shoes but she scarcely gave it heed. She was walking, figuratively, on air. Freedom, blessed freedom was within her grasp.

The bark of a dog sounded. They hastened on. Then came the banging of a door, the sound of voices, angry voices, hammering and shouting.

"Open this damned door!" It was her father's irate tones, so tempered by distance that she could almost afford to force a smile.

Yet she faltered. "Oh, Jack!" she exclaimed. "He's found out!"

"Hurry!" ordered Tempest, and catching her arm, made her run, stumbling over the uneven surface of the tufted meadow. A low whistle sounded ahead. There were the horses, ears pricked, alert, wondering who came out of the darkness until Tempest called in a low voice.

"Jem!"

"Yes, Cap'n."

"They've given the alarm. They'll be making for the stables in a minute. We shall have to ride for it."

"Up with the lady, then," Jem was at the mare's head while Tempest hoisted Celia with scant ceremony into the saddle. "Put your cloak on," he ordered.

Then he swung into his saddle, took the bundle Jem held up to him, and in another instant all three horses were walking quickly to the open gate.

Once in the roadway they broke into a canter, keeping in line ahead along the grass to deaden the sound. It would leave a trail, thought Tempest, but he quickly decided that it was to their advantage to deaden the hoof beats, the sound of which would carry clearly on the night air. The tracks, he argued, would not be distinct until daylight, by which time he hoped to be miles away over the Welsh border. Celia only spoke once. That was when he rode beside her for a moment to see whether she was all right.

"Jack!"

"Yes? What is it?"

"I'd like you to call me Celia from this night."

"*Adieu,* friend Jill!" he said softly. "Greetings, Celia!"

Jem led the way, Tempest came last. Frequently he gave a glance over his shoulder, more than once he touched his pistols to make sure the butts were ready to hand. Once he stopped to strap on his spurs. He let his companions get well ahead while he waited to listen. But there was no sound of pursuit.

When he rode on it was with a puzzled brow but thankful heart. They had made their escape—made it far more easily than he had ever imagined possible.

CHAPTER THIRTEEN

ONCE the urgency and excitement of the escape had passed, Celia began to experience reaction. Elation gave way to weariness. She may have sagged in the saddle. For some reason Tempest drew alongside, glancing into her face with anxiety in his eyes.

"You are all right?" he enquired.

"Oh! Jack. My feet are numb, and I'm almost too cold to cling to the saddle."

He swore softly. "Bear up a little longer. Just till we get to the next cross-roads. Then I will soon have you set to rights. May I leave you a moment?"

He cantered ahead to Jem with instructions. At the crossing Jem pulled his mount into the shadow of the hedge and sat waiting while Tempest and the girl turned southward. Tempest rode in silence awhile and then he said: "Jem is keeping guard in case of pursuit. He will give us ample warning if there is danger."

"What do you mean to do? Oh, Jack, I do not wish to appear ungrateful but I—I can't ride much longer. I feel faint."

He pulled up both their mounts and passed her a flask. She took a sip and gasped.

"Drink," he ordered. "It is rum—finest thing for keeping out the cold."

She drank and felt revived. "Not much farther," he volunteered, and whistled like a screech owl. "There is a secluded dell near here, frequented by gipsies. If they are there now, all will be well. Yes, they are there." A low whistle sounded from the dark trees ahead.

Drawing the horses to a walk Tempest put his arm around the girl, telling her to lean against him. Thus he supported her until a man stepped quietly from behind a broad oak. He was swarthy and ragged of apparel, yet gold ear-rings gleamed, and the silken scarf about his neck was of rich texture. Tempest bent low and whispered in the man's ear. Celia saw the man's attitude change from curiosity to respect.

"This lady is faint and requires rest. May she find it with my friends?" inquired Tempest.

"Assuredly. Come to the fire. My wife will see to her. My name is Jasper."

"We may be followed, Jasper."

"I will send my young brother Gideon to keep watch."

"My man is at the crossing. He will signal if horsemen are sighted."

The man Jasper took the chestnut's bridle and led the animal along a narrow path where the soft earth deadened the hoofbeats. Beyond a spur of rock which jutted across the glade they came upon an encampment. Several rounded huts were made from bent boughs with tarpaulin spread over them. A fire in the centre glowed red, throwing a ruddy reflection on the tree bark, the curving huts, and the dark faces of two women. One, the younger, was rich in colouring, and pretty. She held a baby to her breast. The other was an aged crone whose grey hair fell in snake-like locks to her shawl-clad shoulders.

"My wife, Miriam," said the gipsy briefly. "She will care for your lady."

When Tempest lifted Celia from the saddle she swayed. He took her in his arms as easily as if she had been a child and bore her to the fireside. The warm glow was comforting and Celia stirred, holding out her white hands.

"My feet are like ice."

Tempest placed her on a log and knelt. The girl's red satin slippers were sodden.

He went to his saddle for the heavy boots.

"You think of everything," said Celia.

"I remembered to bring the boots—and forgot to give you time to put them on!" he reproached himself.

"There was no time. How were you to know there would be no pursuit?"

"I can't make it out. It is unaccountable," he confessed. "Get dry stockings and chafe the lady's feet if you would earn my gratitude," he said, turning to the gipsy woman.

The old dame who had not spoken fetched a crock and swung it over the embers, stirring with a wooden spoon a concoction of stew which smelt appetizing to the hungry travellers.

"I have scarce eaten for days," confessed Celia.

"You must eat now," commanded Tempest.

"I want to eat," she exclaimed. "I am hungry, ravenous. I could eat a horse."

"Jasper, you had better remove the animals to a place of safety!" said Tempest.

The gipsy's white teeth gleamed. "I will see to them, Master," he said. "Never fear. Bid your lady rest easy. She must know you are with friends."

The old woman shuffled forward.

"What have you there, Gran?" inquired Tempest.

"A comfrey lotion. The pretty lady has had a blow."

Celia experienced difficulty in preventing herself from shrinking as the claw-like hands came towards her face, but Tempest touched her arm and reassured her.

"Let her apply it," he said softly. "They are expert in the use of herbs. It will ease the pain and speedily allay the swelling."

Celia acquiesced. Before long she was prepared to confess that the stiffness had already gone from her bruised cheek and mouth.

No question was asked, but the shrewd dark eyes which studied her seemed to be capable of reading secrets.

The young woman Miriam, and Tempest, held a hurried consultation. Then they went to one of the booths where a bed of hemlock in the frame of boughs had been prepared. Tempest put the blanket he had brought with him on this, and added his great coat.

"You must sleep," he told Celia, "else you will break down. We have a long ride ahead of us and you are in no fit condition to face it as you are."

"Is there no risk in our remaining here?"

"Yes," he confessed, "there is risk, but it is a risk worth taking. I doubt whether anyone could approach without Jem or the gipsies being aware of their presence in time to enable us to get away. Relax and try to sleep. I shall be on guard."

The words comforted her. As she made her weary body comfortable on the woodland couch she felt the touch of Tempest's coat consoling.

The cheery pipings of small birds greeted Celia's ears when she awoke and lay drowsily in the warmth of the blankets! For a few moments she was unaware where she was. She was conscious only of complete and utter comfort and relaxation after a time of stress. The stiffness had almost gone from her lips but the wound to her pride remained unhealed. Gradually her full consciousness returned. She moved slightly and became aware of her forest bed. Mingled scents assailed her nostrils and they were as pleasing as they were strange. There was the smell of the crushed hemlock, and the blended odour of soil and fallen leaves, while from without, on the cool, keen air of early morning, there hung the pungent smell of woodsmoke from a newly-lit fire. She moved slightly. The old crone was bending over the flame, outlined against a curl of grey smoke, boiling something in a small pan. Behind her stood a youth, possibly the boy Gideon of the night before, holding a horn tumbler in a grimy, or sunburnt, hand.

A little whimper caused Celia to turn. It was then she realized that she was not alone. On a similar bed on the far side of the hut lay the bright-eyed young mother, Miriam, with her babe in the crook of her left arm.

She smiled as her eyes met those of Celia!

"You have slept well, Mistress. You feel much refreshed!" she said, and Celia reflected that the tone was musical though the inflection contained something foreign to English speech.

"I am rested and refreshed," she agreed, "and I thank you."

The old woman turned from the fire, poured something from a skillet into the horn tumbler, and walked towards the hut.

"A drink of hot milk will warm and comfort you, Mistress," she said, placing it on the ground beside Celia.

"Thank you. I must get up."

"Not yet," said Miriam. "The men have not come in yet from their night watch. When they report it will be time enough for you to stir."

Celia was not sorry to remain abed. She closed her eyes and dozed until Miriam aroused her with the warning that her milk was getting cold. Celia sipped and found it good, though the taste was strange.

"Goat's milk," explained Miriam. "We take our goats about with us. The milk is more healthy than that of the cow."

Miriam fed her child, and then wrapped the baby warmly ere she arose and walked across to a tiny woodland brook for her morning ablutions. Celia noted the soft-footed ease with which the woman moved. Gideon was walking apparently aimlessly up and down the narrow path which led from the glade to the lane. At times he would pause to pick up handfuls of dead leaves to scatter over the path.

Interest in the boy fled when Celia saw the stalwart figure of Tempest walk briskly up the path. He paused in the clearing. "Celia. Are you awake? May I speak to you?"

"Come inside, Jack. I am too warm and comfortable to stir. I have slept and am a new woman."

"How does your face feel?"

"Less painful. Tell me—— Am I disfigured?"

He shook his head. "I refuse to be drawn into this! If I told you what I thought of your looks you might become insufferably vain. You would say—'I am far too lovely and radiant to waste my time on a ne'er-do-well like this Jack Tempest.' "

"Jack! How dare you even suggest such a thing, even in fun? I am almost cross with you." She leaned forward and put her hand on his. "Tell me something."

"What is it, fair lady?"

"Why are you so good to me?"

He turned and stared out of the hut. It was almost as if he had not heard.

"The time—and the place," he said softly. "No, not today, and not here. I am too tense. Once I start to talk I shall forget my surroundings, and I must keep my wits about me until you are in a place of safety. Someday I will try to tell you, perhaps, but not now."

"We are not safe?"

"Oh! Reasonably." He shrugged his shoulders and looked indifferent, but Celia noticed that his eyes were never still. He seemed to be watching. And listening.

"We will not be really safe until we are across the Severn. In this land of ours, Celia, in the towns and the villages, and along the turnpikes, there is order and cultivation. People dwell in comfort and live civilized lives. But once you get away from the beaten track, when you get out into the far places where no roads lead and where no people dwell—then you are in a different world. It is to such a region I shall have to take you until we can decide where you can dwell in comfort. Dublin, perhaps, but there is time to discuss that once we are over the border. They are searching for you."

"You are sure?"

"Yes. Jem watched two parties of horsemen pass along the Shrewsbury Road. It is well we turned aside. We cannot cross by the bridges, of that I am certain, but Jasper knows of a ford lower down if the rains have not swollen the river too badly."

"And if they have?"

"I know of a boat in which I can take you across. Then we shall have to decide whether it would be safe to have the horses ferried across at a place I know, or whether it would be more expedient to swim them. But have no fear. We shall cross to safety. Meanwhile Jasper and Gideon have obliterated all the hoof marks of our horses and sprinkled soil and dead leaves over the path. It would take a keen-eyed man to follow our way now."

It was as well that the precaution was taken. The morning was not far spent when the boy Gideon came running in with a message from the vigilant Jem. A horseman was coming up the lane. Miriam acted promptly. "Come, Mistress. There is a little cave beyond yonder brambles in which you must lie concealed. Pray, put on my shoes. Sorry I am to offer such ugly footwear for your dainty feet, lady, but your heel marks would show." Awkwardly shuffling in the borrowed shoes, Celia followed Miriam to the cave behind the bushes. Here she drew her cloak about her, for the damp rock struck chill, and crouched, peering through the screen of brambles while Miriam searched the hut and came forth carrying every article which might incriminate the fugitive. She piled these behind the bushes and returned to the hut.

Tempest was with the horses, farther up the gully, holding their nostrils lest they should whinny.

With something akin to alarm Celia saw a horseman turn from the lane into the woodland path. Jasper walked towards him. Celia's alarm increased. The rider was Guy Goadby. His neat clothing was spattered from hard riding, his horse was mired, his dark face was sour.

"Good morning, Master!" Jasper greeted civilly, touching his forelock.

"Were you encamped here yesterday?"

"Yes, Master, that we were. Making baskets from osiers."

"Have any riders passed this way?"

"Not this way, Master. But when I was down the lane last evening I did see some turn into the lane, and then ride away again."

"How many were there? Which way did they go?"

"Steady now, Master. My memory grows better for the sight of a silver coin."

"What! You rogue. You would beg! I would have you know I am a magistrate."

"Not begging, sir. I know information which is of value to your honour. Why should I not bargain?"

Celia experienced a sickening sensation. Was the man going to betray her? A sense of desperation stole over her. If necessary she would break from cover, take to the woods, and trust to Tempest to prevent pursuit.

Jasper caught the florin which Sir Guy tossed him contemptuously.

"Thanks, Master. Why now, there was a tall man, handsome as yourself, sir, and a lady with him."

"What was she like?"

"That I could not say for her face was hid but she seemed young."

"Well?"

"Why, as I said, they paused and whispered together. Then the man caught hold of the lady's bridle rein and dragged her horse about. And they set off along the Shrewsbury Road."

"They could not have gone that way, fellow. I have asked and no one has seen them pass."

"That does not say they did not start that way, Master. People are not always on the look-out. How far along the road they rode I cannot say but I do know that that was the way the horses were heading."

Without a word of thanks Sir Guy wrenched his steed about and set off at a sharp trot in the direction of Shrewsbury.

Jasper spat on the florin for luck.

CHAPTER FOURTEEN

As soon as Goadby reached the Shrewsbury road, the glade became animated. Miriam and her baby emerged from the hut, the old woman stepped from behind a great rock, young Gideon raised his head from a dry ditch where he had lain with the patience of a wild animal. Tempest came sauntering down the gully from the place where the horses were concealed.

Celia felt it was safe to venture forth, too.

"Let us go," she said when Tempest approached.

"You are safe here, my dear. Danger is past."

"He may return."

"Not for a while. In any case we should be warned of his approach."

"Next time he may search more thoroughly."

"You will be safe. Just because I was out of sight, you did not imagine, I hope, that I was not taking an interest in what transpired."

"Oh no, no. I felt you were near. Though I could not see you I was conscious of your presence. But suppose—suppose he had ventured to the cave. I go chill at the thought!"

"He would not have reached it."

"How could that be?"

"He would have been prevented; he would have stopped short before his foot profaned the rocky threshold."

"I don't understand."

"I exercise magic!" His smile was sardonic, and Celia noticed his right hand was thrust into the breast of his jacket. "Now, don't bother your pretty head about such matters. Just remember that you are being cared for and that there is no danger. I didn't rescue you from your home with the intention of lightly passing you back to the arms of that scoundrel."

"I—know. But, Jack, I should feel safer if we went."

"As you wish. It would be wiser to wait for nightfall, but I will have a word with Jasper and see what we can arrange."

While the men debated, the old woman served some food. Her appearance was unlovely but she had a practical turn of mind.

Before the day was out Celia had cause to remember with gratitude that warming, sustaining meal.

Tempest walked to the group resolutely. "We will go," he
said succinctly, as one whose mind is made up. Instead of elabor-
ating plans he began to eat as one who is sharp set.

Jasper was engaged in cutting sacks into large squares.
Noticing Celia's look of inquiry Tempest paused with the spoon
half-way to his mouth—"To muffle the horses' hoofs," he
explained.

Miriam knelt in front of Celia and spread two of the smaller
canvas strips in front of her.

"I am not a horse!" protested Celia, laughing.

"You are to be treated like one," Tempest assured her. "We
don't want to have the tell-tale imprint of your shoe to incriminate
us should we have to walk."

Celia submitted, noticing how deftly the gipsy woman used
her fingers.

When the horses were brought out, Gideon was sent to
summon Jem.

Celia turned with a smile and held out her hand to
Miriam.

"How can I thank you for your great kindness?"

"Do not thank, pretty lady. We have been paid."

"There are some debts which are too great to be settled with
money. I shall always be indebted to you."

When the packs had been strapped into position, Celia was
lifted into the saddle of the chestnut, and the little cavalcade
moved, Indian file, along a narrow path in the woods, Jasper
leading, and Jem bringing up the rear. The men walked, leading
their horses, pausing whenever Jasper signalled, so that he
might have time to scrutinize the landscape before they ventured
into fresh territory. They avoided beaten tracks and made
detours around every hamlet they sighted. Twice they came
across poachers, and once a farm labourer, crossing a meadow,
stared curiously at them.

"That is a risk we are bound to take," remarked Tempest
when he noticed Celia's concern.

"How calmly you take matters, Jack."

"Oh!" he shrugged his shoulders. "A man has to acquire

a philosophy if life is to be endurable. I never take a needless risk. On the other hand, if a risk must be run, I take my chance and never fret. I am not unduly concerned, Celia. I am pitting my brains against your wealthy but, I say it respectfully, not too intelligent parent, and that libertine he would have made you marry. It may be vanity on my part, but I feel that my wits are nimbler than theirs."

"Oh, I am sure of it. I think you——" She paused.

"What?"

She shook her head resolutely. "I shall not tell you what I think of you, Jack. *You* might become insufferably vain."

They both laughed, and Jasper turned with a frown at their levity. He put his finger to his lips for silence; halted them with a gesture and went crawling up a furze-covered slope ahead. They were almost clear of woodlands now, save for occasional clumps of trees. The spring sunshine streamed pleasantly upon them.

Jasper came cautiously towards them. "The river is ahead, I have brought you to the ford. You can cross here, and I think it is safe. I can do no more. Once across it rests with you."

Tempest nodded. "I ask nothing better. Thank you, Jasper. Now get back to Miriam. If ill befalls you as a result of this day's work, send me word. I will see you are recompensed."

Celia smiled her thanks. The swarthy gipsy bowed and disappeared among the bushes.

Tempest now took the lead and led the way down a sunken road which ran to the river's edge. He made Celia walk. She was glad. It stretched her limbs, which were getting cramped. They halted in the shadow of a hedge at a bend of the river where a bank of shingle jutted into the moving water. Jem mounted and rode into the water, testing the foothold cautiously. The current had eaten into the western bank and Celia watched anxiously as the water rose higher and higher until the foam almost swept the girths. Then the horse emerged and with a struggle and a heave of his haunches, scrambled up the distant bank. They could cross.

Tempest kept his great black horse close beside Celia as they crossed the ford, to give her confidence. Her chestnut found difficulty in gaining the bank so Tempest lifted her out of the saddle and placed her feet on dry land, leaving the animal to scramble up unaided.

They paused to allow their mounts to recover from their exertions. From a cottage near the ford, a pleasant little building of red brick with lozenge-shaped panes in the tiny windows, a woman with two children stood watching their efforts. Celia turned boldly and waved to the children.

"I think you are right," said Tempest, nodding approval. "A friendly gesture is ever better than a furtive look."

There were marks of the scrambling on the muddy bank. Tempest examined them and shrugged his shoulders. "Jasper could read a story there," he observed, "but I fancy that our obtuse friends will not interpret it aright. There are no hoof marks to assist them. Come, let us move. Once we reach the open country we will have these mufflers off the animals' feet. They'll make better progress then."

The party headed southward for a while, Celia noticed that Tempest's policy was to keep as far away as possible from the recognized routes. If he chose a road, it was never a turnpike. Now that the greatest danger seemed to be past, Celia began to enjoy the excitement of the escape. She felt secure, such confidence had she in Tempest's sagacity and courage. Security means much to a woman.

The nature of the terrain began to change the farther west they rode. Distant hills which hitherto had appeared green now began to take on a bluer tint, and to loom higher against the skyline. There were more rocks, more valleys, more streams, more boulders. Red brick gave place to grey stone or lime-washed buildings. White-faced Herefords in the meadows were scarcer, the Welsh Blacks more frequent. The build of the sheep changed. They became lighter in frame, more agile. By unfrequented routes they rode hour by hour. Then Tempest turned to the girl. "You are weary?"

"I am, a little," she confessed.

"More than a little. It grieves me to subject you to this strain but I believe it will prove for the best. If you can hold out another fifteen minutes we will reach a *cwm* where we can rest, reasonably free from prying eyes."

"A *cwm*?"

"A hollow. You should know that, dwelling on the border!"

"Do not stop on my account if you feel we should press on. Freedom means more to me than comfort."

"The horses require a rest. It is time we off-saddled." Whenever they passed beneath trees the girl noticed that Tempest broke off any dead branches which hung within reach. He had collected an arm full. She was curious.

"We shall require firing," he explained. "Wood will be hard to procure on the hillsides. There will be dry furze, of course, but nothing with any substance."

The horses were sweating freely and showed signs of weariness when Tempest led the way up a narrow, grassy path and turned into a small ravine which cut, like a quarry, into the bleak hillside. A pool of water had collected in the rocky hollow, fed by several tiny freshets which trickled down the rockface from a spring in the mossy ground above.

In the short turf near the shelter of the crags, black embers showed that the place had been used for a bivouac on previous occasions. Their horses drew up with the readiness they exhibit when they reach a journey's end. Tempest's strong arms lifted Celia from the saddle and supported her a moment until she felt her feet.

Then the men unsaddled. While Jem prepared a fire, Tempest tossed a tarpaulin on on a low bank warmed by the westering sun, and spread the blankets there for Celia's comfort. But first she chose to stretch her legs, and then went to pat the horses.

She found Tempest squatting in front of the fire frying bacon, the appetizing smell of which made her realize how ravenously hungry she was. A can of water was boiling. "Cut some bread," he ordered, indicating a loaf. Celia searched for a knife. It was her initiation into a mode of life which was to become part of her existence.

Jem joined them, after picketing the horses, and the three ate in silence. When they had finished, Jem walked away to rub down the horses, and Tempest, lighting a pipe, lay back on the rugs and stared at a white cloud drifting across the cerulean sky.

"Jasper was most kind to us," said Celia. "Did you know him of old?"

"No, Celia. I had not met him before."

"Then why was he so kind?"

"His nature, perhaps."

"I think not. You persuaded him in some way."

"I paid him."

"I do not think he would have acted so generously for payment alone."

Tempest smiled. "Not only observant, but curious! I did not know Jasper, my dear, but I know the chief of the tribe. I have the pass-word. Had Jasper not done his best when I asked for aid it would have been counted against him. I did not know of him, but he knew of me."

"You are a strange man, Jack. You have breeding, you are cultured, yet you associate with gipsies and farmers and jockeys."

"They are friends of mine." He was succinct. Celia did not question him further.

"Well?" he demanded as she fell silent. "You want to ask me more about myself?"

"I shall wait until you wish to tell me, Jack. What I am most conscious of is that you have rendered me such unselfish service that no woman was ever treated more loyally and chivalrously. I shall not repay your kindness by prying into your affairs."

"Some day I'll tell you. But the sun sinks and it grows chill. Up with you. Pack these things while I help Jem to get the saddles on."

"You do not intend to stay the night here?"

"You shall have a roof over your head, Celia, even if it be a humble one."

So they rode on at a walking pace, over broad upland heaths, along narrow ways which led through sheltered valleys, until they came to a rippling brook. Beyond it was a hill farm with a curl of friendly smoke rising from a squat chimney and the yellow glow of a rushlight in one of its small square windows.

"Here we stop!" said Tempest. Jem rode ahead and bending from the saddle, spoke to the farmer who emerged as the bark of his dog heralded the appearance of his unexpected guests.

CHAPTER FIFTEEN

SADDLE weariness and a superfluity of mountain air, combined to induce sleep in surroundings more squalid then the delicately reared young woman had ever experienced. The hill farmer and his wife vacated their only bedroom for her use, and though the good woman bustled about providing the best that she had in the way of bed coverings, Celia chose to retain most of her garments rather than come into too close contact with the coarse blankets. The man and his wife made a bed for themselves on the kitchen floor. Celia suspected that Tempest and Jem found what comfort they could in the hay loft, and though at first she sympathized (possibly needlessly) with them, she could not help feeling that the scent of the fragrant hay would be preferable to the musty stuffiness of the bedroom. Folk were stirring soon after dawn and Celia herself was not sorry to get the door open and inhale deep breaths of pure morning air. She was given (doubtless on Tempest's instructions) a bowl of hot water in which to wash.

Breakfast was an unknown luxury, but a mug of hot milk and some bread and cheese satisfied the travellers, who were anxious to be on their way.

The fording of the upper waters of the Dee presented no difficulties. Once the party was thoroughly in Wales, progress was more rapid. Sometimes they glimpsed the turnpike from afar, but for the greater part of their way their track lay across moorlands where the stillness was broken only by the eerie cries of curlew or peewit.

"Are we to return to Mrs. Evans's farm?" inquired Celia.

"No." Tempest was concise. "Your father knows that spot. He is sure to make inquiries there. We must avoid it."

"She was good to me."

"Was she the only one?"

"Jack, I didn't mean that. I merely observed——"

"I think she is trustworthy but she had not been proved. I shall take you only to persons I know, and whose dependability is proven."

He rose in his stirrups and stared fixedly at the mountain rim. "Cattle, Jem, if I'm not mistaken."

Jem peered and agreed. Tempest looked about him and turned aside to a hollow which lay inland, riding alongside Celia so as to interpose his body between the girl and any watcher in the distance. "Go ahead, Jem, and find out what news is likely to interest us."

The little man on the big horse trotted towards the dark mass which loomed in the distance.

"We are near the cattle road," explained Tempest. "Most of the drovers are friends but it would be well if you were not seen until Jem has made sure that there are no strangers with the party. At times, you know, travellers prefer to cross country with the drivers, who go armed, and are more than a match for any footpad."

They waited in the stillness and silence of the moors. Both dismounted in the hollow and Tempest let the horses crop the grass while he sprawled on the bank and looked over the lip of the hollow, his head concealed by a jutting rock. The air now carried a sound, a murmur. The muffled padding of countless hoofs on the mountain turf provided an obligato to shouts, barks, lowing, mingling with the cracking of whips or thwacks of sticks.

"Come here, Celia," said Tempest glancing over his shoulder. He spread a cloak beside him. "Lie here and look upon a spectacle the like of which you have never seen before, if I am any judge."

Across the broad, green undulating moor with its tufts of heather and bracken and gorse, streamed a long, moving column of animals which shuffled and jostled. They were led by an old bull, a black, broad-headed veteran of numerous trips across country. After him came a seemingly endless horde of cattle, black mostly, but here and there the colour scheme was broken by red or white or grey. The tossing horns and swishing tails gave an appearance of animation more pronounced than the moving feet. About the flanks of the column rode ragged men on shaggy ponies, watchfully shepherding back into the ranks any straggler which attempted to break away, or linger to snatch a mouthful of grass. Their efforts were seconded by lean and active dogs which welcomed an opportunity to rush snarling at any animal which failed to conduct itself with desirable docility. The procession moved slowly—two or three miles an hour perhaps. Thus they went past, bulls and bullocks, cows and heifers and runts, heading for the border, for Leicestershire's fattening meadows, and finally Barnet Fair or Smithfield Market.

"Thank you for letting me see such a sight. One might go a lifetime without such an encounter."

"So I thought."

"The poor animals. Are they not weary?"

"I doubt it. They do not cover more than twelve or fourteen miles a day, and the pace, as you notice, is slow. It would not pay to drive them over much. They will be lean enough, heaven knows, when they reach their destination."

"And foot-sore."

"That I cannot say. They are shod for the journey, you know. And along the route are blacksmiths who have specially shaped shoes for re-shoeing as the occasion demands."

"I thought the men looked rough fellows."

"They needs must be. It is a rough life. But they are honest enough in their way. I know them—Evan ap Harry, Tom Bach, and one-eyed Dai."

"Was it necessary for you to hide, then?"

"For me? No. Had I been alone we would have stopped to yarn with them, but I don't want a single eye to rest on you if it can be avoided. Who knows when a chance remark, even from a friend, might set your enemies on your track."

"Enemies! It sounds strange to hear you use that word."

"I look on them as nothing else. A father ceases to be a father when he strikes his daughter in the face."

"I have forgiven him—almost—I think."

"I haven't!" Tempest's tone was grim. "To horse; we waste valuable time. Jem will be waiting ahead."

The two men seemed to have an understanding about their destination. Presently the countryside began to take on a vaguely familiar aspect. When Celia sighted in a depression ahead the small white farm with the spacious out-buildings, and saw the greetings extended, she realized that Jem had led them to his home.

"Is this where we stop?" inquired Celia.

"Until I can find a more suitable, and possibly safer, home for you. You are in need of repose and the horses are badly in need of rest."

"Thank you, Jack, for putting me first!"

His eyes twinkled. "I only transposed the order in the nick of time. You would not be so unkind as to imply that the horses have not earned their rest?"

"They have my gratitude."

Celia thankfully let Tempest lift her from the saddle. She walked stiffly towards the farm door where Jem's wife waited to greet them. The clatter of weary hoofs showed that Jem and his lad Tim were leading the horses to the warmth and comfort of their stalls.

The table was set for a meal, a spotless tablecloth and the best china gracing the board in honour of the occasion.

"My boy saw you coming," said the woman. "He has been on the watch each day."

"You expected us?" Celia's tone showed slight surprise.

"The Cap'n bade me prepare for your arrival. He went out with my man to fetch you back. You'll find, Miss, that when the Cap'n set his heart on doing something he usually gets what he goes for."

"Well, he went for me—and here I am. And so tired. And hungry."

The house was substantially built and comfortably furnished. The splays of the small windows revealed walls a yard thick. Inside the doorway a wooden partition formed a passage, shutting out light as well as draughts. The kitchen was spacious as became the principal room of the house. In the gable end was a fireplace, nine foot wide, in the centre of which a log fire burned, throwing its warm glow on to the contented face of a tabby cat which sat in comfortable meditation. On either side of the hearth shale slabs served as shelves for receptacles. Above the fireplace, in a place of honour, was a cavalry sabre. A wooden mantel, painted black, displayed an array of brass, pewter and copper which glinted with the flicker of the flames. Guarding them two Staffordshire-ware dogs turned their noses to regard all comers with a haughty china stare. On one wall was a rack which held whips and crops and a fowling-piece. To the right of the fireplace a tall settle shut in the warmth. Though its seat was padded by a cushion, the straightness of its back seemed primarily designed to discourage comfort. To the left of the hearth was a rocker which possessed a more inviting appearance.

Celia thought so, as she sat herself down in it, receiving a cold stare of disapproval from the cat whose reverie her intrusion had disturbed.

"What large outbuildings there are," commented Celia when Tempest joined her.

"It was those which attracted me. In the Middle Ages this was the haunt of bandits who required large stables."

"Bandits!" Celia showed her surprise. "And are you—a bandit?" Her tone was mischievous. Tempest did not smile. Slowly he extracted a pipe from his pocket and began to fill it.

"No!" he said deliberately as he picked up a spill and lit his pipe from the fire. "Not a bandit."

Celia's laugh was forced. "What a relief!"

"Not a bandit," he repeated. "But a law-breaker, none the less. One outside the pale. An outcast from society."

"Jack!" She spoke sharply. "I have wounded you with my nonsense. Please, please do not tell me anything you do not wish to. I—I owe so much to you. You are the kindest and most considerate person I have ever met. Let others judge you if they will. By whatever name you call yourself, you are still—you."

He flashed her a grateful glance. Then fell to puffing deliberately at his pipe and stared into the embers as though inspiration lay there.

"I may as well tell you," he said. "Sooner or later I must."

"You are not to tell me anything you do not wish."

"But I do wish! I—I have a feeling that I would justify myself in your eyes, Celia. A month ago I cared nothing about the opinion of anyone. And now! Your presence has a refining influence, my dear." He spoke with forced lightness, but his eyes were sad.

"Celia, have you ever heard of a debtors' prison?"

"I have heard of them, yes. I am afraid I have never given them much thought."

"Few people do! There are more delectable places! I, who have seen the inside of one, can tell you so."

"You, Jack?"

"Precisely. No, don't interrupt. I will tell you about myself and then, if you will, Jem may take you away to some safe place where you can dwell in seclusion. It seems that you have very little choice at the moment—either to be the wife of a rogue or the companion of a gaol-bird."

"Don't, Jack! You grieve me when you talk like that. Your voice—well, it doesn't sound like you."

"My name, let me say first, is not Jack Tempest."

"It is the only one I know you by. I do not wish to hear any other. It is the name of a man who befriended me in my hour of trial."

"My father was a man in comfortable circumstances. I was sent to University and had a promising career ahead of me. Or so I thought. Do you know what is the easiest thing in the world to do? No, of course you don't. I'll tell you. The easiest thing is to fool a person who trusts you. You have them at your mercy. You take them off their guard. I know. I found out to my cost. I was naturally trusting—that's why the blow cut so deep. I never set much store on money. It is surprising how the good news gets around when a fellow is willing to lend to a friend in trouble. I imagined myself in love with a woman who seemed to be perfect. That was the first lesson I learned. When a thing seems too good to be true, usually it is just that—too good to be true. She got money out of me, of course. And there was a fellow I knew. He was one of those honest persons who would never steal as it was against his principles. He just borrowed and didn't pay back! Between the two of them they had me shorter of money than I had ever been in my life. Then, like a bolt from the blue, two men walked into my room, presented a great sheaf of bills, and asked for payment. I told them I had no money at the moment but would settle in due course. They were adamant. They must have the money or I must go to the Fleet Prison. In my dilemma, I wrote to the man who was my friend. He owed me a matter of a hundred guineas. I begged him to raise the moncy somehow and rescue me from my dilemma. The messenger returned. He had, let's give him his due, a sense of humour. He said he had seen my friend who had told him to say that he was 'not at home'. I knew then that his failure was deliberate. So I was dragged off to prison. I won't harrow your feelings with a description of the Fleet Prison! You, bless you, do not know such sordidness exists in this Christian land. I was there, penned in with the scum of the country—men and women, low, mean, debauched, dwelling in squalor and filth. And the worst of them all were the gaoler and his wife—drunken, thieving scoundrels who, if anyone brought money to a prisoner, pocketed it themselves saying it was due for board. I made two friends there. One was a groom—a steady fellow, whose master had committed suicide after losing his estate at cards."

"Jem?" she asked.

"Your perception is keen. Yes, it was Jem. The other man was a seaman, a great burly fellow with a beard, and the heart of a poet. A Welshman, Heilyn by name, who had sailed round the world, and had been at Trafalgar. He, it was, who gave us a glimmer of hope. It is a strange thing how the slightest incident can seem an augury. He was staring out of the window one day when he exclaimed 'See! The rising gull.' A herring gull which had come from the Thames scavenging, had just flown up from the ground and was gliding with the breeze. 'How I want to be free!' he exclaimed. 'I shall be as free as yon rising gull or there'll be murder done.' Then a recruiting sergeant came in and offered us our freedom if we'd enlist for the Peninsular War. Jem and I did! We were with Moore in Spain and I saw enough soldiering to last me a lifetime. I was lucky—I was made a cornet for capturing a French general whose horse had stumbled at a ford. But that retreat nearly killed me. When we got to the shore at Corunna, I was too weak to crawl into a boat and was carried there by a seaman. On board Jem came to me where I lay in my hammock to say that our Welsh friend was one of the crew. It was like old times. But I am making this last too long."

"You are not; please go on."

"I will make it brief. We were struck by a gale in the Channel

and ran ashore off the coast of Cornwall. We got ashore with
Heilyn's aid on the foretopmast which had broken adrift. Half
the company lost their lives. In the darkness and excitement
Heilyn came to us with the news that there was a footpath to
the cliff top. 'So it's Wales and freedom for us, lads,' he said,
'and seeing we have just been decently drowned, the Government
won't be bothering us any more.'

"That, Celia, is how I became a smuggler."

CHAPTER SIXTEEN

As though he regretted the momentary weakness which had caused him to lay bare his past, Tempest rode away without a word of farewell the following morning. For two days Celia watched in vain for a sight of his figure crossing the distant moors, or listened unsatisfied for the click of a hoof which would betoken his return. She had ample opportunity for reflection. The predominant emotion was sympathy. Her sensitive nature appreciated something of the agony of spirit he had been called upon to endure as the result of his betrayal by those he had befriended. If suffering had made him hard of heart she could detect no sign of it. To her Tempest had been gracious, even chivalrous, and her gratitude was something which it was easier to feel than to express. She admired him for his rebellion against a society which had shown him scant consideration. Then she found herself wondering about the unknown woman he had mentioned so casually. He had made no further mention of her perfidy—a sense of chivalry, perhaps, kept him dumb. Celia grew indignant that any woman should allow a man like Tempest to languish in a debtor's prison on her behalf and make no effort to bring about his release. How she would have liked to have given the creature a piece of her mind! Her wayward thoughts went roving until she found herself contemplating her own predicament. The first fierce flame of resentment against her father's callous treatment had dwindled, but the fire still glowed. Instead of being swayed by her emotions she was now submitting herself to reason. Knowing full well her father's intractable nature she was convinced that she had ruined her future by her conduct. He was a man who, while setting emphasis on a child's obedience to a parent, gave little thought to a parent's obligation to the child he had brought into the world. Though a blow in the face had killed her affection for him, the bonds of convention were hard to throw off. She found herself wondering what her father would think, or more particularly, how he would act. Moreover, she was conscious of the fact that she was not yet of age. She had not meant to defy her parent, nor would she have done so if he had not insisted upon that odious marriage.

"I won't be shackled to that lecherous beast!" she exclaimed aloud. "I'll kill myself first."

How could she respect a law which remained supine while a girl's happiness was bartered away by an inconsiderate parent? She felt rebellious. She had a typical English respect for Law, but, she argued, if the Law demanded reverence, surely one must assume that it was a just Law.

This was her frame of mind when, two evenings later, Tempest returned. She experienced a certain feeling of restraint when she greeted him. He, on his part, appeared taciturn. Wisely she did not question him until he had finished the meal which Jem's wife hastened to spread for him.

He lit his pipe and tried to make himself comfortable on the high-backed settle. Celia sat in the rocking-chair and regarded his face as he stared abstractedly into the fire. Usually the expression was one of alertness but there were times when a touch of wistfulness would creep into the keen eyes. It was the look of one who had waited with exemplary patience for something which had not come to pass; for a promise unfulfilled. There was an undefinable sadness about him that night, though he strove to dissipate it and smiled when she addressed him.

"You have basely deserted me for two long days," she said accusingly.

"You were not deserted, Celia, merely left alone."

"The result was the same."

"I had to go away."

"So I assumed."

"I—I was busy."

"I remember having to work on a sampler which said: *The hand of the diligent maketh rich*."

"You shall give me the sampler for a birthday present."

"I can't. I threw the horrid thing in the fire."

"What reprehensible behaviour! May I ask why?"

"I spelt 'diligent' wrong, and spoiled hours and hours of toil."

"Typical of life, my dear. One mistake will undo years of conscientious endeavour. All the same, I'm sorry you destroyed it. I should have valued it all the more for the mistake. I can't say I like things—or people—to be perfect. I feel more at ease when folk have faults, foibles and failures. They seem more human. I suppose it is because I am such a reprobate myself."

"Jack. I'll not have you speak like that. There is nothing reprobate about you. You are a much wronged man."

"I'm a law-breaker. A gaol-bird. I'll not allow you to forget it. There's no gainsaying that, no matter how charitably-minded you may be, I am no fit companion for you, Celia. I ought not to associate with you, but somehow I can't tear myself away."

"Well, that's a relief. Thank heaven for that!"

"You would be better off without me."

"But I don't wish to be better off. I consider I am well off as it is. Tell me something. Why did you run away for a couple of days? Were you sorry that you opened your heart to me and made your confession?"

"Partly, perhaps. I don't know what came over me. I have never talked before. And I sincerely hope I never shall again. What must you think of me!" He turned almost defiantly. "Come! Say you are disappointed in me!"

She was silent for a moment, biting her lower lip thoughtfully. Then she said slowly: "I must confess, Jack, that I'm a little disappointed in you."

"I knew you would be!" he said morosely. "I am outside the pale. What right have such as I to aspire to the friendship of a woman like you? But I had to tell you, even though you were disappointed in me. I think that's what you said."

"Yes, Jack. I was disappointed in you. Often and often I wondered what you were. When you told me you were a smuggler —I could not help a feeling of disappointment. I thought you were a highwayman at least!"

"Celia!"

"So a mere smuggler seems horribly respectable by comparison."

Jack Tempest put down his pipe and stood up.

"What are you implying?" he demanded, almost harshly. "Do you mean to tell me that you are not really ashamed of me? After the way I have acted?"

"Not ashamed. Say proud, rather. And as for the way in which you have acted, I will tell you this, Jack: had I been in your predicament, I should have done much worse things. I should not have been nearly as forgiving or as tolerant. In any case, who am I to criticize you, I, who am so undutiful a daughter? You cannot, even in your most chivalrous mood, say that I have conducted myself with restraint and decorum."

A smile softened his lips. "I like you all the better for it, Celia," he said. "And I—I wish more than ever that you hadn't burnt the sampler!"

"Good," she said, holding out her hands. "So we are neither of us perfect—thank goodness—so we can be friends."

He put first one of her hands and then the other to his lips. "I would do a lot to serve you, little girl," he said.

"I shall take you at your word, Jack. Now sit down. I want to talk seriously to you. I'm puzzled about this smuggling."

"What puzzles you?"

"I thought smugglers were people who brought contraband goods across the sea in ships."

"That is so."

"Then how can you be a smuggler when you are riding about the country on a fine horse?"

He laughed. "I can see you still crave to turn me into a gentleman of the road. I hate to disillusion you, Celia, but I have never held up anyone—yet."

She shook her head reproachfully. "You are being evasive. I must have a satisfactory answer to my question. Is not smuggling done in ships?"

"True, my dear. The goods are brought to this country in vessels. You may remember my mentioning a broad-backed, bearded sailor, Heilyn, who escaped with us? He has that part of the business in his capable if tarry hands. But what would be the use of bringing rich cargoes to our shores if they remained in caves on our headlands? The landing of contraband is only part of the game. Possibly even more difficult and more risky, is the safe disposal of the goods in this country. That is my part of the venture. I arrange for the convoys which go inland by unfrequented paths. I see to the stopping places along the route. I protect the pack-horse trains from possible capture by riding officers. I bribe people to act as agents for us in inland towns. I have much to do, I can assure you, and it is the more difficult because the work has to be done by stealth. And all the while treachery has to be guarded against. Fortunately most people befriend us because it is to their interest to do so. And the free traders are ugly customers if they suspect treachery. Why, only last month a man was seen talking to two excise officers. He may, for all I know, have been commenting on the weather or anything else as innocent as you like. But that evening, as he sat by his fireside, he heard a roaring sound which was not in the chimney, and saw a greater light than ever came from hearth or lamp. Then he realized that his thatch was ablaze."

"Luckless fellow!"

"It was a hint to him to be more careful in his choice of companions."

Her eyes were fixed on his, and he noticed they sparkled with suppressed excitement.

"It sounds risky."

"Yes, it is risky, Celia. That is one of its attractions. I like pitting my wits against people. And the game is going to become increasingly difficult."

"What makes you say that?"

"The presence of this new friend of yours."

Celia looked puzzled. "My new friend?" she queried, perplexed.

"Acquaintance then. By name Thomas Telford, Esquire."

"The great engineer? I cannot claim even his acquaintance, Jack. It has been my pleasure to speak to him, that is all. But how will he interfere with you?"

"He is opening up the country, Celia. His great new road through the mountains will mean that mail coaches, and all manner of traffic, will come this way regularly. Hitherto we have been able to roam almost unwatched and unnoticed about this wild and barren land. Our pack-horse trains have passed in the dark unseen save by cottagers whose mouths are stopped by gifts. The drovers who make their way by lonely moors to the Shropshire border, have carried many a parcel slung on animals concealed in the midst of their herds. But now, with new-comers arriving, with tourists driving along the new road, with officers of the law able to explore new territory, our task will be harder than ever."

"Why, it is almost like a game—a big, dangerous game. First one side makes a move, and then the other does something to counteract it. I had not thought that a road could mean so much."

"The road, my dear, the common road which folk take for granted, is the harbinger of civilization, the fore-runner of commerce. Since the days when Rome thrust its great highways to the uttermost corners of its empire, the road has played a vital part in the life of mankind. If this lonely land, with its silent grandeur, becomes populated; if towns spring up in our valleys and along our coast; if commerce comes to a country which knew nothing but husbandry, it will be because roads have made these things possible. It will be a few years yet before Mr. Telford constructs his great road. If we are quick we will be able to reap our harvest uninterrupted—but there is no time to lose."

"And then, what?"

"For me? I scarce know. Perhaps, with my ill-gotten wealth, I will purchase an estate in some remote part of Britain and settle down to sober respectability. Strange, is it not, how we yearn for respectability? It is almost a patronizing word. Can you picture me respectable, Celia?" His tone held mockery.

"I think you would be bored, Jack."

"You are right. I must have change. I must have adventure. Better risk than boredom."

"I prophesy that you will not be able to tear yourself away from this fascinating adventure on which you have embarked," she assured him. She moved nearer to him, coaxing.

"And now, dear Jack," her tone was mellifluous, "I want you to accept a new recruit."

"A new recruit? I do not understand."

"I want you to let me join your ranks."

"You! My dear Celia, don't be ridiculous. Never would I dream of such a thing. Put the misbegotten idea out of your pretty head."

"It is not ridiculous, Jack. I cannot go home. That surely is obvious to you. I have burnt my boats. I must do something to justify my existence."

"You don't know what you say. Ours is a hard life."

"I have sampled a little of it, and found it anything but disagreeable."

"You have been a guest in, shall we say, unusual places. There is greater risk and greater discomfort to be encountered than living in isolated farms, I can assure you."

"But I am homeless—I was going to say, and almost penniless. If I am not now penniless I shall be before long. How, then, would you suggest that I live?"

"There is no need for you to give it a thought. I have plenty of money concealed in one place and another—enough to keep you in comfort all your days."

"Jack! As if I should allow you to spend it on me."

"I have to spend it on somebody. It is no use in a hole in the ground, and I dare not visit a bank. No, be sensible."

"I am sensible. It is you who are not. Surely I could do something to help?"

He began to pace the room. "You place me in a quandary. I find it hard to refuse you anything. But the idea is preposterous."

"You are weakening! I warn you I mean to have my way. I shall coax you, cajole you, bother you, threaten you, pester you until you agree!"

"But I am not alone in this. I must consult Jem."

"Don't bother about Jem. I can talk Jem round."

"I believe you could!" said Tempest. There was admiration in his tones. "You would talk him round just like you talk me."

"That means you assent? Oh, I knew you would. How sensible of you!"

"Well, just for a short while—as an experiment. I feel I ought not to, yet—heaven help me—I can't bear to contemplate parting with you, and you must either come in with us or depart."

CHAPTER SEVENTEEN

WHEN Harry Standish returned to the road through the Welsh hills, sooner, it must be confessed, than he anticipated—he felt weary but elated. His action at Squire Upton's house though not spectacular had not been without its practical advantage. He was a little apprehensive about the possible outcome of his conduct, but he dismissed this resolutely from his mind, failing to see what good came of thinking about an unpleasant subject when there was one infinitely more pleasing on which the imagination could dwell. The lovely Celia, by some means unknown to him, had managed to effect an escape. She would, he trusted, henceforth be immune from the undesirable attentions of the amorous baronet. From a brief encounter with Sir Guy Goadby, Harry had acquired an antipathy not unlike that held by the fair Celia. More than ever he was on her side. At first he had chosen to espouse her cause from devotion to her; to this was now added her personal execration of the man.

Harry found Mr. Telford in an inn at Capel Curig. Rain was steadily falling and the engineer was glad of an excuse to remain indoors to attend to clerical work which had been allowed to accumulate over-long. On one table was a draft-board and instruments; on another a model of cardboard and string in course of construction. Mr. Telford regarded his young helper quizzically. Despite his fifty odd years his cheeks retained the healthy colour and freshness of youth, and in his eyes, though he did not smile, there lingered the suspicion of a kindly gleam. As a boy he had acquired the sobriquet of 'Laughing Tam' and success had not eradicated the bright twinkle.

"You're back again sooner than I expected, young man," he said. "Has all gone well? I hope you've rescued the lassie from the pestering villain."

"I have done what I could, Mr. Telford," said Harry, and briefly outlined his escapade. Mr. Telford sat with pencil poised, listening to every word.

"So you locked 'em in their own stable, eh?" He gave a

grim chuckle. "It's a pity you did not remain to overhear their observations. Well, you've broken the law, I'm thinking. I trust you will not suffer the consequences."

"It was done without premeditation, Mr. Telford," said Harry earnestly. "And I did so want her to get away. You must not blame me."

"Blame you? Who said a word about blaming you, lad? I'd have done much the same—if I had thought of it—were I in your position. So the lassie is running away? She has spirit! Running away—running away——" He stared out of the window, reminiscent, a dreamy look in his kindly eyes. "I call to mind an apprentice who ran away once, Harry Standish! He was only a wee laddie. His mother was a widow and thought it mighty fine when he was apprenticed to a master-mason to learn his trade. Och! He was a devil, that man!"

"So you ran away, sir?"

"*I* ran away? Who said a word about me?"

Harry gave a superior smile and scorned to answer.

"Well, there's no point in dissembling," went on Mr. Telford. "I was the lad who was articled to the master-mason of Lochmaben. For months he starved me and used me cruelly. So I ran across the hills back home. It was breaking the law, which is hard on run-away apprentices, but nothing came of it and I finished my apprenticeship with a kindlier master. Ah well, it seems long since. And it's long since I came riding to London on a borrowed nag in search of fame and fortune."

"And you've found both, sir."

"Well, I'll not brag too much about the fortune. I'm working for the Government, you notice. And talking of the Government, it is full time I submitted another report, so you can get your quill sharpened and write what I dictate. You young fellows have the benefit of education. I picked up what I could in a parish school, and after that I taught myself."

"You're a genius, Mr. Telford," exclaimed Harry ardently.

"Nay, lad, just a man who'se not afraid of hard work and one who has some spark within him which has for ever told him he was never meant to be a common drudge."

Harry settled to his task and, in his neat calligraphy, copied page after page of a report on the progress of the road. It was no new experience for him. When he had completed the report, Mr. Telford read it through in the deliberate, thorough manner which characterized all he undertook.

"You write a neat hand, Standish. I have little patience for folk whose writing is like that of a spider that's strayed into the ink-well. What's worth doing is worth doing well."

Telford walked to the window and looked across the glistening street, watching the rain drops course down the pane. A shepherd with a sodden sack about his shoulders and a thin hazel switch in his hand, squelched past, herding a small flock of soaking sheep aided by a bedraggled sheep-dog. The patter of the numerous tiny hoofs on the road and an occasional bleat of protest, proclaimed their passing. The great engineer regarded them sympathetically. Something in his blood, perhaps, responded to their plight, for his long-dead father had been a shepherd in far-off Dumfriesshire. Telford stared disapprovingly at the tracks in the mud. It was no road, this! Not what he considered a road. There was no foundation to it, and how could a road stand up to the hard wear of constant traffic if it lacked foundation? There were contractors, he knew, who preferred Macadam's method. They said that the Telford way was too expensive, but Thomas Telford held to his principles. He would admit that the initial cost of his road-making was considerable, but in the long run it would prove the cheaper because there would be less expenditure on maintenance. And there were quarries in abundance in this mountainous land! He had undertaken some mighty works in his lifetime, had this engineer who was to be known as the Colossus of Roads. His mind went back to those early struggling days when he rose to be Surveyor of Public Works for Shropshire. Then his mind drifted to the time when the Government appointed him to report on the public communications of Scotland. He had superintended the construction of nine hundred miles of road in his beloved Scotland and over a hundred bridges. It wasn't only roads which came beneath his spell. There was the Portsmouth dockyard improvement, the Caledonian Canal, the harbour works at Wick, and Aberdeen and Bamff and Leith. . . . So his mind ran on. But this road to Holyhead was to be the greatest feat of all.

Down in the Midlands where the land was level, his task was comparatively easy but here, in rocky, remote Snowdonia, he encountered a task worthy of the skill of a man whose character was as rugged as the hills against which he strove. How sorely his skill was needed here. It was a patchwork roadway, the present one. In sundry places local squires combined to make a turnpike, collecting tolls for its upkeep, but once the road passed beyond their Trust, it lapsed into its primitive state. Perhaps a yeoman farmer would repair a stretch or the owner of a quarry would surface a length for the convenience of his own conveyances. Then the road would return again to an unfenced route across the wild heathland, a miserable track, a succession of circuitous and craggy inequalities, a troublesome, dangerous way, where the wayfarer was at the mercy of the elements.

But Thomas Telford meant to rectify all this. No man was farther removed from vanity of ostentation, but he had a proper appreciation of his calling and he was resolved to build a highway which would be a memorial to his name for all time.

It would be costly, but the Government was behind the scheme and they could afford the cost, despite the war with Napoleon. They would have to afford the cost for he was resolved that his ship was not to be spoiled for the sake of a ha'porth of tar. The route to Dublin from Whitehall must be made smooth not merely for the comfort of Irish Members of Parliament, but for the more expeditious transaction of business of State.

Telford came back from his day-dreaming and turned to his amenuensis.

"What's the distance of the road, Harry?"

There was only one road. "The distance, sir, from London to Holyhead is two hundred and sixty miles."

"And a half," added Telford. "It's a straight road—as roads go. Which means a direct road. And it should satisfy our Irish friends when they wish to hasten to the capital. Or more likely, hasten away from it, to seek the charms of Dublin's fair city. We must finish it by 1825, Harry."

"Yes, sir," replied Harry dutifully.

"It's not the road which will take the time and test our

ingenuity, though there are viaducts and bridges enough required in this wild country. It is crossing the Menai Straits."

"The ferry is not a long one, sir."

"Ferry! There must be no ferry on a Government Road from London to Holyhead. The Straits will be bridged!"

"Sir, it's impossible!" Harry Standish was incredulous. "A bridge of that size could not be erected. No bridge could take the strain of such a span."

He spoke with conviction. The engineer merely smiled; it was a tolerant smile. "I don't think it is impossible, lad. I have a feeling my life will be spared to see the bridge an accomplished fact. A bridge which will be the talk of Europe. I see it already, in my mind. It will be a strong bridge, a useful bridge, and it shall also be a thing of beauty."

A dreamy look came to his eyes. "The human mind is a strange and unaccountable medium, lad. Did it ever strike you that everything that has ever been made by men was first fashioned in the mind? The mind comprehends before the hands function."

He walked to the model and began to touch it gently with delicate fingers.

"The bridge will come," he said softly. "It is bound to come. Not for nothing did I get the idea of suspension. I can see the completed structure. But it will take time. And we must experiment."

Harry stared at the model. It seemed fragile, ridiculously fragile. A toy for a child, perhaps. It was one thing to construct a model; it was another task to fling a gigantic structure across the swirling straits.

Mr. Telford was speaking again. "You know the city of Chester, of course?"

"I have been to Chester, sir."

"You must go again. I want you to follow the course of the turnpikes right through to Bangor. I must make the journey myself the moment I have time. In the meanwhile do you survey it and submit a report. It will interest me to see how you attempt it. Start from Chester. You will travel to Holywell. Then over the moorlands to the city of St. Asaph. From there a new turn-pike goes to the market town of Abergele. Thence over Penmaen

Head—an awkward place—to the ferry of the Conway River. Tell me your opinion of the Sychnant Pass as a coach road."

Telford gave a grim smile. "And don't forget drainage. Road drainage is of vital consequence! We shall meet in Bangor in two weeks' time. At the Penrhyn Arms. I don't want too much detail. What I am anxious to receive is an account of *your* impressions. And if you are dubious about our ability to bridge the Menai Straits, my boy, just tell me whether you consider we can span the Conway River. It is a lesser task than the Menai, but scarcely less important."

Telford bent over his model, and Standish, concluding that the interview was ended, quietly withdrew from the room. He stared through the street doorway into the grey mist at the grey houses opposite.

The rutted roadway seemed to be alive with runlets. The village was deserted. Rain clouds clung to the hills, obscuring their tops. The air was full of the not unmusical tinkle of rain which ran from spouts into water-butts, rain which splashed into puddles, rain which pattered on roofs. Rain! Rain! Rain! And all the while Harry was thinking not of the weather, nor of Mr. Telford's bridges, not of the Chester to Bangor subsidiary road. Harry's thoughts had drifted away from reality into the kingdom of romance. He wondered where Celia was. He wondered whether she was safe and comfortable in weather such as this. He wondered whether she was still enjoying her freedom. Most of all he wondered whether he would see her again.

With an effort he brought himself back into the world of reality. Mr. Telford had spoken kindly, but Harry knew him well enough to know that he was not a man to countenance dallying. He thrust a few clothes into his saddle-bags, struggled into his oilskins, and splashed across the inn yard to the stables, where he proceeded to saddle his reluctant horse.

There were few people about. A stable-man, seated on an oats bin, took a pipe from his mouth and spat into the yard. It expressed his opinion of any man who was unbalanced enough to venture out in such rain.

Harry climbed into the saddle before the rain could damp

it, and pulled his oilskins closely about him, hoping that the downpour would find no penetrable place in his protective clothing. He urged his nag into the village street, turning his head towards Bettws-y-Coed and the Conway Valley, that verdant, pleasant, winding vale which would prove so acceptable a change after the bleak uplands of Hiraethog or the towering crags of the Nantffrancon Pass.

CHAPTER EIGHTEEN

CELIA awoke the following morning with the feeling of mingled uncertainty and excitement which comes to those who are about to embark on an adventure into the unknown. The sun shone and the morning air was broken by the trilling and twittering of small birds rejoicing that winter was past. It was, thought Celia, a happy augury. She lay awhile staring out of the small sun-bathed window into the clear blue of the morning sky, yet she was scarcely aware of the heavens which held her gaze, for her mind was given over to imagery. As one who turns back the pages of a book she recalled the events of the past few weeks—incidents which had changed the entire tenor of her life, events which had metamorphosed her into a woman who seemed a stranger to her original self. The step she was resolved to take would mean a wholly new form of living. This change she had already sampled. Gone was the life of convention, gone the aimless existence in a stately home where servile servants hastened to obey, gone the fastidious care of appearance, the fashionable chatter; gone, too, comfort and security. In its place she was offered privation—and freedom. Never before had she known the true meaning of freedom. As a cage-bird which finds its prison door left open hesitates to take advantage of the liberty offered, so Celia found herself incapable of imagining what manner of life she would lead when she was accountable to no one for her actions. It seemed paradoxical that from people who would have been regarded as uncultured she received greater consideration than from those who prided themselves on their social position. She saw for the first time how thin was the veneer which coated polished society. If going back to the life of fashion meant marriage to Sir Guy, the rough existence of the hills was preferable. A hard look crept for a moment into her eloquent eyes. She shrank back from the mere recollection of Goad by as one would recoil from a poisonous snake.

A soft tapping on the door aroused her from her reverie. It was a strange tapping, either timid or cautious, not the knock with which she had grown familiar.

She drew a shawl about her shoulders and called "Come in."

As the door opened her eyes rested on the swarthy features and large dark eyes of the young gipsy woman, Miriam.

Celia smiled her welcome. "I did not expect to see you. Where have you come from?"

"My husband sent me, Mistress."

"I am pleased to see you again. I do not forget the kindness you showed me at your encampment. How is your little baby?"

"He is healthy and happy, Mistress. I have him downstairs. You may like to see him when you get up."

"Indeed I shall wish to see him."

Miriam lowered her eyes and looked pensive. "May I speak my mind, Mistress?" she inquired softly.

"Of course. What is it you wish to say?"

"The Captain told me how you wished to join our band. Is it wise, Mistress? You have been brought up in a fine home. I have seen it from the park fence and it is great and grand. You do not know what hardship means."

"I have thought of all that."

"You will be taken away from your friends."

"I shall make fresh ones. Perhaps better ones."

"The Law can be hard and cruel."

"Respectable members of society can be cruel also."

"Your mind is made up?"

"It is. My father would force me to wed a man I detest and despise. I will not go back. I prefer my freedom."

"Then, Mistress, if you are resolved, the Captain says that I am to remain with you to serve you. If that is your pleasure."

"How thoughtful of him. And how good of you to consent. You are willing?"

"It would give me pleasure provided I may bring my little son with me always."

"Of course."

"And sometimes I may grow restless for the free life of the woods and the moors. . . ."

"You shall not be tied too strictly. I promise you."

"Then all is good." Miriam smiled and withdrew.

As Celia dressed she mused. Tempest was not only thoughtful but considerate. Of course she must have a woman companion.

I

When Celia reached the kitchen she was aware of a bustling activity which was foreign to the customary leisurely atmosphere of the place. Food was being stacked and packed. There was activity, too, in the yard. The sunlight had something to do with it, for every living creature seemed to be active, glad of the warmth and brightness after the long spell of winter. The cattle were turned out to pasture where sedate cows kicked their heels in joyous abandon with unbecoming lack of bovine dignity. Several horses were in the yard, some drinking at the trough, others dozing in the sunshine. Then Celia's eyes lit on a caravan in the lane—a bright green caravan with red wheels and brass-work which twinkled in the sunlight. There, too, was the gipsy Jasper, and the old crone and the youth Gideon. All showed white teeth in friendly smiles when she appeared.

At the sound of her voice one of the stable doors was thrust hastily back and Tempest strode forth, bare-armed and business-like.

"What a lovely day!" she exclaimed. "I blame myself for being so slothful. I feel as if I had missed something delightful."

"The day is yet young," he assured her.

"Is it the sunlight which is the cause of all this com-motion? Is some big undertaking afoot? I confess I'm all curiosity."

"Let us attribute it to the weather. It drives one out of doors."

He crossed to a bench near the back door. "Sit down," he said, and made a place for himself at her side. For a moment they were quiet, listening to the musical hissing of Jem as he curry-combed Jess, the chestnut mare.

Then Tempest spoke. "You have seen Miriam?"

"Indeed I have. How thoughtful of you to arrange for her to be in attendance!"

"You will find her unused to civilized ways. Do not expect her to act as a lady's maid. But she is faithful and is knowledge-able so far as her limited experience goes. She is the most suitable person I can think of."

"I don't really need a maid, Jack. I have already learned to manage without one."

"You must have a chaperon of some sort, Celia. Even if you choose to lead this unconventional life, there is your good name to think of."

"It never entered my head. You are far-seeing, Jack."

"It would grieve me if any ill was spoken of you. You have talked with Miriam?"

"Yes. It was she who told me of the arrangement you had made."

"Nothing else?"

"No, I don't think so."

"She did not say why they arrived here in the night? She is very discreet. It is a hopeful sign."

"Why have they come?"

"With news which is of interest to you."

"Bad news, Jack?" she asked quickly.

"Not good news. Your father and his undesirable neighbour are not taking your disappearance kindly. They have a number of men, including constables, making inquiries, and are searching the countryside for you."

"Oh! I suppose that is to be expected."

"Jasper found them heading in this direction."

"Bother!"

"That was to be expected. If you are to remain undiscovered we must get you far into the country. You are resolved not to return to your home?"

"Quite resolved, Jack. My mind is made up. Just assume that and it will save time!"

"Very well. That means we must go much farther afield. I shall not be easy in my mind until we reach the coast."

"Why the coast?"

"Because, if they press us too hotly, there is always the sea as a means of escape. We have boats and ships at our disposal. If they find out where you stay we can whisk you off to Ireland or Pembroke Dock, North Devon, the Isle of Man. Oh! anywhere you care to choose."

"What a wonderful man you are. No wonder the smugglers made you their organizer."

"Go to your room and pack."

"We start right away?"

"As soon as you are ready. I feel restless. Miriam will bring you some gipsy clothes—your own are far too conspicuous."

"I am to be disguised? This grows more exciting, Jack. I am just loving this adventure."

He smiled. "I hope it will prove enjoyable. All the way through." His tone was sincere but lacked conviction.

When Celia descended the stairs after Miriam's ministrations she was barely recognizable. Her fair hair was concealed by a tightly bound kerchief of red. She wore a black skirt and yellow blouse, the latter almost concealed by a grey shawl. The Dresden China freshness of her complexion had been subdued to a sunburnt shade. Celia collected everything she possessed, save the money concealed in the Evans's barn.

It was decided to place all her belongings in the caravan in which she was to ride for a while. The party moved forward across the moors with the careful precision of a military advance. Jem rode ahead and Tempest lingered well behind. The boy Gideon on a piebald pony rode well on the right flank.

As the caravan bumped slowly forward, Celia experienced a thrill of excitement. She kept glancing about her, watching first one distant horseman and then another. Progress, so far as she was concerned, was too slow. She wished something would happen!

The old dame nursed the slumbering baby as Miriam chose to walk with her husband at the horse's head. The gipsies had travelled thus so often that the proceeding did not hold for them the novelty which Celia experienced.

By noon they were nearing less wild country where the hollows were darkened by clumps of leafy trees. At one of these, where there was a brook, they halted for a mid-day meal. Celia was glad to stretch her legs. Tempest joined the party. Jasper borrowed the black and rode off to keep watch over the back trail. Miriam lit a fire with the aid of a tinder-box from the caravan and the old woman busied herself preparing a meal. Celia watched the orange flames licking the black crock suspended over them, thinking what a colourful picture was afforded; Tempest, less artistic, wondered how soon it would be before they ate. He was still restless; though Celia endeavoured to engage him in conversation his mind was elsewhere. Several times he walked to the edge of the glade to scan the track along which they had passed.

"Jasper is there, Master," commented Miriam quietly. "Have no fear. Jasper's eyes are keen. If anyone suspicious comes he will give the cry of the curlew thrice."

They gathered around the fire to eat the stew which had been heated. Once the cry of a curlew sounded and Celia put down her spoon to glance about her with apprehension in her eyes. Miriam smiled. "It is the real curlew," she explained. "See," and she pointed to a big brown bird with the long curving bill, which flapped slowly towards the moors.

The next interruption was the soft thudding of galloping hoofs. Gideon on the piebald came up at a gallop, and without dismounting, the boy called out that Jem had signalled him that a stranger was approaching from the west. He was off again promptly. The sound of his pony's hoofs faded, and he was lost to sight in a hollow of the hills.

Tempest took charge.

"Go into the caravan, Celia," he ordered. "Keep in the shadow at the rear. Miriam, you and your mother must remain here, eating and talking. If you are asked you can say your husband is in the woods and will return any moment. I will lie hidden behind that leafy mound in case I should be needed."

As he glided silently away Celia noticed that he looked at the priming of his pistol. Obediently the girl entered the caravan. The old crone followed her to the door.

"Nurse the baby!" she commanded in a hoarse whisper. "It is your child, remember."

Then there was silence until the sound of a slowly trotting horse broke the stillness.

A tall, dark-featured man clad in a blue coat halted, and stared down at the group beside the fire. He had a prominent jaw and a cast in the left eye—an unprepossessing fellow.

"Good day," he began, and his eyes roved over the encampment. "Nice weather we're having."

"We haven't had it long." Miriam was curt.

"That's a fact. Any chance of a bite to eat?"

"You'd better ask my husband."

"Where might he be?"

"Just over there. He'll be back any minute."

"Reckon he'd best keep an eye on his missus, if that's what you be. 'Taint every day one sees as pretty a lass."

"If that's all you have to say, you need not stay any longer. Good day."

The man was not abashed by the snub.

"You haven't by any chance, seen any other pretty gal about these parts?"

"I have not. And if I had I'd not be telling you."

"How's that?"

"I've too much regard for a pretty girl."

"Meanin' I've a way with the ladies. You must put it down to my good looks! Pretty smart-looking waggon you've got! Mind if I takes a look inside?"

He got off his horse and took a step towards the caravan. Miriam was on her feet. "What are you?" she demanded "A cut-purse? Leave our caravan alone. If my husband catches you——"

The man gave a laugh. Putting one foot on the lowest rung of the ladder he thrust back the half-door.

"Ah-ha! There's somebody else here I see."

It was the old dame who came to the rescue. "Shame on you!" she croaked. "Pretty pass it is when a woman can't feed her baby without being pestered by the likes of you."

"We're a hot-blooded race," said Miriam calmly. "If you offend one you offend all. Then watch out for a knife in your back."

"Threaten me, would you? You'll sing small, my lass, if I reports you to the magistrates."

"Try it, and see what happens to you." She raised her voice. "Jasper! Come here. There's a vagabond interfering with us."

There was a movement among the trees.

"Now, there's no need of that!" said the man hastily as he fumbled for his stirrup. "No need whatever. I'm just a companionable passer-by who wants a friendly word."

He rode slowly away. Tempest came quietly from the bushes and stood beside Miriam, staring after his receding figure. "I wonder," he said softly.

Celia came to the caravan door and looked down upon them.

"May I come out now?" she asked. "Miriam, I think you were just splendid. You almost frightened me."

No one spoke.

"What are you all staring at?" asked Celia, perplexed.

Miriam took a pace forward. Her sunburnt hand pointed. Beneath the red kerchief bound about Celia's head hung a strand of golden hair.

"You can't afford to be careless," said Tempest succinctly.

"Oh! I don't know how it slipped. But I am sure he could not have noticed it. I was right in the shadow at the back and he only glanced in for a minute."

"I hope you are right. Now hurry, and finish your meal. No more caravan comfort for you, my dear. I shall feel happier when you are on horseback again. That rogue, if I am any judge, was merely one of the advance party. They are not letting the grass grow under their feet! Our next encounter may be more serious."

CHAPTER NINETEEN

DISQUIETUDE is a strange emotion. There are occasions when it creeps upon one mysteriously as though attuned ears have caught mystic whisperings. Tempest experienced disquietude as he helped Celia into the saddle of the led horse. He kept glancing about him uneasily. Celia, too, felt disturbed, but she tried to make light of her agitation. Why should they be perturbed because a man with a villainous squint chose to make himself objectionable?

The party rode from the wooded hollow and turned southward, moving away from the track which wound across the moors. Tempest called Gideon to him and bade the boy follow in the distance, keeping them in sight.

"I am foolish, I know," confessed Celia as their horses moved silently over the smooth turf, "but the presence of that man has upset me. He seemed evil. Do you think there is any reason for concern?"

"I hope not," replied Tempest quietly, but Celia noticed that even as he spoke he glanced over his shoulder.

"Do you know, I seem to catch, all the while, a soft voice whispering, 'You are followed! You are followed.' "

"Your imagination is running away with you, Celia."

"Yes, of course it is only my imagination. In any case—I have you. You are my comfort and my strength, Jack. You are like the shadow of a tree in a parched land. You are a fortress. A rock."

"I appear to be an assortment of widely-varied things, my dear! By whatever name you choose to call me, I am a friend who is solicitous of your welfare; one who wishes you happiness. One who, if it is humanly possible, means to save you from the fate which threatens you."

"I know," she replied simply. "The mere thought of it sustains me."

It was wild land they were traversing, undulating, the grass broken by outcroppings of limestone, darkened in places by patches of gorse or heather. In moist hollows reeds grew sharp and straight like clumps of lances. They heard the curlews calling overhead. They saw the pied lapwings tumble in the air as they beat the breeze with their broad wings. Beside a foaming stream they would find the lonely stone-built cot of some shepherd, and the hillside round about would be dotted with the nimble sheep which were his charge. The land was well-nigh uninhabited. All the while, whenever they lifted their gaze westward, they saw rough, rugged mountains, dark against the sky, with patches of snow still streaking the hollows and crevices of their gaunt slopes.

"It will not be as bleak as this when we reach our journey's end," he assured her. "You will find it green and pleasant on the coast. The beauties and the charm of North Wales have not yet been discovered by those who dwell in the south."

"I shall be content to follow where you lead."

Tempest turned in his saddle to look back. Celia, too, turned. Like a dark speck on the broad moor they could see young Gideon dutifully following on his sturdy pony, a link between them and the distant caravan.

"What made you bother about the caravan?" asked Celia.

"It is for your comfort. I did not want you caught in a storm in some exposed place. I recollect you had a serious illness. I do not wish you to have another."

So they rode on until the sun sank behind the mountains, throwing their outline in dark silhouette against the flushed sky. The shades of evening gathered in the hollows.

"We had better bear more to the right—over there, where the road runs. There is an inn not far away where you may spend the night. It is small and not much frequented but the people belong to our company and are dependable."

Through the fading light they could see the track in the distance. It was devoid of fence or wall or hedgerow. Its ends were lost in gloom so that it seemed to come from nowhere and to go nowhere. At least that was the thought which passed through Celia's mind, and she was about to say as much when a faint cry caused both to turn. They saw Gideon waving to them as his sturdy piebald approached at a gallop.

"Something's wrong," said Celia. Tempest did not speak until Gideon brought his pony slithering to a standstill.

"That man's come back to the caravan! I saw him. They signalled me to tell you."

"My valise!" exclaimed Celia. "If he searches he will be sure to find it."

Tempest frowned. "I should have brought it away," he said.

"Jack! Don't reproach yourself. You can't think of everything."

"Gideon, you remember the Bedol Inn?"

The boy nodded.

"Conduct this lady there. Watch over her until I return."

Fragments of turf flew into the air as the great black horse leaped forward at the touch of the spur. For a moment Celia watched admiringly as Tempest, straight of shoulder, galloped in the direction of the caravan.

Gideon ventured a proud glance as he drew his pony alongside the fair lady he was privileged to escort.

"Is the inn far away?" inquired Celia.

"Not far, just beyond that hill ahead."

"What is it called?"

"We call it the Bedol. That is Welsh for Horseshoe."

They cantered until they reached the mountain road. Then, rounding a bend, Celia saw that the way dipped, and beside it, sheltered from the winds by a spur of rock, just where a brook crossed the road, was a square, stone-built structure which had a faded sign swinging. On the sign was a crudely painted horseshoe, and at one corner she saw a touch of white paint. Its presence was reassuring. She would be among friends. Gideon held her horse while she dismounted, then gathering both bridles, waited while Celia rapped on the door.

A swarthy, low-browed man opened it and stared.

"We have just been watching the gulls rising," she remarked boldly. "May I have a room for the night? And a meal?"

He nodded his head. "Come inside."

"Take the horses to the stable, Gideon," she ordered, and followed the man into the slate-flagged passage. He threw open the door of a small room. A fire burned in the grate.

"I will fetch candles," said the man. He went outside and closed the shutters, then returned with a brass candlestick in each hand. "To cook a meal—it will take some time," he said, speaking deliberately as though he was not sure of his words.

"I do not mind. Set the meal for two."

The man withdrew and the latch clicked. Celia tossed her gloves on the table, opened her coat and held her hands to the blaze. Now that the sun was down the air was chill. When she had warmed herself she took off her coat. A horsehair-covered chair with a high mahogany back stood beside the fire. She seated herself and put her feet on the black-leaded fender. There was comfort in the fire. She sat staring into the flames, wishing Jack Tempest would hurry back. She missed him. His presence filled her with assurance. When he was at her side she felt care-free—almost reckless. Once she was alone she became a prey to forebodings. A woman entered to lay the cloth on a round three-legged table. Celia was conscious of the clink of cutlery but, absorbed in her thoughts, she did not look up. There was no further sound but the flicker of the flames. Then a horse's hoofs clattered in front of the inn. There was a pause and she heard the animal led away.

When a manly stride sounded in the passage she looked up with an expectant smile.

"How quick you have been, Jack!" she exclaimed, as the latch clicked.

"Oh!"

The door was flung back and Sir Guy Goadby stood, riding-crop in hand, regarding her with a mixture of incredulity and satisfaction.

"Ah! So I have found you. Might I observe that my name is not Jack, and I have not been quick. It has taken me a devilish long time to run you to earth. But I knew that I would get you sooner or later."

"You!" It was all Celia uttered. She stared uncomprehendingly.

"You do not appear pleased to see me!" Sir Guy gave an urbane bow. "I have been to no little pains to find you. That, surely, may be interpreted as a compliment."

"To your own vanity, not to me." Celia spoke bitterly.

"Perhaps you are right. I am, I confess, a proud man—one who is not to be trifled with. I like having my own way.

Woe betide the person, man or woman, who tries to thwart me.
But let us talk of something more pleasant, my dear Celia. You
forget that you are my betrothed wife."

"I will never be your wife."

"Oh, but you will! I must remind you that you are not yet
of age, and it is your duty and your obligation to obey your
parent."

"I am old enough to know my own mind, and I have no
longer any regard for a father who barters his daughter's happiness."

"I think you are treating your father very badly."

"What you mean is that you think I am treating you very
badly. I am. And I shall continue to do so. Can't you see reason?
What prospect is there of a happy marriage? Nothing you could
ever do would make me care for you. You say I treat you badly.
I should treat you worse if you forced me into this odious marriage. If you drive me too far I might even poison you."

Sir Guy chuckled. "A lass of spirit."

Celia turned to the fire as if seeking consolation in its flames.
There was a slight commotion outside. The sound of wheels and
hoofs and voices. Sir Guy frowned.

"Landlord!" he shouted, flinging open the door. "Where are
you, fellow? Here's a sovereign for you. See that I am not
interrupted."

Celia was staring towards the shuttered windows, a faint
hope dawning in her eyes.

If Tempest had returned, or Jasper, all would be well. But
though she strained her ears she could catch no familiar sound.
The new-comers must be strangers. Her spirits sank.

Then the latch clicked and Sir Guy wheeled angrily.

"This room is private!" he said curtly to a man standing in
the passage.

"I was unaware I was intruding——" began the new-comer.

"You are. You will pardon my abruptness, but I cannot
have this interruption. The landlord, doubtless, will attend to
you elsewhere."

The door was beginning to close when Celia started to her feet.

"Mr. Telford!" she cried. "Don't go! Mr. Telford, please
come in."

"Hello. Somebody appears to know me!" said the voice. A friendly voice. A welcome voice. Celia had reached the stage when one clutches at straws, and Thomas Telford, Esquire, was a substantial straw.

"Please come in!" she entreated. "Please do."

"Be quiet!" Sir Guy was peremptory. "I am sorry, sir, but I must ask you to retire. The lady is a little distraught."

"Then that is all the more reason why I should humour her, sir."

"You shall not enter!" said Sir Guy, barring his way.

"You'll stop me? You are uncouth, sir. Your conduct puts a different complexion on things. I have half a dozen sturdy fellows outside within call. Do you step aside and allow me to join this lady, or do I call them, and have you thrown into the roadway?"

"I shall summon you for assault if you lay hands on me."

"You may summon and be damned."

"Mr. Telford," cried Celia. "Please protect me."

"Protect is it? Ay, that I will, lassie. Have no fear."

"This lady is my affianced bride. I would have you know that I shall not tolerate interference."

"You have no say in the matter. Stand aside," said Telford, pushing past. "Now, my dear, what's the trouble? I can plainly see you are upset. Is it your wish that you go with this man?"

"No! No! No! Don't let him take me away, Mr. Telford, please."

"I'll not. Set your mind at rest. It would appear that my arrival was opportune—I might almost say providential."

"You are acting in a most reprehensible manner, sir," said Sir Guy scowling. "I warn you that the consequences will be serious. I am a baronet, and I am also a magistrate."

"Ay, I dare say. It is only the presence of a lady of tender susceptibilities which makes me moderate my language, but let me tell you this. I care not a straw for your baronetcy or your magistracy or whatever other fancy titles you like to adorn yourself with. I tell you that you are a rascal to persecute a helpless, motherless lass! I, for one, am not standing by idle to see injustice done!"

"You will hear more of this!" Sir Guy was livid with anger.

"I gather that you are this engineer who makes roads. I will see to it that your conduct is reported in the proper Governmental quarters."

"Do so. I have some influential friends in those same Governmental quarters. Men who, maybe, hold me in higher esteem than they would a libertine who forces a sweet maid into marriage against her will."

"I have her father's permission——"

"And I have her word that she does not want you. That is good enough for me."

"You shall hear more of this."

"Oh, go away with you. You have told me that twice. Words never hurt any man, and if you want to fight with something more powerful than words, Tom Telford was never a man to shirk danger or difficulty."

Sir Hugo scowled at the girl beside the fireplace.

"I'll get you yet!" His tone was vicious. "You win tonight. Tomorrow will be my turn." He turned his back and stalked into the passage, slamming the door behind him.

"Oh, Mr. Telford, how can I ever thank you?" exclaimed Celia.

"Well now, let's see!" remarked Mr. Telford thoughtfully. "Here's a table set for two. Why not invite me to share your repast with you? It's been dry work telling that fellow what I think of him. Let me say that from the brief glimpse I have had of him, I concur with everything you have said about him. And don't bother to thank me, young lady. It is a real pleasure to prevent such a rascal from having all his own way."

CHAPTER TWENTY

INTO the gathering night went Sir Guy, so incensed that he paid little heed to what went on. He was only vaguely conscious of seeing a covered cart with a tired horse in the shafts, and a group of workmen standing nearby. Nor did he notice a youth on a piebald pony holding the reins of two saddled horses. He blundered towards the stables from the open door of which came the yellow gleam of a lantern's light. The first two stalls were empty, but he saw in the farthest box the hindquarters of his horse. In the dimness of the stables stood a tall man, shirt-sleeves rolled up, bending over the strap of some harness.

"My horse!" shouted Sir Guy. "At once."

The man did not so much as glance up.

"Hurry! Do you hear? Saddle my horse."

"Saddle it yourself!" There was contempt in the tone.

"Why, damn your impudence! You speak to me like that!"

"Damn your impudence!" said Tempest turning.

Sir Guy was taken aback. He stared into Tempest's face. A pucker of perplexity appeared on his brow.

"I've seen your face before. . . . Now, where?"

Tempest walked past the baronet so that he stood between him and the stable door. He turned the lantern so that the light fell on his face. "Take a good look. I would have you remember me."

"You are impudent, fellow. I make people treat me with respect."

Tempest laughed. "Respect! You! The only way to gain respect is to merit it. Now, where have you seen me before? You can't remember? I'll refresh your memory. It was in Shrewsbury. You came inquiring at The Raven about a young lady you were seeking. Did you, by any chance, find her at Ludlow?"

"Ah!" ejaculated Guy deliberately. "I have placed you now. You struck me then as being a smug rascal. It is my impression you sent me on a wild goose chase."

"It has only just dawned on your muddled mind? Lord!

You're a greater blockhead than I thought." Tempest's laugh was mocking.

Up went Guy's riding-crop. "You dog," he cried with an oath, "I'll teach you manners."

He aimed a furious blow. Tempest, watching him, ducked his head and diverted the blow with his left arm. His right fist crashed into the distorted face, and as the baronet staggered back, Tempest leaped forward. Left, right, left. His fists, propelled by passion, smashed into the man's face so that the blood ran down Goadby's chin. Sir Guy flung up an arm to guard off further blows. Then his crop cut a weal on Tempest's cheek. The pain maddened Tempest and he rushed forward hitting harder than ever. The horse in the stall snorted and plunged, sensing anger in the atmosphere. With a terrific upper-cut Tempest sent the baronet staggering against the horse's flank. The frightened animal kicked. The next instant Tempest instinctively leaped forward to rescue his enemy from the flashing hoofs. Sir Guy's unconscious body was flung on to a pile of straw. Tempest stood for a moment, breathing heavily, gazing down on the prostrate form. Then he gently raised his fingers and touched his burning cheek as if previously he had been too intent upon strife to give it a thought. He was standing thus, motionless, when the door swung noiselessly open and Jasper crept in.

"So soon?" he asked softly.

"Yes. I hadn't half finished with him. He has got off too lightly. I knocked him against his horse and he got kicked."

Jasper knelt beside the man, felt his heart, and ran his practised fingers over his bones.

"There is not much amiss," he said. "Nothing broken. He will come to when he gets over the crack on the head."

"We had best get him away quick, then. Where is the caravan?"

"In the yard."

"And the men with the cart?"

"They have all gone inside to eat."

"They did not hear anything then?"

Jasper grinned. "They could not help but hear a swear or two, but they did not interfere. Their boss came out and told them to mind their own business."

"It's as well. I don't want them implicated—for their sakes as well as ours. Let us get the rogue away while we are not observed. Catch hold of his feet, Jasper."

Between them they carried the unconscious man into the yard and stretched him on the floor of the caravan. Jasper led the patient horse out on to the moors again. Tempest stood watching until the gay vehicle was lost to sight in the darkness.

First Tempest went to the pump to wash the signs of conflict from his face. His arm was bleeding where the whip had struck it. He had this bandaged by the inn-keeper's wife. Then he donned his coat and tidied his hair. In the kitchen he came across the surveying party in the midst of a meal.

"Hello!" Stephens, who was the leader, glanced up. "Was it you who was milling about in the stables?"

"Found a tramp there," said Tempest coolly. "He was trying to steal some harness so I gave him a lesson."

"Ay! We heard you." Stephens seemed intent on his plate. "Well, it's an interesting story. I'll remember it. A tramp, I think you said? You heard, fellows, it was a tramp trying to steal harness."

Tempest tried to grin, but his cheek distorted it by a painful twitch. "I think I'll join the party in the parlour," he observed.

He found a cosy scene. The room was well lit by candles. The meal was over and Mr. Telford had half-turned to the fire-place, contentedly sipping a glass of port. Celia sprang to her feet with an exclamation of delight as Tempest entered.

"Jack, I'm so glad you have come. I've so much to tell you."

"Something interesting?" Tempest was laconic.

"But first let me introduce you. This is Mr. Telford, the great engineer."

"Come in. I have heard so much about you, Mr. Tempest. Help yourself to a glass of wine. When I came here for the night I little expected to find so charming a visitor awaiting me."

"Oh, Jack, it was so fortunate that Mr. Telford put in an appearance. I am sure it was providential. Jack—he's been here!" She lowered her voice and the laughter faded from her eyes.

"He?" Tempest looked mildly interested. "You mean . . .?"

"Guy Goadby, of course."

"Think of that! What made the man come here?"

J

"Just my bad luck, I suppose. It was awful. I was expecting you and—he walked in. I nearly swooned."

"And was he offensive?"

"Not particularly so. It was the old story, you know. I had to tell him bluntly that I would never marry him, and he was growing awkward when Mr. Telford arrived and . . . and . . . put him in his place. Bless you, Mr. Telford. I shall never forget what you did."

"I am inclined to think I acted a trifle impetuously, my dear, but I could not stand idly by and watch you being carried off without raising my voice in protest."

"Oh dear. I hope no harm comes of it."

"To me? I'm old enough and big enough to take care of myself. Don't go wasting sympathy on me. My concern is what is going to happen to you. It seems to me, Mr.—Mr. Tempest, that either you have to return this young lady to her father——"

"I'll never go back, never," interposed Celia vehemently.

"Or else remove her to a place of safety so remote that there will never again be the possibility of a chance encounter like this. The next time this Sir-what's-his-name may not depart as docile as a lamb."

"I'm proposing——" began Tempest. The engineer held up a protesting hand.

"Provided you're not proposing to this young lady I do not wish to hear a word. The less I know the better. Keep me in profound ignorance. I don't approve of interfering with other folk's concerns. If I have been of assistance this evening I am gratified, but I have a big task on hand and I must not be deviated from it by petty annoyances or trivial disturbances. This is my life's work. I shall build a highway, the like of which this country has never seen before. And I must not be distracted because an amorous baronet chooses to make a fool of himself."

"You are right, sir," said Tempest. "The less you know about this the better. Let me thank you for what you have already done. Let me also assure you that I will do my utmost to protect this young lady's interests."

"If you are short of money——"

"I'm not." Tempest was emphatic. "Tonight's encounter was

unfortunate. A hundred-to-one chance. It is not likely to happen again."

"Well, if you take my advice you remove this lady before the scoundrel returns."

"I don't think he'll return for a while," observed Tempest with simulated indifference. "It's a long, dark ride over the moors, and he could not be back here with any helpers for some days at least."

"I hope you're right. Now you must excuse me. I've a report to make out and already I'm a weary man. Good night."

As soon as the door closed Tempest seated himself at the table. "I will change my mind," he said. "I am hungrier than I thought."

"Let me serve you with something. Some cold ham?—oh, Jack, what have you done to your cheek?"

"Struck it against something in the dark. It's nothing."

"It looks sore."

"A mere graze. It serves me right for being so careless. Now, tell me about yourself."

"There's nothing much to tell, except that I have sustained a shock. I wonder how Sir Guy knew I was here?"

"A lucky chance, I expect."

"Maybe. But perhaps that man who came to the caravan told him."

"Perhaps. In any case you have come out of it well."

"How thankful I was to see Mr. Telford."

"Yes. You owe him a debt of gratitude. But how was it he knew you were being forced into a marriage against your will?"

"I—I wonder? Perhaps Harry told him."

"Harry? Oh, that fatuous boy who works for him."

"Don't speak so disparagingly. He is quite a nice boy—only young for his years and somewhat impetuous. I'm sure he means well."

"Lord! The amount of trouble in the world which is caused by people who mean well. Anyhow, Mr. T. saved the situation and I'm grateful to him."

The girl shuddered "Brr! I'm glad Guy's gone. The more I see him the more I detest him. Though I stand up to him it is a sort of artificial courage, Jack, all the stronger because I am desperate. In my heart I am frightened of him. Horribly frightened."

"You poor girl. I'll try to arrange that he does not frighten you again. To think this is a civilized, Christian country and such things are possible. Do you know one thing that troubles me, Celia?"

"What is it?"

"That you are still under age. I don't know the law, in fact I have such an aversion to it that I keep as far away from it as possible, but I have an idea that until you come of age you are legally under the power of your parent. So we must arrange to keep you well concealed until you are twenty-one."

"It won't be long, now. In two months and eight days I will come of age. I have been counting."

"Then you will be a real woman! And I shall have to be very respectful and address you as 'Miss Upton'."

"If you do, I shall call you Mr. Tempest. Or should I say Captain?"

"The problem is rather complicated. I think it would be simpler if we retained the Jack!"

"It will depend on whether we retain the Celia!"

They both laughed, but the laughter was a trifle forced.

"We have a long way to go tomorrow. It is time you thought about retiring."

"What of my things? Were they in the caravan?"

"They were. All safe and sound. I have had them brought to this inn, and already they are up in your bedroom. And— shall I tell you a secret?"

"Please do."

"I bribed the good woman to light a fire in your room and to run a warming-pan over the sheets! If you don't sleep well I shall accept no responsibility."

"Of course I shall sleep well. Only, Jack——"

She hesitated and he saw the old strained look of apprehension creep into her eyes and it filled him with a fierce anger that men should persecute a girl so.

"What is it?"

"Is it safe? Suppose Guy returns."

"He won't."

"But he might."

"I assure you it is extremely unlikely."

"You say that just to cheer me. You can't be certain what a man like that will do. I should sleep more soundly if I knew that he would not come knocking at the door."

"Will you sleep soundly if I promise you that I shall stay on guard all night?"

"Of course I should feel secure then. But I won't have it."

"Why not?"

"You'd be too tired. I can't let you."

"When we are disposing of a cargo of spirits I assure you I stay awake all night for a far more ignoble purpose. But if you will go to bed and put your head on the pillow and sleep until morning I will undertake to share the night watch with Jasper. Do you agree?"

"Yes, I will agree to that. How condescending I sound, when all the while my heart is full of gratitude to you for your consideration and kindness."

"You may reward me by going to sleep. Pleasant dreams. I will join Jasper. He will keep me company."

CHAPTER TWENTY-ONE

AT the entrance to the gully, the caravan came to a stop. The tired horse stood patiently in the darkness. Jasper gave the curlew call and then he and Tempest awaited in silence until two men came towards them, approaching silently among the boulders with a certainty which bespoke familiarity with the route.

"We did not expect you so soon," said the leader.

"A new cargo this time, Gwilym," replied Tempest. "No kegs. We have a prisoner."

Instead of answering, the man walked to the open door of the caravan and looked inside. Guy was conscious enough now, but he maintained a silence enforced by a scarf across his mouth. Legs and arms were pinioned. "Go back for a hurdle," ordered Tempest, and the second man disappeared up the gully. When he returned the bound man was lifted out of the caravan and laid on the improvised stretcher.

"I could bring the horse no farther," said Jasper.

"It's a marvel you got him so far—and in the dark, too," said Gwilym. The track was littered with boulders deposited by the glacier which, countless centuries before, had gouged the scar across the face of the mountainside. No vehicle could have made its way farther over so rough an approach. The bearers walked with caution until they came to a long, low stone building which blended with the cliff-side into which it was built. The walls were of boulders. Only a door and window gave it the appearance of a habitation. In addition there was a stone-built chimney from which a curl of smoke ascended—smelt rather than seen. It was a place which would have escaped the notice of any but the most discerning eyes. They carried the man into a room with a wooden floor on which they laid him. When door and shutters were fastened, Gwilym struck flint and steel and lit a hanging lamp.

Gwilym looked down upon the pinioned man. "Spy?" he inquired succinctly.

"Poking his nose where it wasn't wanted," replied Tempest. "We'll have him in the inner chamber."

Tempest walked to a rough dresser which occupied one end of the room and grasped a hidden lever. The dresser swung noiselessly back. The second man lit a lantern and carried it ahead. Following his lead the hurdle-bearers bore the inanimate man along a passage cut in the rock until they reached a door which opened into a cave in the hill. A broad tarpaulin was spread over boxes stored in the far corner. There were shelves and a few empty cases.

"Go and get something to eat, Jasper," ordered Tempest. "I want to have a word with this fellow alone."

When the door closed he untied the bandages and propped Goadby against the wall. The baronet did not open his eyes but sat gasping for breath. Then his tongue moistened his lips. Tempest fetched a glass and gave him a drink. Goadby looked about him.

Seating himself on a box, Tempest proceeded to fill a pipe.

"You'll live to curse the day you ever laid your hands on me," muttered Guy, scowling. "I'll break you for this."

"A prophesy of longevity," remarked Tempest lightly.

"I am a Justice of the Peace," said Sir Guy with dignity.

"My condolences to the luckless prisoners who come before you."

"I'll see you get a stiff sentence."

"When?" asked Tempest, coolly.

"When you answer for this outrage, you rogue."

"What gives you the impression that you'll ever sit on the bench again, Goadby?"

"Damn you! How dare you address me thus? Treat your betters with respect."

"I never fail to do so, Goadby. You have not answered my question yet! What makes you think you will ever disgrace the bench of magistrates again?"

"You shall release me instantly or you'll regret it."

"You appear to be particularly obtuse, Goadby. I don't intend to release you. When will it penetrate your thick head that you are not in a position to dispute with me. I hold the cards."

"Release me. Release me instantly. Do you hear?"

"I intend to release your hands shortly. It will be to sign a document."

"I sign nothing."

"You may make a cross for your mark if you are too illiterate to write!"

Tempest walked from the room and returned carrying a pad of paper, an inkwell and a quill.

He dragged a second box before him to serve as a desk and then set to work. There was no sound but the scratching of his pen.

The captive on the floor watched him furtively. Tempest was engrossed. There was an intent look in his eyes. Goadby moved slightly. Tempest took no notice. Slowly the man raised himself up. When he was able to kneel he made an awkward hop forward.

"Please lie down and keep still," said Tempest without glancing up. "Your fidgeting distracts me. If you contemplate attacking me from behind let me suggest that you don't expend your strength in unprofitable effort. Not only are my hands free, my feet are also and, let me be candid, my right toe is itching to apply itself to your posterior."

Goadby scowled and subsided. He was powerless. He knew it. Moreover, he knew that Tempest knew it. The thought maddened him. He was not used to being thwarted.

"I should have finished this quicker if you had behaved yourself," observed Tempest, carrying the document nearer the lantern. "Now, Goadby, pay heed to this:

"*I, Guy Goadby, Bart.*: you notice how courteous I am, Goadby, giving you your full title as if you were a man of consequence——

"*I, Guy Goadby, Bart., being in my right mind* (but, let me add, in a vile temper, but we need not include that) *do hereby confess that I have schemed with my neighbour, W. Upton of Upton Hall, Esq., to marry his daughter, Celia Upton, well knowing that on account of my dissolute life, I am unworthy of such a woman. Realizing that my presence is obnoxious to her, and that she abominates me, I hereby declare that the contract I have made with her father, W. Upton of Upton Hall, Esquire, to be null and void. I hereby promise and undertake to release her from all obligations to me and will, moreover, not molest her, pester her,*

*follow her, or interfere with her happiness in any way whatsoever.
Signed by me———"*

"Well, I'm damned———!" ejaculated Goadby.

"I'm sure you are. Or at any rate will be. But why comment
on the obvious. I will now release your arms so that you may
sign that document. After which you will be free to depart."

"I sign that!" Goadby gave a laugh which was supposed to
be ironic. "I'll see you in hell, first."

"You'll not sign?"

"You're mad to think it. I'll make you suffer for this affront,
this intolerable insult. . . ."

"When?" Tempest raised his eyebrows impudently.

"Let me go!" shouted Goadby. "Let me go, damn you!"

"Ah! You have changed your mind. You are prepared to
sign."

"I will not sign. Never."

"I am sorry," said Tempest with a sigh. "Truly sorry. The
document is, I know, not worded with legal precision, but you
must attribute that to my lack of training. If there is any word
you would like altered, any phrase you would like embellished,
do not be afraid to let me know. I am ready to oblige."

"Damn you. I will not sign. Damn you!"

"Please do not keep repeating that. It may relieve your
feelings but I find it monotonously boring. As you are unreasonable, there's no more we can do about the matter."

Tempest stood up, carefully folded the paper and placed
it in an inner pocket. Picking up pen and inkwell, he turned
towards the lantern.

"Apart from practising penmanship I appear to have wasted
my time. Or rather you have wasted my time, you thick-headed
oaf. You may now have time to meditate. I shall return in a
couple of days." He picked up the lamp.

"Stop!" shouted Goadby. "You think to intimidate me. I
tell you I will marry that girl. I am more resolved to marry her
than ever I was if only to punish you for your intolerable
behaviour. I will marry her. I vow by all the devils of hell I will
marry her. You hear me."

"I hear you, you fool. My answer is that you'll never marry
her. When I heard of your conduct I disliked you, Goadby. Now

that I have met you I find you loathsome. At first I was prompted to act solely in a lady's interests. Now, I act for myself alone. Creatures like you merit a lesson and you shall have one. Lie there and cool your hot head. When next I condescend to speak to you—keep a civil tongue in your head."

He picked up the lamp and walked towards the door.

"Come back!" raved Goadby, struggling into a sitting posture. The door shut with a slam. The baronet was left alone in the darkness of the damp and chilly cell.

.   .   .   .   .

When Celia descended to the parlour the following morning, she found the sun streaming through the small-paned window, brightening the table on which an appetizing breakfast was set forth. The covered-cart with the surveying party had departed. There was no caravan to be seen. She walked to the door. Apart from the tracks in the mud there was no sign of the visitors of the previous night. The place seemed less dismal in the light of day, but it still retained its air of isolation. Before her stretched the undulating moor. She noticed that the gorse was showing yellow. A cockerel in the inn yard sent forth a clarion challenge. Celia heard her host carry something to the room, and returned.

She was hungry. "Am I permitted to ask where—anyone— is?" she inquired.

The man lowered his voice. "He will soon be back," he said. "I was to tell you as soon as you came down. He will come to you." With that she had to be content. She ate in silence until she heard hoofs. Moving hurriedly to the window she saw Tempest ride up with the led horse. He handed the animals to the care of the inn-keeper and came striding towards the door.

"Good morning, Celia. You have saved something for me, I hope? I am sharp set." He dropped into a chair. "You have slept well, I trust?"

"Very well, thank you, Jack. I had no qualms, so great was my trust in you."

"I had a conviction that you would not be disturbed."

"You do not look very sleepy, Jack. Have you had any rest during the night?"

"Oh, Jasper and I managed to pass the time not unpleasantly."
He spoke lightly.

"Where is Jasper?"

"He has gone on ahead. I suggested he made for the first
town and purchased some paint."

"Paint? Why should he buy paint?"

"My idea was that he should paint the caravan. I suggested
yellow with blue wheels."

"But it did not require painting. I like its present colour.
Why——" She looked at him closely. "You usually have a
reason for what you do. Is it because you wish to change its
appearance?"

"I think it is desirable that the caravan should not be easily
recognized," he said. "My precautions may be needless, but,
well, we do not wish to run risks."

"You are right. We must run no risks; Jack, if that wretch
got me in his clutches I should go mad, I think. I detest him
worse than ever."

"I am not enamoured of him," agreed Tempest, putting
down an empty cup. "I hope he will not trouble you again.
But if you have finished, please get ready for the road. Or rather
the moors. It is time we were off. Get your coat on. I will see
to the horses."

Celia responded to the glad spirit of the morning as they
cantered over the short-cropped turf, but Tempest was more
reserved than usual. He appeared abstracted.

She teased him. Tempest smiled, but it was a sombre smile.

"I feel the burden of responsibility, my dear," he remarked.
"Your welfare is at stake. I will do my utmost to save you. I
will try to protect you. But should I fail, by some mischance. . . ."

"Oh, you would not fail. You couldn't."

"Life is quite unpredictable, Celia. I want to ask you this.
If I should fail, will you believe that I did my best? And, remember always, that the man whose life you saved has tried, to
the best of his ability, to repay a little of the debt."

"Oh, Jack, of course I promise. But why have you grown so
serious? It is not like you. As for saving your life—you make
too much of what I did. All I did was to jump out into the mud.
Oh, such mud. I am glad from the bottom of my heart that

good Mr. Telford is going to give us roads along which travellers may go without risking their lives."

"Well, you did save my life. I know how I felt as I lay in the mud and cold and rain and blackness, with my leg numb and my strength ebbing. I verily believe that in another fifteen minutes I should have been dead of exposure. You saved my life. I believe it was saved for a purpose. My task is to save you, and never was a man allotted a more privileged task. The service itself is its own reward."

His mood changed. "Let's have a gallop," he cried with simulated enthusiasm. "Faith, I was getting sentimental. A fatal mistake. You ride well, Celia. There's something invigorating in this mountain air. Roads may serve mankind right nobly. They open the way for commerce and help travellers on their way, but with a good horse between my knees, give me the heath and the wind in my face and the feel of the springy turf. Make the most of the land, Celia. It may be that before long you will turn into a seafarer. We are getting nearer the sea every day, my fair lady! I have sent Jem on ahead to arrange preparations for your arrival. You are going to be happy, Celia. Happy and free and safe!"

He reined in his horse and as she drew up beside him he pointed.

"See!"

"What am I to see?" she asked. "Those birds?"

"Gulls, my dear, gulls. We are nearing the coast at last."

"The Rising Gull," she quoted, hardly knowing why.

"Why, yes. An augury. A happy omen. Freedom under the blue of heaven. Soon you shall feel as free as the gull which rises from the foam."

CHAPTER TWENTY-TWO

AFTER a long sojourn inland the first glimpse of the sea arouses a feeling of exultation. Both Tempest and Celia were conscious of a stirring of the emotions when they crested a grassy rise and saw between green-topped promontories ahead the blue-grey sweep of the ocean. The moving waves spouted white against the foot of limestone cliffs. About the crags, like flecks of white, moved restless seagulls. Several vessels were in sight, three ketches and a cutter which appeared to be fishing, a coasting brig under easy sail, and afar off, a three-masted ship which by the cut of her canvas, might have been one of His Majesty's frigates cruising the Irish Sea.

Celia took a deep breath as though she could already inhale the ozone. "How glorious!" she exclaimed. "It is years since I saw the sea. Thank you for this rare sight, Jack."

"I am glad the sun shines," he replied. "I have seen that same sea look sullen enough in a winter's gale. We near our journey's end."

So they rode on until they looked down upon the valley of the Conway, where the river broadened. On the one side was the massive peninsula of the Ormeshead, seeming severed from the mainland but for a narrow neck of sandy marsh. Farther off lay the green expanse of Anglesey, and in the offing was the long islet of Priestholme with the pointed tower of its tiny ancient ruined church upthrusting its dark point. Farther west rose the ponderous bulk of Penmaenmawr. At the edge of the estuary Celia could see the homely outlines of the snug, grey-walled town of Conway and its venerable castle with eight round towers. In front of the castle a wooded islet rose firm amid the swirling river. At the anchorage coasting vessels rode at their moorings. A few small boats gave animation to the scene as they plied between the town and the Deganwy shore. After lonely moorlands and bleak hills the scene appeared sequestered and tranquil.

"So it is to Conway you take me?" she inquired.

"No, fair lady." Tempest shook his head. "You must endure

157

solitude awhile. I dare not let you mix much with the madding
crowd lest word reach your father that you have been seen. We
must descend by stealth and cross the turnpike which leads to
Conway Ferry. Our destination is the Ormeshead. You will dwell
in a cottage set in a green hollow of the hillside. It stands high
enough to permit us to watch the approach of strangers, but
being in a depression and almost surrounded by trees its stone
walls render it almost unnoticeable."

"What is it called?"

"A quaint name, 'The Rising Gull'."

"Oh! That sounds like a vessel. Why did you choose it?"

"I did not. It was so named when I bought it. No one knows
how it came by its name. You don't like it?"

"I think it charming. But I pictured a ship—Heilyn's, perhaps."

"She is named the *Gwynedd*. He has a new vessel just launched.
Maybe he would name that the *Rising Gull* if you asked him
nicely."

"*Gwynedd* sounds pretty! Is the boat named after his sweet-
heart?"

"So I concluded at first. He tells me that *Gwynedd* is nothing
more sentimental than the ancient name for the Principality.
See! That looks like his craft; that one with the patched
foresail."

"You persist in disillusioning me, Jack. I thought all smugglers
had luggers. I long to see a lugger."

"You won't find one off this coast. A lugger, my dear, would
be conspicuous. Our aim is to avoid attention, not to attract it."

"Then," she said triumphantly, "why has Heilyn that conspicuous patch on the sail. Even I noticed it."

"I am glad you did. The patched sail is only used when we
are bent on honest business. When we embark on less reputable
but more lucrative ventures a different one is substituted so that
we will not be easily recognized."

"Jack, there is no trapping you!"

"Not as easily as that, I hope."

They were riding down an old narrow road which led from
the moors to the wooded slopes which skirted the shore. Ahead
of them at a road-crossing Celia could see a small inn set high
on the western bank.

"The Four Crosses," said Tempest pointing. "We will rest here. The old highway crosses at this point but it is not much used now that the turnpike has been made lower down. There's good food to be had here. We'll risk a meal before we complete our journey."

He returned to say that there were no travellers at the inn.

"Then we may venture indoors," said Celia, dismounting. "I'm famished."

So long as she was out of doors Celia was conscious of freedom and lightness of heart. No sooner did she find herself within four walls than she became ill at ease. Her mind was teased with possibilities. She had the feeling of being hunted. Her nerves were tense. She was alert. No sooner had Tempest departed to arrange for a meal than she walked to the window, pulled back the curtain, and stared down upon the road. There was little to cause her anxiety. Two boys in ragged clothes were playing tip-cat. A man went by with a barrow which rumbled noisily over the stoney way. Then came a wagon drawn by two horses, bearing sacks of grain for the mill. A dog-cart with a fast stepping horse went down the highway without pausing. It was followed at a more leisurely pace by a farmer's trap. Her eyes noted everything within sight. The lilacs and pinks and London Pride in a ragged garden beside the inn, in various stages of budding.

Her ears caught the clip-clop of a weary horse. It was a bay horse with a rough coat which came into view, walking with hanging head. Its rider sat long-legged in the saddle, staring moodily before him. She recognized Harry Standish. He looked paler, she thought, and older. The animation which characterized him when first they met had disappeared.

Before she realized what she was doing she tapped on the pane. Feeling sorry for her impetuous action she dropped the curtain, and stepped back into the room, but not before she had seen Standish rein in his horse and look back inquiringly. She hoped he would ride on, but he did not. Instead, he turned his horse and came to the gate where he methodically tethered the somnolent animal (possibly needlessly) and walked stiffly up the path and into the flagged passage. There was a silence as though he looked about him. Then a knock. She heard him inquire if anyone had summoned him. The landlord replied that he knew nothing about it.

"I may as well have a mug of ale now I am here," replied Standish. "I could have sworn somebody tapped on the window as I passed by."

"Children, maybe." The landlord seemed unconcerned. "Unless it was the lady?"

"The lady?" Standish spoke quickly.

"A young lady who has arrived for a meal."

"Where is she?" The listening girl noticed the eagerness in his voice.

"In the parlour."

The door swung open. Celia saw Harry's eyes grow wide with surprise; saw the colour flood his cheeks. The weariness of the jaded horseman vanished.

"You! Really you! It seems unbelievable!" He hurried across with outstretched hands. "I have wondered and wondered what had become of you. Everywhere I have gone I have looked out for you. I have made discreet inquiries. I thought I was never going to see you again. And now, just when I least expected it, I encounter you. Tell me, was it you who tapped on the window?"

"Yes. It was foolish of me. I did it without thinking."

"It was adorable of you. How can I thank you. I might have ridden on without ever knowing you were here. I should never have forgiven myself."

"But if you hadn't known I was here you would not have known you had not seen me!"

"No, I suppose not. But let's talk about yourself. Tell me, are you well?"

"How do I look?"

"Radiant! Lovely! Beautiful! Perfect——"

"Please. Please. You mustn't talk like that."

"You asked me——"

"But I meant did I appear in good health."

"Oh, that. I suppose so."

"So my health is not of any great concern to you?"

"Of course it is. I am delighted that you look so well. That night—you escaped—how did you manage?"

She looked at him curiously. "What do you know about an escape?"

"Didn't you know? No, I suppose you could not know."

"Know what?"

"I called at your house that evening."

"What on earth for?"

"To try to rectify the wrong I had done."

"What wrong?"

"It was I who told your father where he could find you."

"You!"

"Great heavens! I didn't know you were running away. I thought I was rendering you a service. When I learned the truth—— Well, I decided I would seek this man Goadby and plead with him not to force you into this hateful marriage."

"So you actually called! I need not ask what manner of reception you were accorded."

Harry made a wry face.

"They were going to make me convey my apologies to you. That fellow, Sir Guy, seemed to think the situation would prove amusing. But your door was locked and they thought you had —had—done something to yourself. Your father was upset. Then the butler told them your window was open and everyone rushed out of doors and made for the stables to start in pursuit."

"Oh!"

"When they were inside I slammed the door and locked it."

"Harry, how clever of you!"

"Well," he said bashfully, "it wasn't very brilliant but I couldn't think of anything else at the time."

"It was most practical. I wondered how there was no hue and cry."

"There was cry enough—your father's language——"

"I can quite imagine it. Give me your hand. You have proved a real friend."

Harry seized the outstretched hand in both of his and seemed reluctant to let go.

He was standing thus when the door was pushed open and Tempest came in.

"Damn!" said Harry forgetting his manners.

Tempest was suave. "I trust I do not appear inopportunely."

K

"Not if it is to tell us the meal is ready," said Celia brightly. "Have you two met before?"

"We have met, but we have not been introduced formally," Tempest gave an ironical bow. "I was unaware that you had company."

"I saw Mr. Standish passing."

Tempest shrugged his shoulders. "Why not let him pass?"

Tempest walked nearer. "You know that we do not seek company," he remarked meaningly.

"Oh, but this is different," said Celia hurriedly. "I know we can trust Mr. Standish."

"I would like to be certain of it."

"Oh, but we can. He has rendered me good service. You have wondered why there was no pursuit on that memorable night. It was Harry who stopped my father and Guy. He locked them in the stables."

"Commendable. In view of that I should like to waive our wager."

"Wager?" Celia and Harry looked puzzled.

"Your young friend and I had a wager, Celia. I wagered five guineas that although he knew your name and address, I would rescue you before he did. I won my bet."

"You!" Harry's face showed his amazement. "You got her out of the window? But how the deuce? How did you get there. How did you know where she was?"

"Someone showed me!"

A look of understanding crossed Harry's face. "You followed me!" he said accusingly. "I call that cheating."

"All's fair——" began Tempest.

"Well, this is neither," interposed Celia brightly. "Now, you two must be friends. We are all striving in a common cause."

"Not common," observed Harry with attempted gallantry. "Anything but common."

"Yes, common. Very common. We are all of one mind in our detestation of Guy Goadby."

"I'll agree to that," conceded Tempest.

"I loathe the beast," added Harry with fervour. "By the way, I wonder where he is?"

There was a silence.

"You've seen him," said Harry impetuously, turning to Celia. "Where? How? Has he molested you?"

"He came across me when I was in a lonely inn, but fortunately Mr. Telford arrived and persuaded him to go."

"Excellent. Good for Mr. Telford. He's a stout fellow. And then what happened to the rogue?"

"He seems to have disappeared," said Tempest blandly. "You haven't set eyes on him since, have you, Celia?"

"I don't know what's become of him! I sincerely hope he will not trouble us again."

"It is to prevent that possibility, Mr. Standish, that I am escorting Miss Upton to a place of greater security," said Tempest suavely.

"Where?" demanded Harry.

"Somewhere in the vicinity of Caernarvon."

Celia opened her mouth to speak but Tempest silenced her with a quick glance.

"Then I shall see you again, I feel sure," said Standish, "for our road—both our roads—concentrate on the ferry near Bangor."

"Both roads?" Tempest was curious. "I was only aware that one was contemplated."

"Mr. Telford intends to bring a subsidiary road from Chester down the coast. That is why I am here, making a preliminary report on it."

Celia detected a note of importance in Harry's voice as though he would impress Tempest. But Tempest did not seem impressed. "You'll have your work cut out crossing the Conway," he said.

"Nothing is impossible to Mr. Telford." There was hero worship in Harry's voice.

Tempest showed a touch of impatience. "You must not let us delay you, Mr. Standish. A task of such magnitude must call for all the time and energy you can devote to it."

"I am not in so great a hurry——" began Harry.

"Let me be more explicit as you do not take a hint. You may not be in a hurry but we are. It is most essential that Miss Upton should not remain near a public road longer than is necessary. While we stand gossiping here, her enemies may be on her track.

If you have any regard for Miss Upton you must allow me to escort her to a place of greater security."

"If it is in her interests I will go immediately. But I must keep in touch," said Harry, turning to Celia. "Now I have found you again, I really must. You—you might need my help."

"If we do I will notify you. I give you my word, Mr. Standish," said Tempest curtly. "Good day."

Harry turned to Celia, who added: "I think, Mr. Standish, that you had better ride on your way. As Mr. Tempest observes, every minute spent in this public place has an element of risk. I am so pleased to have seen you again, and I thank you for all you have done to aid me in my dilemma."

"There's nothing in my power I would not do for you if I could," said Harry, and hurried for his horse.

"Thank heaven he's gone," said Tempest with fervour.

"You are hard on him."

"There's one good thing about his visit."

"What might that be?"

"In his infatuation he has forgotten to drink his ale." Tempest laughed and emptied the tankard.

"Yes, Harry is absent-minded," said Celia sweetly. "It seems he forgot to pay for it, also."

CHAPTER TWENTY-THREE

CELIA and Tempest made their way along the beaten track which led across the sandy waste just as the sun, visible behind Penmaenmawr's crest, was throwing a long red ripple across the waters of the Conway estuary, deepening the shadows which lurked on the massive sides of the Great Orme. A cluster of white-washed cottages high on the slope showed where the fisherfolk and miners dwelt. There were scattered farms, small of size, where the soil of the headland was fertile enough for cultivation.

Tempest led the way, his tired black pressing forward with eagerly pricked ears as though it recognized the approach to its stable. He took a path which led away from the cottages to where one dwelling stood in dignified isolation. It was surrounded by a neat garden with clipped trees which almost hid it from the plain. The boy Gideon ran out eagerly to secure the horses as they paused panting from the ascent. Tempest lifted Celia from the saddle. The girl walked stiffly up a path bordered by a low box hedge. The cottage door stood open and at the porch Miriam, baby in her arms, smiled a welcome.

The arrival savoured of a home-coming. The place, at close quarters, proved larger than it had appeared in the distance. Celia kissed the child, greeted the mother, and dropped into a chair beside the cheery fire with a sigh of thankfulness. She looked about her, curious as a child. There were flowers on the table, a polished Welsh dresser with rows of plates and jugs, a model ship, a cutlass, a telescope, a fowling-piece. She was conscious of Tempest smiling down upon her.

"You like your new home?"

"Is this where I am to live, Jack? Of course I like it. Every-where is spotless. Oh, and there are some of my things. How thoughtful of you. I suppose you brought my valise in the caravan. And is the caravan painted blue? There are so many questions I want to ask."

"You shall talk all day tomorrow. For the present I suggest that you go to your bedroom and change into comfortable clothes. You must be weary from so much riding."

"A little. But I'm too excited to be weary. I'm happy. I feel safe. Safe. And I am so much indebted to you, Jack."

As she rose to go to her room she glanced out of the open door. The whole world seemed bathed in peace in the quietude which came with the going down of the sun. Far off, all about the face of the cliffs, the sea birds were wheeling and crying. Mellowed by distance the sound was not unmusical. Celia felt she was going to be happy in her new home.

When they dined they were served by soft-footed Miriam who had proved herself no mean cook. The gate-legged table was covered by a cloth and Celia was quick to notice that the glass, the cutlery and the china were as fine as any she would have had in Upton Hall.

"You show admirable taste, Jack," she observed. "I need not ask if these are your choosing."

"I am glad they please you. I do not covet much of this world's goods, but I like those things which come my way to be of the best."

Celia understood. Quality meant so much in life. What was it which left a person of refinement dissatisfied with the second-best? What was the hidden spur which kept on striving to attain the highest? It was not ostentation, but a love of the beautiful which made her want that which was good. There could be beauty in simple things. There was strength and balance in the homely furniture of the room which glowed from constant polishing. There was grace in the lines of the miniature ship which had been carved by the rough hands of some man who loved his calling. She walked across the room to study the model more closely. Tempest's eyes followed her.

"How beautifully it is executed," said Celia. "Some clever person has taken infinite pains to fashion that."

"It brings back memories," said Tempest. "That is a copy of the ship which was wrecked on the Cornish coast when we were brought back from Corunna. You recollect my telling you of the memorable occasion when I was officially drowned?" There was a touch of irony in his voice. Then he added quietly. "Heilyn made it."

"How clever of him."

"Those great fists of his can become as dainty as a woman's," added Tempest. "Every knot in the minute cordage was tied by his supple fingers. I could not do it. A rare lad is Heilyn. He has the shoulders of a prize-fighter and the heart of a poet. He catches fish for a livelihood—and looks on life with an artist's eye. He is bold as a pirate and gentle as a mother. You'll like Heilyn when you meet him."

"I like him already," replied Celia. "When do I meet him?"

"As soon as he comes ashore. I have sent him a message."

Tempest walked to the door and looked out. It was dark. No lights twinkled in the bay beneath.

"I think I can see the *Gwynedd* at anchor," he said. "I know her moorings though it is too dark to be certain. Heilyn should be with us shortly."

"What a pity Jem is not here. You could have a reunion. You three, who escaped when this ship was wrecked." A dreamy look came into her eyes. "Is not imagination a remarkable thing, Jack? I stare at this toy ship on the shelf but I hardly see it. Instead I see a dark, heaving, tempestuous sea and cruel glistening rocks, and white-faced men clinging to the rigging, torn sails fluttering, the crash of spars. Men struggling in the water, engulfed by the cruel, pounding waves. . . . Oh! Jack . . . if you had been drowned . . . !"

She turned impulsively as a child and put her cheek against his shoulder. He patted her head but would not look at her. Instead he stared hard before him.

"Well, I wasn't," he said with a forced laugh. "You mustn't distress yourself by thinking what might have been. You are a quaint girl, Celia. You describe the scene almost as if you had been there."

She drew away and walked towards the fire, holding out her hands to the blaze as though the experience of the wreck had left her chilled. "I was foolish," she said. "It seemed all so real. I'm glad Heilyn made the little model."

"You may tell him for yourself that you admire his handiwork. I hear his step on the garden shingle."

The latch clicked, the door swung wide. Celia, watching with curious eyes, saw the aperture blocked by a broad figure. A thick jersey of blue wool, wrinkled with age, and dark trousers tucked into sea boots formed the man's apparel. His eyes were brown, so dark that they sparkled like jet in the lamplight.

"This is Miss Upton, Heilyn," explained Tempest. "I told you she would be here."

"Not Miss Upton—Celia," added the girl with a friendly smile. "We have dispensed with formalities."

Heilyn did not reply for a moment. When he spoke his voice was rich and musical. Life in England had given him mastery of the tongue but he retained sufficient of his native accent to lend character and expression to his words. He spoke dramatically as though upon a stage.

"The blue of the speedwell is in her eyes; the sunbeams are ensnared in her hair."

Tempest laughed. "No poetry yet, Heilyn. Not so soon!"

Heilyn brushed his friend aside with a contemptuous gesture. "Pay no heed to him. He has no soul. For years I have tried to arouse a sense of awareness in his sluggish mind. He has eyes which see not and ears which hear not. Man! We have the Queen of the Fairies come amongst us. And, damn me, I arrive smelling vilely of fish!"

Celia laughed. "If you had seen the meal I have just eaten, Heilyn, you would not confuse me with a fairy."

When she held out her hand, the man shook his head solemnly. "I must wash first," he said. "Never till this moment did I regret being a fisherman."

He vanished into the rear of the building and there was the sound of vigorous cranking as he worked the pump handle.

"You'll get used to Heilyn. He's not as mad as he appears."

"It is a nice kind of madness. I like him. It isn't every day a girl gets mistaken for Titania."

"You must overlook his eccentricities."

"I would forgive him much—has he not saved your life? I grow cold when I think I might never have met you."

When Heilyn returned, his hands were pink from scrubbing. He had changed into a white jersey and canvas trousers which had once belonged to the Royal Navy. Evidently he regarded white as appropriate for such an occasion.

"Some day," he said earnestly, "I will write you a poem. A poem to you. About you. But not yet. I must wait until the divine fire has loosened my lips. The words of my own poor brain are not sufficient. And then I will sing it to you. Can I not sing, Jack?"

"You can sing, Heilyn, but not here. The room is too small."

"So small a room is unworthy of me. I can fill a great hall. I can sing. I can compose. That fellow——" he pointed a scornful finger at Jack Tempest, "can do nothing but ride a horse!"

"Never mind. He rides a horse very well."

"Heilyn's jealous. He couldn't ride a clothes-horse."

"We have not all the same gifts. I have been admiring the little ship, Heilyn."

"Little ship!" Heilyn's tone indicated disapproval. "Little ship! She is a ship of the line, a seventy-four."

"You must admit you have made the model of her very small. I do not know how those big hands of yours managed it."

The man coloured with pride. "Wait," he said. "Wait!" He lowered his head and hurried out of doors. In a few minutes he returned with a block of wood.

"You see?" he exclaimed holding it forth. "A block of wood. So long, so wide, so deep. Nothing more. I will show you. I will bring it to life. It will have shape, design, beauty. I create. My hands work a miracle. I will go to my workshop and begin it this very minute. You shall see the hull before you go to rest."

Eager as a boy he hastened from the room.

Tempest drew a chair nearer the hearth.

"The calm after the storm," he said. "Heilyn sweeps through life like a tornado. You will grow accustomed to his ways. There are no level sands in his life, which is like the heaving ocean. Sometimes he is on the crest of the wave as he is tonight; sometimes he is in the trough. But his sea is always tossing; it knows no tranquillity or calm."

"At least he must live life to the full. I think I should prefer to dwell amid danger so long as I was always alert, rather than endure the humdrum placidity of a protected cow in a field."

"You will not complain of monotony now you have cast in your life with us."

Tempest fumbled in his pocket for his pipe and reached for a tobacco jar on the shelf. As he stood up a paper tumbled from his pocket to fall, unnoticed, to the hearth-rug.

"I wonder what Heilyn intends to make from that piece of wood?" said Celia.

"A ship model of some sort."

"Of course, but what ship?"

"You must wait. You notice his sense of the dramatic? You must see the rough, raw material as it looked, shapeless and void before his hands had touched it."

"I think he is very clever."

"Heilyn, I am sure, would agree with you." He pressed the tobacco into his pipe bowl and looked about him for a spill to thrust into the flames.

Celia's eyes noticed the paper on the hearth. "Will this do for a spill, Jack?" she asked bending down. "Unless," she added, glancing casually at it, "it is anything of value."

Tempest glanced down. "Give that to me!" he said sharply.

"Jack." Celia drew back and looked at him in amazement. Never before had he used so peremptory a tone.

"I mean it." He held out his hand. "Please, Celia. That is not for you."

"You are not emulating Heilyn and writing poetry?" Her voice sounded strange to her own ears. She was conscious of an increase in her heart beat.

"This isn't an occasion for frivolity. Please, Celia! You are not to look at that."

She held it behind her. "Would you take it from me by force?"

"If necessary. You are not to see it."

"Very well," she said coldly. "You shall have your paper. I suppose I have no right to pry into another's affairs."

She held it to him. "But, Jack——"

"Well?" said he, folding the paper and thrusting it hastily into his pocket.

"I have seen it."

"What!"

"At least I have seen a few words. I did not mean to, but as I picked it up my own name caught my eye."

"Yes," he said quietly, "your name was mentioned. There is nothing surprising in that."

"I saw the first few words, too. . . ."

He looked at her keenly, but she averted her eyes. "They were," she said slowly, "'I, *Guy Goadby, Bart*.' . . ."

"Damn!" Tempest turned away with a gesture of annoyance. For a moment there was silence, broken only by the solemn ticking of the grandfather clock in the corner, or the fall of a cinder into the pan beneath the grate.

"I don't know what to say, Celia," he said presently when he had control of his voice. "You will be all curiosity now. Can't you let well enough alone?"

"I confess I am curious. The writing was not Guy's."

"No, it was mine."

"But I don't understand. Why should you write *I, Guy Goadby, Bart*. . . . It sounds like a will, or a confession, or, or something. I don't understand! Jack?"

"Yes."

"Did you see him without my knowledge when you were on guard while I slept. Did he come back?"

Tempest gave a grim laugh. "He never went away!"

"What do you mean, Jack? That bruise on your face. I understand now. You met him and—and fought him?"

"I gave the rascal the thrashing he well deserved. I feel better for it."

"I wish you hadn't, Jack, he'll never forgive you. He was a dangerous enough enemy before. He will redouble his efforts to harm us both now. It was brave of you—but so foolish."

"Don't worry. He'll not harm us."

"You haven't—done—anything to him?" Her voice was awed.

"Not killed him, if that is what you are hinting at. You may as well know. I have the devil in safe keeping and I mean to keep him there until he signs a declaration that he will give you your freedom and never molest you again. He either signs it or stays where he is for the rest of his days! And I know which he will prefer."

Celia was staring at him, wide-eyed.

"Oh, Jack!" said Celia. "I foresee all manner of trouble. Oh, Jack!"

CHAPTER TWENTY-FOUR

FROM a building in the rear of the house came the sound of a saw cutting through wood. Heilyn was singing as he worked on the hull of his model craft. The song sounded happy. Its joyousness struck an ironical note, for within the room there was tension. It was as though Goadby, even when absent, could cast an evil spell. They could not escape from his machination.

Celia was almost tearful. There was a stubborn look on Tempest's face; a hard gleam in his eyes. It was an unaccustomed look to Celia, who had grown used to his devotion, his patience, his consideration.

"You are not cross with me, Jack? You look—different."

He waited a moment before replying. When he did so his voice modulated as if under restraint.

"I am not cross with you, Celia. I could curse myself for dropping that paper. It was my intention to spare you any anxiety. Now, through a moment's carelessness, I have undone all. Of all the cursed luck!"

"I do not believe in luck. It may be the result of some wise purpose."

"Wise!" There was a curl of his lip and a sneer in his voice.

"Yes, wise. It may have been intended so that I might prevent you from doing something which would cause you incalculable harm."

"My dear girl, what happens to me does not matter. I am an outcast, a law-breaker. One who dwells outside the pale. I shall probably end on the gallows, and the contemplation of the possibility does not cause me to lose a wink of sleep. My only thought is to save you—you, who prompted by your gentle, kindly heart, braved the elements to rescue an unknown man from a death from exposure. Your happiness and welfare mean everything. I do not count in the scheme of things."

"You count for much in my eyes, my benefactor. I would not have harm come to you."

He laughed. "So it is *you* who would protect *me*? And all the while I am under the impression that I am protecting you."

But Celia did not laugh. She sighed. "Oh dear, what are we to do?"

"So far as you are concerned, my dear, the issue is simple. You just dismiss an unfortunate occurrence from your mind. Relax in this safe and delectable spot. Recover your health. Enjoy life. Be happy."

"But I can't, Jack. Not in the circumstances."

"What circumstances are there to prevent your so doing?"

"You know perfectly well. You are only pretending that you don't. That paper."

"Forget about it."

"As if I could! I can't forget. I shall never forget. I am troubled."

She looked troubled. Her eyes were glistening as though tears were ready to brim over. She bent forward and laid her hand timidly on his sleeve. "You will not be cross with me?"

"How could I be?"

"But you might. And I don't think I could bear it. Everything you have done has been for my benefit. I know that. I know it so well, and yet—I feel it isn't right."

"What isn't right?"

"Treating Guy as you are doing."

"I have treated him more lightly than he deserves. There are men I know who would have finished him off with no more compunction than one would wring a chicken's neck."

He stared grimly in the fire. Like a background to their conversation sounded the muffled voice of Heilyn singing.

"*Drink to me only with thine eyes. . . .*"

He was using a plane now. Celia could hear the firm, swift cuts. She could picture his capable, strong hands as they shaped the hull. The shavings on the floor. . . .

"But you wouldn't be the man I honour if you acted like that. Those men are cruel."

"I could be cruel when I think of how you are being persecuted."

"Forget all about me. Let us think about this problem of ours dispassionately."

"Don't say 'ours'. It is my problem, not yours."

"What concerns you concerns me, Jack. We haven't travelled

together all these days for nothing. I am going to take my courage in both hands, now. Will you allow me to read the paper which my eyes unwittingly rested on?"

He sat so motionless that she half wondered whether he had heard. She watched him timidly, a little apprehensive. Slowly his hand sought his pocket. He drew out the paper and handed it to her without taking his eyes off the fire.

"Yes. You may read it."

Celia read it slowly. Then the hands which held the paper fell to her lap.

"Oh, Jack! Has he seen this?"

"Yes, he has read it."

"Did he refuse to sign?"

"In emphatic terms."

"And then?"

"I merely told him that he remained where he was until he changed his mind."

"May I ask where he is?"

"In a secret depot of ours in the hills. A place where we store contraband when we carry it overland."

"He may betray you."

"He has no notion where he is. His eyes were blindfolded. Jasper and I took him there on the floor of the caravan."

"So that is why the caravan had to be painted a different colour."

"I thought it expedient. And Jasper is to move to another part of the country."

Celia read the brief agreement again.

"To think you would do this for me."

She folded the missive. Folded it again. She was breathing hard. Her eyes were on Tempest as though she feared an outburst,

Slowly she stretched a small and shapely hand towards the fire. As the tip of the paper touched the bars she paused as though she expected it to be snatched from her grasp. Tempest did not move. Celia thrust the paper into the flames and watched it flare. She glanced at Tempest's face. It was expressionless.

"Jack," she said softly, "do you know what I am doing?"

"Celia," he said, "do *you* know what you are doing?"

"I have burnt the paper."

"Yes, you have burnt the paper. And I vowed he should not go free until he signed it."

For a moment she stared uncomprehending. Then her hands flew to her mouth as though to stifle a scream.

"Jack, what have I done? Until he signed it! You wouldn't . . . wouldn't. . . . Have I killed him?"

She was so distressed that Tempest crossed to her side. He touched her cheek affectionately. "My dear, you must not distress yourself. Does this man mean anything to you?"

"Mean anything? No, I detest him. But he is still a human being. It is you I think about most. I do not want you to do anything you would afterwards regret. You want me to be safe and happy. Believe me I want you, equally, to be safe and happy."

Tempest forced a smile. "Well," he said briefly, "I can always write out another. That one wasn't particularly well-indited. It was drawn up in a hurry."

The distress left her face. In its place was a look of determination, of resolve.

"No, Jack. Not that."

"I don't understand," said Tempest. "You are not suggesting, are you, that I leave him to rot in his cell? He'll give in and sign in time, never fear. But he's not getting his freedom until I have some hold over him."

"That's just it, he must not sign."

Tempest was incredulous. "Must not sign? When I have been to such pains to get the scoundrel where he will do no further harm!"

"No, Jack. Don't you see that to make a person do something against their will is wrong. It is one of the worst sins— I think."

"You had better convince him of that."

"But it is, Jack, and two blacks don't make a white. If you were to force him to sign, where is the dignity of the human personality?"

"There is no dignity in Guy Goadby."

"You are trying to distract me. You know what I mean. I am not thinking of him. I am thinking of you. Of your dignity, your self-respect. You, the man I admire more than anyone on earth. You would go down in your own estimation if you did anything so vile."

"And in yours, I suppose?"

"We are not talking about that. I am jealous only for your good name."

"I haven't one."

"Would I have trusted myself to you if I had not honoured you? You are worth a million men like Goadby. That is why I do not wish you to sully your honour. I know, oh, Jack, I know so well, that all you do is in my interest."

"What do you suggest? I can't keep the fool there for ever, and I must not kill him."

"You must let him go free."

"Never. You have taken leave of your senses. He would hound you down and force you into marriage without compunction."

"No. You must appeal to his better nature."

"He has none."

"When he sees how chivalrously you have treated him he will appreciate it and reciprocate."

"You dear girl. What little you know of the world. You judge others by your own sweet disposition. You can't appeal to the honour of a man who has no honour. If I let Goadby go free he will consider it weakness on my part. He will think that his threats have intimidated me. And he will be more remorseless than ever."

"All the same I wish you to set him at liberty. If not for his sake, then for your own. You have suffered injustice and my heart aches for you when I think about all you have been called upon to endure. There is cruelty and injustice in the world. Far, far too much of it in this so-called Christian land. How can we remedy it? By continuing it? By perpetuating it? By rendering evil for evil? We must rise above it. Even if we suffer for so doing, let us respond to the highest that is in us. You will let him go free?"

Jack turned away. "I am a fool," he muttered. "An accursed fool. A weakling. Deprived of my reason. To free that rogue would be the most insane thing I have ever done. But if you wish it I will do so."

L

She caught his hand and raised it to her lips.

"Jack dear! I never admired you so much as I do this minute."

But he turned from her and walked out into the night.

. . . . .

Guy Goadby was in no gracious mood. It was dark in the cavern and he had lost all count of time. To judge by the gnawing pains of hunger, he had lain bound an unconscionable time. The dank place chilled him. His pinioned arms were numb. A small swinging lantern shed a feeble glow. Beside him was a bowl of water which he could drink by lapping. There was also a trencher containing bread cut into large cubes. It was meagre fare for one accustomed to high living. For hours he had cursed and execrated Jack Tempest until he felt weak from the intensity of his rage. But it is a strain to keep up any emotion indefinitely —even hatred—and as the weary hours dragged by he lapsed into a sullen state which bordered on torpor. Then he became amenable. He would sign. He would sign anything, if only he could get his teeth into a steak, if only he could sleep warm and drink deep. Anything was preferable to this.

His gaolers visited him periodically, either to trim the lamp or to see that he had not upset his water bowl.

When the door creaked open he was surprised to see Tempest standing there. He looked pale and travel-stained.

"Well, Goadby, I have returned sooner than I intended. It was my original intention to give you three days in which to make up your mind to sign."

"Three days? Fiends of hell. Haven't three days passed yet?"

"From your tone I gather you have not been comfortable. But I must remind you that you made the bed on which you lie."

"Damn you," muttered Goadby.

"Still in no amiable frame of mind? I'm sorry. I am going to loosen the cords which bind your legs. You may be tempted to kick me as I know you would like to do, so I must call your attention to the unwisdom of yielding to any such impulse."

"Loosen these damned ropes, I won't kick," said Goadby sullenly.

Tempest's fingers worked on the knots until they were loose.

As the strands unwound, the bound man groaned and squirmed with pain as the blood circulated freely again.

Stoical of face, Tempest stood aside while the man grew accustomed to the freedom he had acquired. Goadby slowly exercised first one leg and then the other as though nothing else mattered.

"Now my arms," he ejaculated once his legs were resuming a more normal feeling.

"Not so fast," remarked Tempest. "We have a few matters to discuss first."

"I'll sign that damned paper."

"There's no need."

"What?" The man glanced up quickly as though suspecting a trap. "Ah, ha! You're coming to your senses. You are beginning to realize your folly in imprisoning a magistrate. Getting nervous, eh?"

Tempest sighed. "I said so! I prophesied it. No gratitude. No sense of appreciation. No, Goadby, you are wrong. Quite wrong. What I am doing is against my better judgment. But it is at the request of a lady. The woman whom you persecuted has pleaded with me to give you your freedom without humiliating you by signing that document."

"Shows her sense."

"It shows her charity which, to my way of thinking, indicates that her heart is more active than her head. But you ought to appreciate her clemency, you rogue, for you'd have got little sympathy from me. So you do not have to sign."

"Then loose these cords. They're cutting my arms like hell. Let me get out of this."

"First I want your word that you will abandon this iniquitous marriage."

"All right. Let me go. I give you my word. Now, let me free."

"It's not so simple as that. Neither am I so simple. When you depart you go blindfolded, and you will ride in my company —on your own horse—until we come to a lonely place. When I release you it will be because I am convinced that you will never be able to find this place. I have no illusion about your sense of honour."

"Loose these ropes."

"In my time, not yours. Stand up! I'll help you, though I feel contaminated by touching you. Now, Goadby, swear that you will never follow Celia Upton, never persecute her, or interfere with her happiness in any way whatsoever."

"I swear," said Goadby sullenly.

"On my undertaking to give you your freedom without any conditions other than these, you swear that you will release her from all contract of marriage."

"I swear."

Goadby was docile. Tempest regarded him suspiciously. Suddenly he grasped the man by the shoulders and shook him. "Damn you," he cried. "Don't take this lightly. I'm giving you your chance. Don't abuse it. Keep those promises or it will be the worse for you. And don't harbour any idea in the back of your mind that you will get the better of me and will marry Celia. You'll never marry her. Never! I'll kill you first."

CHAPTER TWENTY-FIVE

TEMPEST returned to his cottage on the Great Ormeshead in a sombre mood. He was full of misgivings. His mind was troubled, not for himself but for the magnanimous girl whose future was in jeopardy. In order to please her he might have harmed her. He had loitered for a day or two on the moors, a prey to his own black mood, alone with his gloomy thoughts. In passing he had called at Jem's lonely farm to bid him and his son be vigilant; more than ordinarily vigilant. He had sent a message by some gipsies to Jasper. And now he had come back to the cottage which, to him, represented home. The nearest approach to a home he was likely to attain. Or so it seemed to him. It was a bright spring day when he arrived. The sun was brighter than his mood. The cottage appeared deserted. There was no welcoming Celia at the garden gate as he walked wearily from the stable. The silence left him uneasy. It was with a feeling akin to relief that he heard Heilyn's voice uplifted in a cheerful song.

He found the seaman seated, knife in hand, inside the big kitchen whittling the hull of his model which was already nearing completion.

"Where is Celia?" was his first question as he crossed the threshold.

Heilyn held up the miniature vessel. "Isn't she a beauty?" he asked, surveying her lines with appraising eye. "Look at the curve of that cutwater."

"Very nice, Heilyn. But you have not answered my question."

"There's impatient you are, Jack. Did you imagine that I should let her be kidnapped the moment your back was turned? She and Miriam have gone down to the sands with the little one. She is like a child herself, collecting shells and seaweed. Ay, she has a love for things beautiful. She has poetry in her heart."

"Put your ship aside, Heilyn. I want to talk seriously to you."

"Why should I put my ship aside? I can listen while I work, can't I? I hold the knife with my hands, Jack, not with my ears."

"Well, carry on if you must, but listen attentively. I want

your advice. First, let me tell you where I have been, and what I have been doing."

"I know where you have been. The little lady told me. And I know what you went for. All you need tell me is what you have done."

"I have done what I set out to do. Let loose a savage wolf to raven on innocent lambs. Fool that I was."

"That's right. Call yourself names. It is sensitive you are if I should say them."

"I tried to gratify her, and I fear I have harmed her. I acted against my better judgment."

"How would you have acted if you had had your way?" Heilyn held up the hull and took stock of its symmetrical lines, head on one side. "She's about ready. Just a shaving off the starboard beam, and she should be ready for rigging. Well, Jack, tell us, man, how would you have acted, on your own, as you might say?"

"I would never have let him go until he had signed that paper."

"That's what's fretting you?"

"Yes, I feel I have no security: no hold over him. I made him give me his promise that he would neither molest her, nor go through with this marriage agreement. But I do not trust him. I do not believe him even though he swore. Once free—he'll soon forget. I ought to have made him sign."

"And hurt her feelings? No, Jack. Let's talk sense. Just for a change, isn't it? You say he will not keep his promised word?"

"Not if I know the man."

"Well then, it is clear, isn't it, that if he would break his spoken word he would also break his written word?"

Tempest stared at his friend as though he found this difficult to comprehend.

"I believe you are right, Heilyn," he said slowly.

"I know I am. Well then, let that comfort you. How do we stand? You have done what you have done to please the lady. That is right. There is not much chivalry left in the world. It is good to find a touch here and there. You think you have been a fool because you have done the honourable thing. Maybe you are right. To put your honour first is the act of a fool. So the world thinks. But I have a notion that things will work out all the better for it."

"I wish I thought so. All I can foresee is that he will start his search for her again and drag her back. This next time there will be no easy rescue. She will be doomed to a life of hell. I'll kill him if he harms her, Heilyn. I haven't much to live for."

"There you go, talking like a fool. Getting all dramatic instead of deciding what to do next. Should I rig this as a tops'l schooner, or fore-and-aft?"

"Oh, put your confounded ship aside and listen to me."

"It is not a confounded ship; it is a model of my new schooner which was finished not long since on the banks of the Conway. And when she is rigged and painted I shall give her to Celia. The model, I mean."

"You think of your silly ship instead of putting your mind on what I am telling you."

"That's where you are wrong, Jack. I may not put my mind on what you are saying because there are times when you talk like a fool. But I am putting my mind on what you are going to do."

"And what might that be?"

"You are going to make plans for getting the little lady out of this country in case things get too hot."

"I have thought of that. Do you mean Ireland?"

"To tell you the truth, the place I had in mind was Halifax."

Tempest looked dubious. "Do you think she would be safe, or happy, on the Yorkshire moors?"

"There's a man you are! Didn't I tell you that you talked like a fool? Your mind runs in terms of horses. Can you picture me sailing my new schooner across the Yorkshire moors? There are times, Jack, when I doubt if you use your brain. I mean Halifax, Nova Scotia, man!"

"Good heavens!"

"There will be no half-measures about this business, lad. If I know the type of men you are up against they will have the Law on you, and the best way of dealing with the Law is to get so far away that it can't reach you. It's sense I'm talking, isn't it?"

"You have taken me by surprise. Would she like it in that distant land?"

"Would she like it, married to that rascal?"

"It's a matter which needs thinking about."

"I have been thinking about it for months, Jack, while I have been whittling away at my models of an evening. You should do something useful with your hands, Jack. It gives you time to use your brain."

"But you didn't know Celia months ago."

"There's a man you are for twisting words. I never said I did. I said I had been giving the matter thought. So I have. That's why, long since, I ordered the schooner to be built. We have made a lot of money, you and me and Jem, out of our free trading, haven't we?"

"We have."

"And we have had one or two close shaves of late?"

"Yes."

"Why not stop the game while it is safe? We are not misers, Jack, you and me, wanting to get gold because we like the nice clinky sound the guineas make. All I want is freedom to do what I want, and no debtor's prison in the background. I should be surprised if there were debtor's prisons in Nova Scotia. There are pine woods, and rivers, and lakes, and clean, pure air. It's a man's country. Anyone who will work must succeed."

"It's very cold, isn't it? Have you been there?"

"I've been there on four voyages, Jack. I know a bit about the land. A fine harbour there is, too. Ay, it's cold in winter but it's a dry cold, and it's hot enough in summer, and the mosquitoes are the devil's natural children. But there's freedom there, Jack. I tell you what is in my mind. Do you stay here, with the little lass, and hope for the best. Meanwhile, now the schooner's ready, I'll buy a cargo of sorts—at Belfast, maybe— where it will not attract attention. Then I'll sail her across and do a bit of trading. And if things seem fair, I'll buy a bit of land with a shack on it, perhaps, or maybe a small store. I can't tell you yet. But I'll get a foothold there somehow. Then, if you want, you can come out and join me. If not, I will go by myself, for I tell you Jack, the Riding Officers are getting more active, and the revenue cutters are staying in these seas longer than I like. It's a long voyage, I know, with maybe a bit of risk if the weather breaks, but I've seen the inside of a prison once, and sink me if I want to go there again; whether it's for debt or for free trading. Stone walls don't look pretty when looked at from the inside."

"I don't see the way clearly yet, Heilyn."

"Maybe you can't, Jack, but I can, and for myself, my mind is made up. Mind you, the schooner isn't really shipshape yet. Now, not a word of my plans."

"Not a word."

"Not even to the little lady. We must keep watch over her, and ensure her safety and happiness, but she need not know as much as us. And here she comes, Jack. Mum's the word." He picked up his model ship and resumed his whittling.

Celia, flushed and radiant, came up the garden path, followed at a distance by Miriam, with the child in her arms.

"Oh, I'm so hot from the climb," cried Celia, flinging her hat on a settle. She stared at the litter of shavings on the floor.

"Oh, Heilyn!" she exclaimed aghast. "What a mess!"

"Now, isn't that a woman all over!" protested Heilyn aggrieved. "Never a word of praise for the beautiful model I have made—only (because there are a few shavings on the floor) what a mess!"

"The little ship is wonderful, I don't know how you do it, but you must admit, Heilyn, that there are rather a lot of shavings on the floor."

"They can be swept up," he said with dignity. "It was in my mind to present this model to you, but——"

"To me! How wonderful of you. Thank you. When will it be finished?"

"It cannot be finished. I make a mess!"

"You have my permission to be untidy—until it is finished. What shall we call it?"

"This is a miniature of my new schooner. It was my intention to name her—guess?"

"*The Rising Gull.*"

"No. The *Celia.*"

"I think *The Rising Gull* is more pleasing."

Tempest had remained silent. He was still morose. Heilyn swept the wood chips on to a shovel and flung them on the fire. Then he picked up his model. "I will go and fit the masts in her," he said, making for the back door.

The animation faded from Celia's face as the door closed. She crossed to Tempest and laid her hand on his arm. "I am glad you are back, safe and sound," she said. "I know you have done what I asked."

"Yes. I have let him loose. We shall suffer for this."

"I am so glad you've freed him, for your sake. I do not fear him. Right will always triumph over evil; light is stronger than darkness."

"A comforting philosophy which is not endorsed by results." Tempest's tone was bitter.

"It was for your sake, not his, that I wished you to do it. I could not bear to think of you doing anything which you would afterwards regret. You are so wonderful."

"I?" Tempest's tone was incredulous.

"The grandest man I have ever met—Mr. Smuggler. Far more honest than many honest folk."

Tempest sighed. "I do not trust him, Celia. He is a petty-minded, selfish, conceited man whose vanity is wounded. But he had better beware. If he breaks faith I shall show him no mercy."

"He won't break faith, Jack dear. Why should he? By this time he must realize that he is only making unhappiness for himself by dragging an unwilling bride to the altar."

"An altar is a place of sacrifice!"

Celia looked concerned. "Jack, dear, this isn't like your usual self. Why have you changed? Have I hurt you?"

"You? Impossible. No, I am worried about your safety. I'm very concerned. It seems so unreasonable, so unfair, that you should be pursued and persecuted merely because you do not wish to be tied for life to a man you hate. I cannot see any way of escape except to continue this life of evasion, living like a hunted creature, always alert and apprehensive."

"But, Jack, I am not worrying. I am happier than I have ever been in my life. You are all so good to me, so amazingly kind. I know it is a rougher existence than the one I was accustomed to at Upton Hall, but it is far more varied and much more wholesome. Believe me, I am happier as I am."

"You would not like to reconsider your decision and return to your old home and your father?"

"No. I do not want to go back. For one thing it would be an admission of defeat. For another thing Guy would pester me, and my father would insist on my being a dutiful daughter. And, Jack, I cannot forget his striking me in the face."

"It was abominable. Perhaps he regrets his hasty act."

"It did something to me. It killed that feeling we call respect. I could not live in the same house. I should only run away again. I will not go back, so the only thing is for me to stay here. Provided, of course, that you will have me."

He answered her with a smile.

"We may not be able to remain here, much as I should like it." he said soberly. "If they discover our *pied à terre* we shall have to seek another dwelling place. You may have to go to all manner of rough places."

"You will be with me?"

"Yes. Or at least I shall not be far away. I will watch over you, Celia. I have dedicated my life to that task."

"Your nearness will make the rough places smooth. I shall not mind where we go provided you walk beside me."

CHAPTER TWENTY-SIX

To make a report on the Turnpike Trusts from Chester to Bangor was a task which pleased Harry Standish mightily. For one thing the country was more pleasant and populated than the wild, barren, inhospitable route which ran from Llangollen to Bangor across some of the bleakest and most mountainous country in the Principality. He was purposely riding from Conway to Chester before surveying the route from Chester to Conway so that he could be familiar with the way from both directions. His task, he well knew, was only in the nature of an experiment. The great Engineer himself would examine the route with meticulous care before any official report was prepared, but the preliminary attempt proved as absorbing to the pupil as, doubtless, the finished report would be to his expert master. The road he followed was some seventeen feet in width, hedged in many places. Already villages had begun to flourish as the result of the influx of trade and traffic. Inns at convenient stopping places, some of them newly completed, showed where enterprising landlords were seeking fresh custom. Occasionally some small, plainly-constructed chapel, told of the endeavours of some members of the community to cater for their fellows' spiritual needs. In the old market town of Abergele Harry dined and slept at the Bee Hotel. With its spacious stables this was much frequented by travellers and was a posting station on the route from the little cathedral city of St. Asaph to the ancient borough of Conway. While his nag rested Harry laboured with pencil, entering his impressions in a notebook.

Normally Harry prided himself on his powers of concentration, but now, when most desirous to win commendation by his survey of a prosaic turnpike, he found his wayward mind preferring to stray along the primrose path of recollection. Instead of remembering toll-houses and milestones, he lingered fondly on the cerulean eyes of the fair Celia, the unwitting disturber of the even tenor of his life. He found himself rejoicing that she had escaped from the net which had enmeshed her. Curiosity took possession of him and he fell to wondering just what had transpired since that eventful night of her escape. He resented the assumption of possession which the man Tempest chose to assume as though he had some prior claim. Harry felt that he had at least an equal share in the fair Celia's regard. If locking the stable door after the horse had gone was a reproach for dilatoriness, surely commendation was merited by one who locked the stable door when the horses—and their riders—were still inside!

Rescuing damsels in distress was a more exhilarating occupation for a young man with romance in his blood than this task of creating highroads for the use of posterity. Dissatisfaction with his chosen profession took possession of Harry. He began to abominate the shaggy, sturdy, shambling nag he had been given as a means of transport. Why should that fellow Tempest bestride a blooded animal while he had to jog along like a farmer on market-day? Harry was a thrifty soul who had spent little of his wages, partly perhaps, because the district in which he worked had offered few temptations to squander. He went in search of the landlord to bargain with him for the hire of a more spirited animal for a few days on the excuse—possibly with reason—that his own mount was in need of rest.

When he set forth, the morning sun was brightening broad fields and showing up the tall chimneys of the numerous old manor houses (some converted into farms) which were scattered about the neighbourhood. He would, he resolved, ride to Chester, making what speed he could, trusting to his quickness of mind to memorize sufficient of the route to enable him to write some manner of report. Once at Chester, he would take a fresh horse and ride for the Salopian border. Something within him told him that he would never be able to settle to the daily routine his profession demanded until he had seen Squire Upton again, and had it out with him, once and for all, about his daughter's welfare. The idea was doubtless ridiculous. To an infatuated young man things which appear absurd to others, seem possessed of a logic not to be denied. He experienced a sense of righteous indignation that this young woman of culture, of refinement, of delicacy of thought, should be harassed and harried for no other reason than that her unsympathetic parent wished to force her into an obnoxious marriage. He rode beside the marsh

of Rhuddlan beyond which the round towers of ruined Rhuddlan
Castle rose in sturdy, if shattered, strength. Then on until he
crossed the river by the arching bridge, to climb the steep ascent.
He glanced up at the squat tower of St. Asaph's diminutive
cathedral. Then he moved along the road to Holywell. He
paused once he was well over the river. His conscience demanded
that he must, at least, make some notes for his report. For a
short while he allowed his horse to graze the roadside grass
while, pencil and pad in hand, he made observations of the
area. There came to his mind a sketch he had noticed on one
of the maps of Flintshire which worthy John Speede had prepared two centuries before. It depicted the little city of St. Asaph,
but there was no bridge at the foot of the hill where the cathedral
stood. Instead, the crossing was lower down stream. Through
Harry's mind there flashed the thought that the road from
Holywell could be shortened if the site of this now vanished
bridge could be discovered. Quickly he made a drawing of the
present rivers and bridge and marked his suggested route. The
idea, he felt, would have sufficient originality to commend
itself to Telford even if the Engineer did not adopt the suggestion.
Engrossed in his task Harry did not notice the approach of a
horseman until the rider paused. His shadow, falling across the
page, caused Harry to glance up. He was a tall, cadaverous man
in a blue coat. The rider was lean of jaw, with a cast in one eye.
For a moment the thought flashed through Harry's mind that
it might be a highwayman, yet St. Asaph was still reassuringly
near at hand and he could not imagine a knight of the road
operating so close to the haunts of men. To his surprise the man
revealed no hostility; he was, indeed, remarkably civil.

"A nice morning, sir," said he, giving a half-salute with his
riding-crop. Harry responded to this civility.

"An artist, maybe?" resumed the man, nodding towards
Harry's sketching pad. "No. I have it. 'Pon my soul, it's dense
I am this bright morning. You must be one of the Government
surveyors at work on this new highway. Yet, pardon my
presumption, you appear mighty young for so responsible a
task."

"I am merely an articled assistant."

"One of Mr. Telford's men? Now, this is fortunate. I have

been sent to seek one of his young men, but I doubt not that he will be up in the mountains somewhere, difficult to find."

"Who was it you were looking for?" inquired Harry, ever ready to assist.

"Name of Harry Standish."

"That's my name. What could you want with me?"

"Your name? Now, isn't Lady Luck smiling on me. My good sir, you have saved my horse many a weary mile."

"And what brings you in search of me?"

"Ah! That would be telling. There's a gentleman—I name no names—who is mighty desirous of making your acquaintance."

"You fill me with curiosity."

"A roadside is not a convenient place for a conversation. Not a conversation of such consequence. What I suggest is, let us turn back to St. Asaph. A short distance, my good sir, a very short distance. There, at the top of the hill, is a hostelry I can well recommend. Now, over a glass of port, we two might converse in private, and in comfort."

Harry frowned thoughtfully. "I have a long ride ahead of me."

"It might be that I might save you some of your exertions. Come, young sir, I know you are a busy man, and for that matter so am I, but the hour spent now may save hours later on."

"You are very mysterious."

The man looked about him. "I am a man who likes things thorough," he said, and looked about him restlessly. "This chat by the wayside is not my idea of doing business. Also, what I might say to you is neither here nor there for I am but a messenger, sent on ahead, as it were. The gentleman who sent me has a proposition to make. Now, we waste time talking. Get to your saddle. We'll be back in St. Asaph in a brace of shakes."

Harry put away his sketching-pad and mounted. He was, it must be confessed, curious. A messenger? From whom? He glanced at the man. His lantern-jawed face was expressionless; enigmatical as a Chinese idol. Had they been riding to a lonely place Harry might have felt ill at ease; as it was, travelling back to the placid city of St. Asaph where the cathedral provided an atmosphere of benignity, he felt that all must be well. Moreover, Harry was curious, and curiosity is a subtle snare.

The man led the way, not to one of the chief posting houses, but to a small tavern which stood a little way back from the road. He slipped a coin into the hand of an unkempt hostler who strolled from the rear premises and the man led the two animals stable-wards. "You'll have a glass of port, I'm sure. So you shall. For me, I'll take rum. Warms the heart on a fresh morning after a ride." He turned into a low-raftered room which looked out upon a back courtyard, the high walls of which were covered with lime-wash now turned into a streaky grey. A man wearing a soiled linen apron, placed two glasses on the table and added two bottles.

The man with a cast favoured Harry with a knowing wink. "One glass," he confided, "is a sociable chap who calls for another to follow. Drink your fill, young sir, my employer will pay the bill, so let's make it a proper handsome one."

"Who is your employer?"

"All in good time. You shall know. Just another minute or so to wet the throat. A man talks better when he has had a drink even as a machine runs smoothest when oiled. Here's to your health, young sir." The man seemed in a good humour. Harry sipped his port, but the man did not set his glass down until it was empty, and then he reached for the bottle and refilled it. "Ahh!" he said, and there was satisfaction in his voice. "Now to business."

He bent confidentially. "It is information I am seeking," he said. "And I have been told that you are the man who can help me."

"What information?"

"It's about a young lady."

Harry straightened his shoulders and the expression on his kindly countenance changed to stubbornness. The man's eyes were quick to notice the change.

"Ay," he said, with an attempt at gentleness in his tone. "A pretty young lady, a charming young lady who is fair breaking her old father's heart by her wilful ways. She has run away from home, poor child. Tempted away, most likely."

He emptied another glass. "It's a sad story," he said with a sigh. "A mighty pitiful story did you but know the truth."

"I'll do nothing to harm her. I tell you that straight and plain," said Harry defiantly.

"Ah!" said the man. "So you know the young lady I speak about?"

"Well . . . I . . . do know a young lady."

"Like as not you know more than one, a fine handsome upstanding young fellow like you."

"Have done with that kind of talk. Tell me who you are, what you want and who pays you."

"Who might I be? What might I be wanting? And who pays me?" The man weighed the questions solemnly and then reinforced himself with another glass of rum. "Who pays me? Let's have first things first. I've not been fully paid yet. Just a little to go on with, as it were. Payment, you see, is by results. 'Bring my poor erring daughter, my poor misguided child back to me and I will reward you handsomely,' says her sorrowing father."

"I can't imagine Squire Upton speaking like that."

"Upton, that's the name. Now that's fortunate for there'll be no misunderstanding. You are a bright young man, sir. Those words were not, as you surmise, the actual words he uttered, but just, as it were, my presentation of them. If there is any fault, let the blame be laid to my account." He waved his hand with a gesture of magnanimity. He bent forward again and the cast in his eyes seemed the more pronounced as he stared into Harry's face.

"Where is she?" he asked with soft intensity. Harry was fascinated. He kept wondering which was the eye at which he ought to look. His gaze shifted restlessly from one to the other. They were bright eyes, unblinking like those of a snake.

"I do not know."

The man spread his hand deprecatingly. "Oh, come, come, don't go wasting my time. It was you, wasn't it, who said that time was precious, or words to that effect?"

"Yes, and it is time I was on my way."

"Sit down. This conversation is just growing interesting, but let's get this straight and plain. Don't go wasting time saying you don't know where she is, and don't tell me lies."

"I never tell lies." Harry flushed. He wished now that he had not turned back. "What are you? What's your name? And why do you dare to question me in this impertinent manner?"

M

"Name of Thomas Black," said the fellow. "To my friends, Black Tom. Why do I dare question you? I question you because a fine gentleman pays me to do it. And I dare to do so because I have never yet found nothing I dare not do if anybody dares me to do it, see?"

He looked, Harry mentally decided, what might be called a rough customer. Black Tom grew insistent. "Come, out with it. Where is she?"

"I do not know, I tell you, I do not know."

"Lies."

"Damn you, you ill-bred lout, haven't you the wit to understand that to say that to a gentleman is about the worst insult you can offer? Stand aside."

"Easy now, sit down."

"Let me pass." Harry tried to thrust past. Black Tom was on his feet with a rapidity which sent a glass tumbling to the floor.

"Now then, now then! None of them tricks. Sit down when I tell you, and keep quiet."

"Quiet. If you don't get out of my way I'll shout for help."

There was a quick movement of the man's right hand and Harry found himself looking into the menacing barrel of a pistol.

"Now will you sit down? I don't want any fuss and bother, my lad, but on the other hand you have put me to a sight of trouble tracing you. I've ridden hundreds of miles, I might say, trying to catch up with you, and now I have you, I don't mean to let you get away. Oh, no, not on your life! Now, where do I find the lass?"

"Wherever you can! What scoundrels you all are persecuting an innocent girl who never harmed you. Take your pistol away and put up your fists like a man and I'll fight you. You scum. You don't play fair."

A sardonic smile crossed the man's lantern face. "Very pretty. Now, in my game, I get lots of abuse and it don't mean no more to me than water on a duck's back. I've been called worse names, far worse names. So save your breath. Now, where is she?"

"I don't know, I tell you. I wish I did. I've only glimpsed

her once. If I knew where she was, wouldn't I be with her, you fool?"

Black Tom stepped back and stared thoughtfully. "Ay," he said, "there may be something in that. Damn my luck. Well, anyway, I've got you and that's a start. Half's better than none. They want you, my pretty fellow, and you're in for it. There's a charge out against you for attempted assault, and for conspiracy in kidnapping. Well, let's have no ill-feeling. Sit down and have another drink while you can. I've a rendezvous here with Sir Guy Goadby who might be due most any time now. Drink up while you may."

Black Tom picked up the fallen glass which had splintered and regarded it sadly. It was too far chipped to use, so he raised the rum bottle to his lips.

"Look," he said, with a shrewd look creeping into his eyes. "I'll make a bargain with you. Tell me where she is and I'll let you go free. After all, I don't want to see a bright young lad like you clapped in gaol. Not a bit of it. I'm being quite frank and above board. The big money comes when I return *her*. Give me just a hint as to where she might be and I'll let you nip out the back way and off with you while the going's good."

"I don't know."

"Quick man, quick, where is she? There's Sir Guy's horse just pulling up."

"I don't know. And if I did I wouldn't tell you. You think I'd purchase my freedom at the expense of betraying her? You scum, you do not know the meaning of honour. Put me in gaol. Let me rot there until I die. I'll never divulge a thing which would harm a hair of her head."

CHAPTER TWENTY-SEVEN

THE days passed pleasantly enough for Celia. It was the most glorious period of the year, with wild flowers in profusion, sunlit seas, and yellow sands. The days were all too short. On several occasions Heilyn had taken her out in the *Gwynedd*. Though they did little fishing, principally because it troubled Celia to see the fish gasping, they found pleasure cruising off the rocky coast. Sometimes they sailed up the Menai Straits so that Celia could look across at the old grey castle which kept a sleepy watch over Beaumaris.

Once they penetrated deeper into the Straits, past Bangor ferry, and Celia gazed with awe at the wooded cliffs. As her eye measured the breadth of the crossing she almost laughed at the absurdity of any man thinking of building a bridge across so formidable an obstacle. Of course it was impossible! No man could do it. Not even Mr. Telford.

Once, when Tempest considered it safe, she, with Miriam to bear her company, visited the old walled town of Conway where from the Castle walls she looked far up the verdant vale. It was all new to her. Each day brought a fresh interest. She had meditated inside the tiny church of St. Tudno which had bravely withstood the gales in its lonely hollow on the headland. She had climbed to the top of the Orme to marvel at the panorama of the mountains about Snowdon which lifted their formidable peaks against the southern sky. She glowed with health. So interested was she in this new life that she scarcely noticed the absences of Tempest when he disappeared for several days at a stretch.

Heilyn always bolted the shutters when night fell. The door, in addition to its bolt, was kept on a chain. They rarely had callers for the pathway up the cliff was uncertain, especially on nights when there was no moon, but if, by chance, a knock did come at the door, Tempest would noiselessly guide Celia into the back room. He would stand, peering through the crack of the door, his right hand inside the breast of his coat, and though he gave no sign, she knew that he grasped a pistol.

So happy and carefree was her life on the green headland which overlooked the crescent bay, that she would have forgotten the menace to her safety had it not been for these occasional reminders. But Tempest never relaxed his vigilance. He was like some creature of the wild, continually alert for possible danger.

One night they heard the call of the curlew, thrice repeated. When Celia rose, Tempest's hand restrained her. The knock on the door differed from the previous knocks. Heilyn dropped the chain and flung wide the door. Jem glided quietly into the room, and stood, screwing up his eyes in the lamp light, while Heilyn re-bolted the door. The night was dark outside.

The former groom touched his forehead to Celia, an instinctive gesture of respect.

"News, Jem?" inquired Tempest with assumed indifference. Jem turned his hat nervously in his hands and glanced towards Celia.

"You may tell me," said Celia. "There are no secrets now."

Tempest nodded. "You may talk in the presence of Miss Upton freely, Jem. All our cards are on the table. Out with the message."

"There's more'n one message, Cap'n. First, one for Heilyn, particular. There'll be a cargo for the White Chapel cave the first night of the new moon."

Heilyn looked up from the model schooner he was rigging and nodded his massive head. "First night of the new moon," he repeated. "We'll be there." His nimble fingers were fixing the fore-shrouds to the hull as neatly as a woman would knit.

Jem looked towards Tempest, cleared his throat, and appeared ill at ease.

"Out with it, man," ordered Tempest.

"We've been across into Shropshire," Jem said. "There's a fine 'ow-d'-yer-do there, and no mistake. First thing I saw was a notice stuck on a barn door. Reward of £100 offered for news of the whereabouts of the Squire's daughter."

Celia forced a laugh. "I had no idea I was so valuable."

"The local constables have been called out. So have the constables of the nearby counties. And Squire Upton has paid some men to go out prying and searching."

"We have encountered one beauty!" Celia spoke calmly. "This is the sort of thing we might expect."

"Trouble is, miss, they seem to be making this way. You remember the Bedol, that lonely inn where you saw the—er—gentleman who—who——"

"Who wanted to marry me. Go on, Jem. What next?"

"One of 'em has been up there again. Tall man with a squint. 'E put a mighty lot of questions. And 'e's been 'anging around them men who work on the new road."

Tempest scowled and rose impatiently. "They don't let grass grow under their feet."

"Is it serious?" asked Celia.

"Heavens, no. Only irritating. We were comfortable here."

"And happy, Jack. Very happy. I shall be sorry to leave."

"There's no need for that yet. Only, no more trips to Conway, my dear. And shun strangers. I think you might spend more of your time out in Heilyn's boat. You will get fresh air then without much risk of being seen."

"I think so, too," remarked Heilyn. He paused from his activities to nod his head approvingly. "We get on famously, don't we, Madam Mermaid, provided I don't catch fish?"

Jem moved towards the door. "I'd best be getting back. My boy Tim is holding the horses at the foot of the hill. I want to get across the turnpike and make for the hills before the night stage from Bangor goes through."

Heilyn moved to open the door. Jem paused. "I'd nigh forgot. When I was talking to one of Telford's men 'e told me something about that young fellow——"

"Mr. Standish?" asked Celia.

"Ay. That was the name. Well, 'e was sent on a job to Chester a week since and there's no word of 'im. I don't say as anything's wrong," added Jem hastily, "but I'm just telling you!"

When the door was bolted Tempest swore softly. "I was wrong!" he said. "I knew I ought never to have let that scheming devil go loose. Now we pay for it."

"Jack, please. My father is doing this. You must not put the blame on Guy. I dislike the man but we must be fair."

"You will find it difficult to convince me," said Tempest sceptically.

Heilyn picked up his model, held it to the light, scrutinizing it critically. He nodded his approval and placed the ship tenderly on a shelf.

"I think," he observed, dusting his hands, "it might be wise to take the little lady still further into our confidence."

"What do you mean, Heilyn?" demanded Tempest.

"It would be as well if she knew our line of retreat. If one of us is here, we could soon whisk her away as neat as if the fairies had collected their queen, but if by some mischance she was caught unawares, it might be awkward."

"I agree, Heilyn. Come, my dear. And Miriam, you had best come, too."

He led the way across the kitchen, and into the scullery which was small and partly hollowed out of the rock of the hillside. At the far end was a home-made dresser. Tempest opened one of the cupboards, thrust in his arm and grasped a lever. The dresser swung outward, revealing a tunnel cut in the rock. Heilyn lit a lantern, and he led the way, throwing the yellow beams into the cavity. He beckoned to Celia and Miriam to follow, and once they were well inside, Tempest turned a wheel which drew the dresser back into position again. "Try this," he said to Celia. "You must know how it works."

Fascinated, Celia watched Heilyn's moving legs silhouetted against the yellow light of the lantern as they went down the tunnel. Heilyn stopped and concealed the lantern in a cavity.

"Its beams cannot be seen from outside," he said. "We must go cautiously now as we are nearing the entrance."

He gave Celia his massive hand and slowly they moved forward. The girl felt the cool night air on her face, and then caught sight of a cluster of stars. As her eyes grew accustomed to the darkness she could discern the shadowy bulk of the headland towering overhead and was conscious of the murmur of the waves washing far below.

"I think that is far enough for tonight," said Tempest in a low voice. "We had best point out the way in daylight. That will give them greater confidence."

"Yes, please," said Celia earnestly. "I feel as if I was stepping into space and would go crashing from the rocks into the sea."

"I can understand that," replied Tempest. "It is, in reality, quite safe provided you keep to the pathway. What we call fear is usually the result of not knowing. Tomorrow we will try again. There is a cave at the bottom where you can hide, and near it a little cove from which a boat could carry you out to safety."

Cautiously the two women were guided back to the tunnel entrance. The yellow glow of the lantern gave a feeling of warmth and security.

Tempest persuaded both the women to work the lever which opened the secret door and, once they were through, made them close it.

"That secret way is the chief attraction of this cottage," confessed Tempest as they relaxed in the comfort of the kitchen. "Made by smugglers for smugglers!"

Filling the kettle from a huge beaker, Miriam placed it on the fire. "We will have a warm drink," she said. "The tunnel was chill."

"Yes, I am cold," said Celia, holding her hands to the blaze, "but it is partly excitement, I think."

Heilyn picked up his model and, bowing, presented it to Celia. "She is yours," he said. "Made specially for you. There is still a coat of paint required, but I give her to you now as I go away tomorrow for a while."

"How good of you, Heilyn."

"To go away?"

"Don't tease! It is good of you to make this lovely model for me. I shall value it far more than anything bought in a shop. Whenever I look at it I shall picture your strong hands shaping it."

"And making a mess on the floor!"

"It's most ungallant of you to remind me of that, Heilyn! Tell me, may I ask, where do you go tomorrow?"

"To Beaumaris. Thence in my new schooner, to Belfast. I wish to try her out to see how she behaves, and also I want to purchase a cargo."

"A cargo? Do you mean——" Celia hesitated.

"No. You do me an injustice, Fairy Queen. This time I shall be respectable—for the first time for years. The old game grows risky. I have decided to become a legitimate trader. I must, I think, be growing old. I become cautious."

"I hope you will be successful, Heilyn," said Celia slowly, crossing and staring into the fire.

"Celia," remarked Tempest, "you sounded positively regretful. Don't say you are deploring our worthy Heilyn's commendable resolution to reform!"

She turned with a laugh. "Yes—almost. I did so much want to participate in the excitement of landing a cargo."

"So you shall, my lovely Naiad," cried Heilyn. "The change to respectability must not be accomplished too speedily lest the shock prove too great for me to bear. If the wind holds fair I should be back in time for the next landing. If I am not, why we will arrange matters so that you shall have your adventure the following trip."

"No!" Tempest spoke abruptly.

"But, Jack, why not?"

"There is no point in your taking unnecessary risks. We have not had a brush with the Excise people yet, but there is no guarantee that they may not get wind of our venture and raid us. In that case there might be shooting."

"Poof!" exclaimed Celia. "They couldn't hit anyone in the dark. You must let me join in, Jack. I want to. I want to prove to you that I am one of your people, ready to help, ready to take chances."

He shook his head.

"I support the Fairy Queen," said Heilyn. "Jack, I think you are at fault. You spoke of risks. Then let Celia get accustomed to risks as soon as possible. There may be greater risks ahead."

Tempest glanced at him inquiringly.

"And, Jack," resumed Heilyn, "I throw back your own words in your teeth. 'What we call fear is usually the result of not knowing.' The time may come when these devils press us so close that our little lady may have to take to the boat and make her escape by sea. If it is her first experience she may falter. Let her try a landing or two with us. It will test her. She will know better her own feelings. And if the time of testing comes she will move with greater confidence because she knows what lies ahead instead of embarking fearfully because she dreads unchartered seas."

Celia watched the expression on Tempest's face, afraid to speak lest she should say the wrong thing.

"I want to do what is best," said Jack soberly. "I feel my responsibility. I want to do what is best for her. I believe you are right, Heilyn. Celia may be all the better for running risks. Get back from Belfast as soon as you can, Heilyn. As for you, Celia, if you are resolved to turn free trader, you shall have your wish. You shall help to land our next cargo, and I hope the Fates will be gracious to us for your sake."

CHAPTER TWENTY-EIGHT

THE following morning as soon as the wind got up, the *Gwynedd* cutter turned her bowsprit towards the Menai Straits where the new schooner rode at anchor in Beaumaris Roads. Heilyn was proud of his new vessel. Celia had coaxed to accompany him, and was excited at the prospect of inspecting the ship which she had hitherto seen only in miniature. When the *Gwynedd* had anchored, Heilyn stood critically eyeing his new craft with an expert's eye. The sails were bent and the canvas gleamed white in the morning sunlight. Every rope was new and though some required tightening, they gave a smart appearance to the craft. The yards on her foremast suggested the stability of an ocean-going vessel. His eyes satisfied, Heilyn unfastened the painter of a small boat they towed, and bringing it alongside, helped Celia to clamber in. Thus they went on board the new schooner. Several local men were serving as crew. Celia was as curious as a child, gazing up at the tapering masts or down into the dark hold. The cabin fascinated her. Lockers had recently been installed and some chips of wood still lay on the deck.

"When will you learn tidiness, Heilyn," she said reprovingly.

"A fair tyrant; that is what you are! Give a man a chance. She will be all ship-shape presently. Visitors are not expected aboard yet, and if you criticize I shall have to turn you adrift until we are ready to receive callers."

They examined the stores, the water tanks, the lockers, Celia as eager as a housewife in a new house.

"I think I shall enjoy life in a ship," said Celia enthusiastically.

"I hope so, Queen of the Ocean, but you'll not find the deck always as steady as you do at present."

"And you really mean to start trading, Heilyn?"

"I have had it in mind for several years."

"You are tired of smuggling?"

He leaned on the bulwarks and stared dreamily towards the green slopes of the hills. "Life changes," he said, "and we change with it—if we are wise. I seem to have been many men. At first I went in for smuggling because I rebelled against the Law. I stayed because I liked the excitement. Then I became purely mercenary, wanting all the money I could get because I found out that money could get me things which, without money, I would have to go without."

"And now?"

"Now I have discovered that there are things which money cannot buy. I have found that my tastes are simple; that I should never be at ease in a fine house like the one they tell me was your home. I like creating. I like making things with my hands. I like looking on Nature and wondering what secrets she withholds from mortal eyes. I want leisure to dream—and, to write my thoughts. Lord, I was never meant for this life. It was necessity, not choice, which forced it upon me. I wanted to be a student and go to college but it was denied me. There was no money in the house to provide for both my brother and me. I want to capture, if I can, a little of what I have been denied, while I am still young enough to find enjoyment in it. And I cannot be at ease in my mind while I am continually looking over my shoulder to see if there are any Riding Officers on the cliffs or Excise Men in the offing. So I am going to turn respectable. Not because I am reformed, my dear, but because, having gained freedom, I want to keep it."

"Thank you, Heilyn. I know you better now. And like you even more. It was like you to let your brother go to college!"

Heilyn looked embarrassed. "He was weakly," he explained.

He roused himself from his reverie. "Into the boat with you," he cried with a show of energy. "We must take advantage of the tide. I shall make a mariner of you yet."

As they idled back to the sandy bay beneath the shadow of the Ormeshead, Celia stared up at the massive promontory, fascinated by the wheeling gulls, and the serried rows of guillemots on the cliff ledges.

"They look like French grenadiers of the Guard, don't they, with their white waistcoats?"

"I will take your word for it, Sea Maiden, not having seen the Old Guard. You'd better ask Jack. He's fought them."

When the *Gwynedd* reached her moorings Heilyn rowed his fair passenger ashore and they climbed slowly up the winding path until the cottage came in sight. They found Tempest standing patiently at the gate awaiting them.

"How good to have you with us again," cried Celia.

"I shall have to postpone the trip to Belfast," said Heilyn, dropping into a chair. "I cannot get the stores aboard in time to get back here by the new moon. I want to be here when the next cargo is run."

"Yes, I should like you here," agreed Tempest. "If it is to be landed at the White Chapel Cave it would be better if you had charge of the landing."

Two days later Celia was informed that the appointed time had come for the arrival of the cargo from Roscoff. The hours passed slowly. To Tempest and Heilyn the occasion was a matter of routine; to the girl it was the eve of a new adventure. In some mysterious way word had been passed around among the fisher-folk and miners on the Ormeshead, many of whom had shares in the nocturnal ventures which brought to their pockets more money in a single night than they could earn by many weeks' arduous toil. Most families were connected by marriage or ties of kinship, thus the secret was safe in a community which laboured for the common weal. The men sauntered down to the marsh when night had fallen, making their way among the sand dunes, familiar to them since boyhood, to places where their rowing-boats were concealed among the grass. These were carried to the incoming tide across shingle and sand which, by light of day, would have incriminating traces obliterated by the wash of the waves.

Three shadowy figures were at the oars of the boat in which Celia was placed. Before Tempest took his seat beside her in the sternsheets he wrapped her in a boat-cloak. She was trembling, but it was more with excitement than cold. No word was spoken. Muffled oars were dipped into the water almost noiselessly by hands of men familiar with the task. As the girl felt the boat move under her she was conscious of other stealthy shapes gliding eastward. The bulk of the Little Orme was faintly illumin-ated by a pale light thrown from a crescent moon.

It was a time when smuggling was at its height, not merely along the Channel coast but in the Irish Sea. A regular (or irregular) trade in contraband was carried on between Anglesey and the Isle of Man which was the principal depot for these seas. The rocky coast of North Wales, and particularly the sea caves in the Ormes, proved an attractive haunt for smugglers. There were good anchorages, scattered villages, and other inducements. Hardy fishermen, accustomed to the moods of the sea, found a lucrative employment in disposing of the goods which astute mariners brought through the blockade. Preventive measures were left largely in the not-too-efficient hands of the pressed crews of revenue cutters whose movements were well known to the free traders. The revenue cutter *Viper*, stationed off the North Wales coast, had an area which stretched from Anglesey to St. Bee's Head, so that it did not call for any high standard of seamanship to keep out of her way, and detection by the Excise authorities depended more on luck than efficiency. A second cruiser, the *Speedwell*, patrolled from Holyhead to Land's End. The smugglers as the result of years of tradition, handed down from father to son, had innumerable ways of avoiding detection so that many a suspect, overhauled by the revenue cutter, was found to carry no prohibited cargo, no matter how many suspicions might lurk in the mind of the cutter's disappointed skipper.

Celia noticed that the boat was pulling farther and farther from the land. Presently she became aware of stealthy movements ahead. She saw the tracery of a ketch's rigging silhouetted against the sky. The other boats were already busy alongside.

Tubs of spirits, small enough for a man to lift with ease, parcels of merchandise wrapped in tarpaulin, were handed over the low bulwarks to be stowed beneath the thwarts of the waiting boats. There was no talking, only a whispered order when occasion demanded. As one rowing-boat pulled shorewards with its precious freight, another took its place. Celia could see Heilyn's massive figure towering above the other sailors. He was balancing, one foot on the boat's gunwale, handing down the tubs as they were passed to him from the ketch.

When his boat pushed off, Tempest steered alongside. They were the last in the little convoy, having been delayed by waiting to take Celia on board.

The girl sat motionless in the stern, holding the tiller which Tempest had relinquished, while the men worked methodically as they stored smuggled merchandise in the bottom of the boat. The sea was calm, save for a slight swell, which set the blocks of the ketch creaking. From the distant shore there faintly sounded the cries of oyster-catchers, disturbed, possibly, by the movements of the boats.

Tempest came walking aft, balancing carefully on the thwarts. He grasped the tiller, and the bowman thrust off from the dark side of the ketch. The oars dipped. Celia looking back over her shoulder, watched until her neck grew stiff as the vessel's outline grew more and more indistinct until it disappeared from her gaze. She leaned against Tempest's shoulder with a wriggle of excitement. The new life undoubtedly had its compensations. Thus the boat moved rhythmically shorewards until, through the gloom ahead, Celia could discern the white splash of waves, and heard their soft hiss as they broke in regular ripples against the glistening crags at the foot of the headland. The oarsmen pulled for the eastern side, and presently she saw Tempest lean forward and grow tense as he steered the boat until it ran its nose on to the shingle at the mouth of the great sea-cave which loomed ahead. Several men waded into the sea to hold the gunwale steady. A chain of men was formed and the tubs were passed from hand to hand until Celia was unable to see what became of them. When the boat was emptied, Tempest gave Celia his hand and helped her on to the shingle. Another man took his place in the stern. Packages were loaded into the boat ere it was turned back for another load. The girl was impressed by the utter silence. The men worked as though frequent practice had taught them just what was expected of them. Orders were superfluous. The wet shingle crunched and slid under Celia's feet, and a discourteous wavelet washed into one of her shoes causing her momentary discomfort. Jack's firm hand under her arm aided her until she found herself within a spacious cavern. Shadowy forms brushed past her. A faint yellow glow showed ahead. Behind a projecting rock which concealed the light from the sea, she came upon a scene of activity. The cargo was spread out on the shingle while an inventory was taken of its contents as methodically as a shopkeeper would take stock of his stores. Tempest bade her sit upon a bale of merchandise, while he joined in the work. It seemed so quiet and orderly that Celia felt that these men could not possibly be breaking the law. Then she noticed that each man had a brace of pistols thrust into the broad leather belt with which he was girt, and that a sentry with cutlass and musket stood motionless guarding the entry from the sea. The men, she noticed, were stacking the goods in separate piles, and Tempest, his work completed, sat down beside her and spoke in a low voice. The cave, he explained, was only the clearing depot. From this spot the cargo was dispersed in several directions. One load would be sent inland on the backs of pack animals. Another smaller cargo would be taken by water to the shores of the Menai Straits. Another would go eastward down the coast to be landed at the foot of Penmaen Headland from which spot it would not be difficult to dispatch it inland by unfrequented routes over the uplands until the Denbigh Moors could be reached and the way opened for the journey to the English border.

His explanation was interrupted by the arrival of a fresh convoy from the ketch, and all hands were busy handing in the tubs and bales as they were unloaded from the boats. Celia took her place in the chain, passing on the goods until her fingers felt raw from the rough cordage and the salt water. She scarcely heeded the smart, so ardent was she for this exciting occupation. It seemed a pity, she thought, that so enthralling a pastime should be regarded by unsympathetic authorities as breaking the law of the land. When the last boat was unloaded and the last outward-bound cargo sent off, a lantern flashed a message to the ketch. The landing of the goods had been accomplished. A weary fisherman seated himself on a bale, and drawing out some bread and cheese began to eat.

"Oh!" Celia held out a hand with the impetuosity of a child. "Just a small piece, I'm ravenous!"

The man gallantly offered her all but she was content with a little.

"Come my dear, it is time we took you home," said Tempest. "You not only need supper, but bed. For a first experience you have been out long enough."

"The others?"

"Remain on duty until the dawn begins to show. The work is not half done. We must get the tubs distributed. This cave must be empty before we leave it. Now, into the boat with you."

He helped her aboard and then, running the boat into the waves, leaped in and felt for the oars.

"Are not the others coming to row back?"

"They have too much to attend to. I can manage. It is a heavy boat to pull but I can manage for a short distance. There's no hurry. You must steer. It will be good practice for you."

It was a fresh experience for the girl as she sat with her hand on the tiller watching Tempest as, with feet extended against the boat stretcher, he put his back into the work. Once they were well across the bay he made her steer the boat in with the waves. When she grounded, Tempest leaped into the water and dragged the bows ashore. Then he stuck the boat's anchor in the sand and lifted his weary passenger to dry land.

"The lads will see to the boat when they return," he explained. "Give me your arm. You'll find it hard going in this soft sand."

The girl was indeed glad of assistance as they ploughed their way between the dunes until they reached a firmer path. A candle was burning in the back room when they let themselves quietly into the house. Miriam was abed, but a kettle was singing on the hob, and there was a cold meal spread on the table.

Celia sank into a chair and extended her feet while Tempest removed her sea-stained shoes.

"Tired?" he asked.

"Almost too tired to talk, Jack, but I would not have missed it for the world. It is something I shall never forget until my dying day. You must let me help when the next cargo arrives."

"We'll see. I fear I let you run too many risks. When I brought you away with me it was with the intention of providing for your safety, and now I find myself turning you into a law-breaker!"

"You didn't!" protested Celia sleepily. "I did it myself. And don't argue with me because I'm going to fall asleep."

N

CHAPTER TWENTY-NINE

THOMAS BLACK, *alias* Black Tom, was of unprepossessing appearance. To have told him so would have provoked no resentment. His was no susceptible nature and he had no illusions about his looks. His character, too, was unlovely, but no person is wholly devoid of some commendable characteristic. His outthrust jaw was suggestive of determination, and pertinacity was a quality to which Black Tom might justly lay claim. Having, as the result of many miles cold riding through the Welsh hills, traced Harry Standish, he now turned his powers of patient investigation to a more profitable cause. There was still the missing heiress to be found. The reward of one hundred pounds offered by the squire was an inducement. He regarded it as his. Moreover, as an additional stimulus, Sir Guy Goadby had offered to double the amount should Black Tom prove successful. Though mercenary motives were not to be despised there was an even stronger urge. Black Tom disliked abandoning a chase until he had pulled down his quarry. There was nothing vindictive about this. It was the age-old hunting instinct. Others might grow weary, faint hearted, or fall by the way, but to Black Tom there was no respite until his objective was reached, the prize gained. Once Harry Standish had been handed over to the ungentle hands of Sir Guy Goadby, Thomas Black automatically returned to the scene of his investigations. Roving the land were several of his satellites who reported periodically at a rendezvous on the results of their search. Black Tom listened patiently to all they told him—and reserved judgment.

Patient observation was one of his methods, but his most successful procedure was simplicity itself. He asked questions. Moreover, he asked them in a manner which he considered to be polite. He never raised his voice as ill-mannered men might do. He put them in a wheedling, coaxing tone, nor was he in the least disconcerted at rebuffs which came his way. His logic, like his *modus operandi*, was simple. If people spoke the truth he got to know what he wanted to know. If they lied, it meant there was a purpose for their prevarication. In which case there was need for more questioning.

During his interview at St. Asaph he discovered with little difficulty the route which Harry Standish had followed after he had been briefed by Mr. Telford.

"You haven't, by any chance, recently seen this Miss Upton who is missing?" he had asked unexpectedly, knowing, from his experience of human nature that Harry Standish was an upright young man to whom lying was abhorrent. Harry had coloured so violently when he stammered a negative—adding, as though to assoil his conscience "not for a long time". Whereupon the astute Mr. Black had changed the subject. Much, he reasoned with himself, depended how long a long time might be. To a young man in love a few hours might appear a long time. So Black Tom set off without any impetuous haste back along the way which Harry had taken.

He stopped at the Bee Inn at Abergele and found in the stables Harry's shaggy nag. The creature was not a thing of beauty but its presence afforded Black Tom no little pleasure. So far he had not gone astray.

When he reached the village of Llanddulas he paused to water his horse in the stream. Black Tom was averse to speed. He reasoned that unless there was urgency, a man was more likely to overlook something by too much haste than miss something by being too slow. He conversed with a villager, admiring the bridge of stone which spanned the stream. Had anyone ever made a picture of the bridge? Yes, he was told, a young man had stopped not long before to make a sketch, or some sort of drawing. Just so!

He walked his horse considerately up the turnpike as it climbed the hill behind the great headland of Penmaen Rhos. There was, he knew, the remains of a rocky pathway cut in the cliff face, but the danger of it was such that no one frequented it now that the coach-road had been made. He paused at the hamlet of Colwyn beside another stream, but he could gain no tidings here. Patiently he rode on until he came to another inn. Here, at the Four Crosses, fortune smiled upon his perseverance. The young man with the shaggy horse had been riding past when a lady tapped on the window and called him inside. The hostler knew no more, save that the lady was accompanied by a handsome gentleman who wore a bottle green coat and rode a black horse. Which way did they leave? The hostler was not sure. It was not for Conway. Maybe they went towards the Ormeshead. Black Tom rode out of sight and the way he took led to the Ormeshead also.

.   .   .   .   .   .

Sand dunes provide admirable cover. Black Tom discovered that. Not only do they conceal one from sight, but the grassy crests permit one to lie full length in the sand and observe without exposing the head. In the comforting sunlight of a pleasant May morning, Black Tom stretched his ungainly length upon one of the dunes, and contemplated the tranquil scene ahead. There were several fishing smacks at anchor in the bay. Some fishermen were erecting herring nets, for the tide was at the ebb. Others were engaged in hauling a row-boat across the sands to the water as if they meant to row out to one of the anchored ships. It was a pleasant picture, calm and innocuous, with not so much as the flutter of a petticoat to reward a man for his persistence. Black Tom felt drowsy. The sun was so strong upon his blue-coated back that he grew somnolent. This was not surprising. He had spent long hours in the saddle and his night's repose had been brief and fitful. His cheek settled against his coat-sleeve. The cries of the gulls provided an obligato to his snores.

Black Tom came to himself with a start. Had he been asleep? There was no one to ask. He felt guilty as if he had done a discreditable thing. It was impressed upon him that he must have dozed, for he felt rested and energetic. The men with the boat must have reached one of the smacks for he heard the creak of blocks. Glancing seaward, he saw that a mainsail was being hoisted. As if to make up for precious moments lost, Black Tom got to his feet, dusted the sand grains from his blue suit, and made his way to the depression among the dunes. It was impressed upon him that if dunes provided good cover they also left a record of footprints. This caused him some disquietude. So much of his life had been devoted to following people that he had acquired a horror of being himself followed. So he walked in the softest sand, shuffling his feet so that the outlines would be indistinct. He came to a firmer trackway near the edge of the dunes where the sand was beaten hard. It was much used and as he regarded it, more from force of habit than from hope of finding anything of interest, he stared incredulously. A woman's shoe was plainly outlined. Robinson Crusoe never contemplated the imprint of a human foot with greater amazement—or with greater pleasure. Black Tom seated himself on a sandy bank and proceeded leisurely to assess the footprint. It was a stylish shoe which was recorded, not a peasant woman's footwear. A man's footmarks were beside the tracks, which went forward in a straight line towards the Ormeshead. He shook his head incredulously. Diving into one of his capacious pockets he fetched out a small piece of brown paper, neatly folded. Carefully he spread it on his knee and smoothed the creases. The pattern was shaped to the outlines of a woman's shoe. He took off his coat and spread it on the sand. Walking cautiously across this so as to leave no footmarks behind, he stooped and placed the paper pattern over the imprint of the shoe. The size was identical. Black Tom folded the pattern, picked up his coat and brushed it carefully. He was a methodical and tidy person.

Withdrawing to the seclusion of the dunes he sat himself down to think what his next move should be. Once more his hand disappeared into a capacious pocket. This time he drew out a small telescope. Sprawling full length, concealed by a thick tuft of marram grass, he drew out the brass sections of the glass, polished the lens on his handkerchief, and began to take stock of the scene ahead.

A faint movement seaward attracted his attention. The cutter had slipped her moorings and was heeling to the morning breeze. As his glass became focussed he saw first a burly, bearded sailor in a blue guernsey. Beside him was a man in a bottle green coat. They were both waving to someone ashore.

With surprising rapidity Black Tom turned his face from the ship and, raising his head, stared ahead at the promontory. He was rewarded by the flutter of a white kerchief which showed clearly against the green of the hillside. He trained his glass on the spot. He saw a low stone house, clipped shrubs, a garden gate, and a girl in a print frock. Her hair looked as bright as the morning sunshine where the sunbeams were tangled in its mesh. It looked fair enough to Black Tom; very fair indeed! Carefully he shut the telescope and replaced it in his pocket. Then he lay thinking what he should do next. He liked to plan his movements carefully. Motionless he lay, intent, concentrating. He was nearing the journey's end, and there must be no false move. Subtlety would accomplish what threats and force could not. So he thought deeply, but though he lay very still, this time he did not sleep.

.   .   .   .   .

He knew that Celia Upton had seen him at the caravan. Only for a brief while, it is true, but she would not be likely to forget his ugly face. That cast in his eye gave him away. Black Tom nursed a grievance against life on that account. It had embittered and hardened him. Had he been of good appearance he might have cherished less rancour; as it was he considered that Nature had treated him scurvily and he retaliated by venting his spleen on his fellow men. Whatever happened, Celia Upton must not see him. She would be frightened. She would know that he was sent to capture her. Either she would refuse to accompany him or else make a scene! The men who had carried her off—if that was what had transpired—were no weaklings, and Black Tom was aware that he was in the enemy's country. Let her raise an alarm, and he would be attacked—perhaps killed! He was one among many, Subtlety was obviously required.

She was tender-hearted, susceptible. Of that he was certain. He must play upon her weakness. She would prove vulnerable if he appealed to her compassion. But how?

For a moment he cherished the idea of sending her a note to say that her father was dying and called her to his death-bed. He discarded this as unworthy of his astute mind. It was too obvious a plot. Moreover, from what he gathered, she was no longer attached to her father: not since he had struck her.

No, he must think of something else. The sending of a note was shrewd. Black Tom brought his hand down on his thigh with a slap. "Fool that I am! Of course!" he exclaimed, and began to hasten back to the inn where he had left his horse.

Once he was settled in his bed-chamber, he bolted the door and took from his case a writing-pad, a stoppered bottle of ink, and a quill. Before he unscrewed the top of the inkwell he drew out his pen-knife and sharpened the pen. This was a momentous occasion and there must be no blundering. Everything must be done with deliberation.

He began to write slowly, carefully, pausing between each sentence to weigh carefully the words before they were set down.

Miss Upton.
Dear Madam,

It is with great reluctance that I write to acquaint you of an occurrence which will grieve you as much as it has occasioned me distress. You will recall, I am sure, that most promising young gentleman, Mr. Harry Standish, who was embarking on a professional career of rare promise under my supervision. Some days ago I sent him on a mission to survey a new portion of this territory over which I trust some day to build a subsidiary road. For some reason which is, as yet, unexplained to me, he chose to make his way to your home. My own impression is that he, being a generous-hearted young man, and touched by your unhappy fate, resolved to visit your parent so that he might personally appeal to him to bring about a happier state of affairs.

Nothing could have been more unfortunate. I am told that, by some unhappy mistake, he has been accused of kidnapping you, and, as such, has been cast into prison, where he is likely to remain.

Moreover, it is rumoured that as no trace of you has been discovered, the impression is that you have met with an untimely end, and that the charge against him may well be altered to that horrible and detestable crime of murder. It grieves me to write thus, but my opinion is that his promising young life is in jeopardy unless you appear in person, not only to prove that you are alive, but to assure the authorities that he is innocent of any participation in kidnapping or any other unworthy act, and that anything he may have done has been prompted by his warm and generous heart, and his chivalrous nature.

I, myself, am making what protestation I can, but my efforts, I fear, will be insufficient to save him. Only you can do that. But hasten, dear madam. Let not a day—an hour—be lost, if you would

prevent a most horrible miscarriage of justice which we would
all lament until our dying day.

I have the honour to be, Madam,

Your humble, obedient Servant,

Thos. Telford.

Black Tom read the effusion through critically twice, inserting a comma or two. He sat tapping the quill against his blackened teeth. If Telford's writing was known to Miss Upton his labour would be in vain. But it was worth the attempt. He called the inn-keeper's son, gave the lad a shilling, and explained where the note was to be delivered. The boy knew the house well, he said.

"Tell the young lady that it is urgent," said Mr. Thomas Black, impressively, "and should she ask who sent you, you must say—'*Mr. Telford*'."

CHAPTER THIRTY

THE maiden voyage of the *Rising Gull* had proved a triumph. The vessel behaved beautifully. Apart from the re-setting of some of the canvas, there seemed nothing requiring attention. Twice they had been struck by squalls, but the *Rising Gull* had risen in all her strength and beauty, and though her white wings were slightly ruffled, she rode out the storms with ease and grace. Heilyn was enraptured and apostrophized the vessel in the poetical tones of a lover. At Belfast, too, they met with success. There were men there who were eager to trade, particularly when they saw the gold coin which Tempest and Heilyn produced. With a small experimental cargo for North Wales ports, the *Rising Gull* soared seaward. They stopped at Douglas and went ashore on the Isle of Man—a place with which they were by no means unfamiliar, though as they walked the streets with their newly acquired respectability, the place acquired a new aspect. They were held up in port for two days, for the wind dropped; but on the morning of the third day a breeze blew from the west, and the *Rising Gull* resumed her homeward flight. They had to drift with a spring tide up the Clwyd to unload a cargo at Rhuddlan Quay. When the ebb had carried them clear of the bar they turned homeward. Already the great bulk of the Ormeshead gave a friendly appearance to the coastline. So they idled along with an easy breeze. Heilyn, pipe in mouth, a huge hand on the tiller, dreamed, as contented as a cat on a hearthrug. Tempest was equally happy but less complacent. He was impatient to be back home.

"I had not thought to be so long away from Celia," he said, moving restlessly. "Can't you get more sails on this slow sailer of yours."

"She's doing very nicely. I never thought she would respond so grandly on her maiden voyage. It's delighted I am with the little lady. The best ship I have ever sailed in, and that's a fact, Jack."

Tempest stared towards the Orme as though its friendly outline afforded comfort. "I hope Celia is all right," he said. "I feel my responsibility."

"Miriam is with her. And Jem is not so far away. The lass

will be all right. Stop worrying." Heilyn puffed contentedly at his pipe. "It's very much in love you are, I'm thinking." For a moment Tempest did not reply. "Yes, I love her. Perhaps worship would be more appropriate. There is nothing I would not endure to give her happiness. Never have I been nearer to death than I was on the night of that storm—lying there with a crushed leg, soaked by the downpour, dazed by the darkness, feeling my strength ebbing, and experiencing the humiliation of dying not like a man in action, but like an unwanted mongrel in a pond. And then—she came! When a man is near to death, Heilyn, I suppose his senses and perceptions are more acute. I know that I felt that some mysterious Force or Being had sent her to save me. There and then I dedicated my life to her service. I will care for her and protect her as long as I have strength. Women like Celia are few and far between."

"Her disposition is as sweet as her face," said Heilyn, "but it seems to me that you waste too much time, Jack. You are a laggard in love."

"Would you have me abuse my position?" demanded Tempest, almost fiercely. "She is but a trusting child who has fled from a marriage which she abhors. She looks to me for protection. And you want me to make love to her!"

"I don't, Jack, but maybe she does."

"I'll wager the thought has never passed through her innocent mind."

"There's no knowing!" said Heilyn looking profound. "I'm a sailor, and it may be that I know more about what women like than you."

"What am I?" Tempest spoke bitterly. "A law-breaker, an outcast."

"Just like me. When have you heard me calling myself hard names, eh?"

"I am no fit husband for a woman of Celia's quality."

"You are good enough for me to have as a friend. It is possible that she thinks the same."

"As a friend, why yes!" And Tempest as though to keep in step with his restless thoughts walked forward to where two of the crew were leaning over the bulwarks, pointing out landmarks as the vessel's bows rhythmically rose and fell.

Tempest's impatience did not forsake him. Presently he returned aft.

"Heilyn," he said. "I think we will have to get her away from here."

"Celia? She is happy here. I should leave her where she is. There is always the secret path down to the cave should anything go wrong. Stop worrying. You would search a long way to find a pleasanter or a safer place."

"I think we ought to smuggle her out of the country. It was to look round Belfast to see if we could make a home for her over there that I came with you on this trip. Tell me, Heilyn. Do you think that rogue Goadby will honour his word?"

"No, I don't."

"I ought never to have let him go without signing the paper."

"Put that out of your mind, Jack. I've told you that he would dishonour his written word just as casually as he would break his oath. Rakes like him have no principle. The alternatives, as I see it, were to finish him off, or to keep him in prison for life. Failing those—get the little lady out of his reach."

"How could I keep him in custody for life? It's not feasible. I might just as well murder the devil in the first place. No, the only thing was to get Celia beyond his reach."

"Which is what you have done."

"Which is what I have tried to do. I'm not easy in my mind. I don't know what is going on but I feel that something is happening. That man will be plotting and scheming; I don't think he wants her really, but it wounds his pride to be worsted."

"Very well, Jack. Ireland it shall be. Nova Scotia, if you like! I will get ready a few bits of furniture and things I think she would like. Her chair, now, would just make a place seem homelike. We'll buy or build a cottage somewhere where the rascal will never find her. Now are you satisfied."

"Yes. I feel it would be a wise move from all points of view. You see if Goadby outwitted us and stole her away, rather than let her suffer I would kill him. And I don't want to be driven to do that."

"You won't be. We'll get Celia across to Ulster next week."

They were off the Little Orme now—Rhiwleden, Heilyn called it, preferring its ancient name. Tempest fetched a glass from the cabin, and steadying it against the shrouds, levelled it at the cottage on the Ormeshead.

"There's smoke coming from the chimney. And—yes, I can see a woman's dress."

He shut the glass and returned it to the cabin. "They'll be watching for our return. I expect they have had the ship under observation for hours, wishing, like I wish, that she would make better speed."

"I'll not have the *Rising Gull* slandered. There's only a capful of wind and she's making good headway considering."

Once they were in the bay the moorings were soon picked up. Heilyn ordered two of the crew into the boat and left the rest stowing the sails. As he and Tempest were rowed ashore they could see Miriam hastening across the shingle to greet them.

"I don't like the look of things," said Tempest uneasily. "Where's Celia? Why hasn't she come? She is either ill or hurt."

"She may have gone a walk!" suggested Heilyn hopefully, but, he, too, looked troubled.

The moment the keel touched the sand both men leaped over the gunwales and hurried to Miriam.

"Where is she? Where's Miss Upton?" demanded Tempest.

"Gone!" Miriam's dark eyes were distressed. Tempest caught her by the wrist.

"Quick. Tell me! What's happened?"

"She had a note from Mr. Telford giving her bad news."

"Mr. Telford? He did not know where she was. Why should he write to her?"

"A lad brought it."

"Why should Telford employ a lad? But, go on. What did it say?"

"Miss Celia was that upset when she read it! She told me that the young man, Mr. Standish, had been arrested, and was charged with kidnapping her."

"I can see Goadby's hand in this," commented Tempest. "And then?"

"That as no trace of her could be found it was thought she was murdered, and he was to be hanged."

Tempest had gone strangely calm. His jaw set with determination. When he spoke his voice was controlled. "I knew something would go wrong. But I did not suspect this. And of course she rushed to his rescue?"

Miriam nodded. "She said she must go home. I begged of her to wait until you returned but she said that delay might cost the young man his life. Then I asked her to wait for Jem to accompany her but she would not. She went to the stables and took the chestnut horse which she rides, and off she went."

"No message?"

"She said I was to thank you for all you had done, and that she'd never forget your goodness. She asked your pardon for disobeying you, but she could not let an innocent man suffer on her account."

"Where's Jem?" Tempest shot out the words.

"Getting the horses ready, Captain."

"Good man! He knows there's some hard riding ahead. Coming, Heilyn?"

"No, Jack. I would like to, but I'm no horseman. I would only be a hindrance. I'll get the *Rising Gull* ready to put to sea. We'll be waiting here, fresh-water tanks filled, stores aboard, ready to sail night or day the moment you bring her back."

"I mean to."

He strode away. Heilyn turned to the gipsy woman. "Put her things together so that I can get them aboard—and pick out everything you think she would wish to take."

He walked with bent head back to the waiting boat. Tempest set off for the stables at a run. It cheered him to see the faithful Jem waiting near the door. The little man looked troubled. There was no need for instructions. Jem had anticipated everything. Three horses were waiting saddled, riding-capes rolled across the cantles, pistols in the holsters.

"Well done, Jem!" That was all the commendation the man got—or expected. Tempest swung into the saddle of the black, and Jem with the led horse, followed close at his heels as he cantered along the sandy road which led inland across the marsh. Tempest did not show too much speed. They had a long ride ahead and he knew that he must husband the horses' strength.

"Cap'n."

"Well, Jem?" Tempest reined in slightly so that the man could draw alongside.

"I 'ave your duelling pistols 'ere, loaded."

"You read my thoughts."

"I'll give 'em you when we stop to change 'orses. I've got 'old of every good animal I could lay 'ands on, and 'ave posted 'em in relays along the route."

"Good man."

"I've told our lads what's afoot. They are all on the look-out. They'll 'elp in any way they can, if there's a chase."

"There's likely to be, Jem," said Tempest grimly. "I mean to get her away if I can."

"You'll do it, Cap'n. She's a sweet young lady and we've got to save 'er. My missus would never speak to me again if I didn't back you. We'll do it, Cap'n, but ride easy, for it will be the pursuit as'll test the 'orses' staying powers."

So they rode on. The flat coastal country gave place to hills, so steep that they had to walk their horses. Day turned to night but there was no pause. They reached the high ground where the mountain air was keen on the moors.

"D'y' think this young man really is in prison, Cap'n, or is the whole story a 'oax?"

"It's a hoax, sure enough Jem, but they might quite easily have clapped the lad in gaol."

"Then I'm sorry for 'im. You and me knows what gaol is like."

"We do, Jem. But we can't waste pity on him now. We've a bigger task before us. Jem!"

"Yes, Cap'n?"

"This will be my last adventure. No more free trading for me. My smuggling days are over. I shall live on my illegal gains—and turn honest. You must take charge of the gang when I depart."

"I'll talk it over with the lads. You're really going for good?"

"I must get her out of this country. I'm sorry, Jem, it will be a bit of a heart-ache but I see no other way. Happiness and freedom come first in the list of life's values."

They were riding across the moors now, the dark, broad moors which rolled on and on into the blackness ahead. Across them, like a white ribbon, went the rough turnpike. Poor though it was, it followed an ancient track, a track on which mailed feet had marched. But there were no ghostly warriors along it. Nothing broke its outline but clumps of furze and dark patches of heath.

"We're making a mistake, Jem, keeping together. You know my aversion to having all my eggs in one basket."

"Meaning as we ought to go different ways?"

"Yes, Jem. Do you take to the moors. And slacken the pace to spare the animals. You remember where we forded the Severn? Wait at that ford with the led horse. If I break through that's the spot I'll make for. If you say there are relays ahead I may as well ride hard. The black will have rested by the time I return. Time is precious. I feel that every hour, every minute, counts. It is as if Celia was in despair and was calling to me for aid. Give me the pistols, Jem!"

"Good luck to you, Cap'n. You'll find Jasper's Gideon at the farm where you swap 'orses. Take 'im with you. 'E'll be useful."

Tempest did not reply. He used his spurs. The great horse sped forward, its hoofs drumming a stimulating tattoo in the darkness long after Jem's straining eyes failed to discern the dark figure against the white of the highway—the figure of Jack Tempest who rode and rode, fearing all the while in his heart that he might arrive too late.

CHAPTER THIRTY-ONE

THE ride through the night left an indelible imprint on Tempest's mind. He was a man who had always considered his mount, but that night in his impatience, he urged his powerful black horse onward with a remorseless persistency. He felt fevered with anxiety and, chill though the mountain air was in the early hours of the morning, he found it refreshing. For the greater part of the time he kept on the turf at the track's margin where the going was easy for the black's hoofs.

A medley of thoughts surged through his mind. His emotions and his reason were at variance. He wondered whether he had acted wisely in leaving Jem behind. It was a wise precaution to keep the led horse fresh for the escape, but this was only part of his purpose. In his heart Tempest knew that he wanted to be alone. He planned a deed of daring and he wished to perform it unaided. It was as though he threw down the gauntlet, prepared to challenge all-comers for the love of a lady.

Often he had tried to convince himself that he did not love Celia. He told himself that he acted from motives of chivalry in serving as her protector. Now that she was in danger, perhaps lost to him, he no longer deluded himself. He loved her with every fibre of his being. Fierce surges of emotion swept over him. He could not endure life without her. All the womanly qualities he admired were concentrated in the person of that gentle girl.

How typical of her to jeopardize her own welfare in order to help someone in difficulty! Why (he demanded of the starry skies) should a woman so rare and choice and lovely be sacrificed to a scoundrel like Goadby merely because the man had rank and wealth? Throughout his association with Celia, Tempest had been oppressed by the conviction that he was unworthy of her. The most he could do, he felt, was to offer her his devotion. He would be her votary, worshipping from afar: expecting nothing in return. But in this crisis the old sense of social values had been swept away by the rush of events. Primitive instincts were at work. He wanted her, and he meant to have her!

His horse stumbled in the darkness and he jerked the rein

angrily. It was not like the sure-footed black to stumble. Then
Tempest reproached himself. He had pushed the animal hard.

The country grew rocky. He was compelled to slow to a walk
for safety's sake. Presently they descended a rough path which
led to a ford across a sparkling streamlet. Here the horse halted
of its own accord to drink. Tempest had difficulty in dragging
its head up. As they climbed the slope the animal again struck a
hoof against a rock. "Pick your feet up!" shouted Tempest
impatiently. Then a feeling of gratitude swept over him as he
thought of Jem's thoroughness in arranging for relays of horses
along the route to the Border. The isolated farm which the free
traders used as their private post-house lay some four or five
miles away.

Again the horse stumbled.

"Keep up, you clumsy lout!" cried Tempest, furiously.
"Get up!"

He used the spurs. The burst of speed was short lived, and
when the animal slowed down, Tempest was conscious of a
limp. At least he fancied the horse was limping, but he tried
to pretend that it wasn't. It would be too exasperating if the
brute fell lame!

The limp grew more pronounced; so pronounced that
Tempest eventually had to dismount. He groped anxiously for
the injured hoof. It was only when he stood beside the animal
that he fully realized its condition. The sleek coat was ruffled,
streaked with sweat and splashed with foam, the nostrils were
extended, the animal's sides heaved. Never had he ridden it so
hard before. His conscience smote him. As he fumbled in the
darkness with the muddy hoof his fingers found a stone wedged
in the shoe. He tried to remove it but without avail. With a groan
he dropped the hoof to earth and stood up. There was no help
for it. He must walk to the farm.

He patted the broad neck. "Sorry, old lad. I'm treating you
cruelly, but it's for a lady's sake."

He grasped the bridle and started to walk the desolate moors.
How slow progress seemed. He felt that he was now carrying
the horse instead of the animal carrying him. Impatiently he
tugged at the bridle; there was no response. The black had reached
a stage of exhaustion when nothing would hurry it—when nothing

o

could hurry it. It seemed an interminable time until Tempest, peering anxiously into the gloom ahead, detected the pale glimmer of a rushlight.

Loyal confederates were watching for his arrival. Feeling nearly as spent as his horse, he stumbled into the farmyard, where two men awaited him. While one led the spent black to the stable, another brought out a sleek bay mare, ready for the road.

"You'll have a bite to eat?" inquired the man.

"No. Time's precious."

"Well, have a drink of this," he thrust forward a bottle. "And shove some food in your pocket. You'll be glad of it."

It was good to feel a fresh horse between the knees, thought Tempest as he took to the moors again. His heart smote him as he thought of the condition of the faithful black. It was his favourite horse: one which had served him on many a dangerous venture. The bay was not so well bred, a useful animal, but without speed or spirit. The walk to the lonely farm had wasted time, and time was of incalculable value.

There was a faint light in the eastern sky when he neared the next stage. As he approached his notice was attracted by a movement in the gloom. He dropped a hand on a pistol-butt. A curlew call reassured him. There was a faint thudding. Something white moved. It was a piebald pony. The gipsy boy Gideon came riding to greet him.

"I've been watching for you, Cap'n," said the boy. "Jem sent me on ahead, day before yesterday, in case I might be of help."

"Thank you, Gideon," said Tempest dismounting, "but your pony's legs are too short to keep pace with me."

"I've got a horse, of course," said Gideon, almost scornfully. It offended his intelligence to suggest he would ride his pony on an occasion like this.

"I shall want the horse for myself," said Tempest succinctly.

"I don't mean that I'll ride the horse you want, I've another one—and a led horse. Jem said I was to go with you. You remember the encampment? There's some more gipsies there. I could wait with them. Maybe you'll be glad to swop horses. You ride 'em hard."

"Very well." Tempest climbed into the saddle of the fresh horse. "You may come that far. No farther."

The journey to the gipsy encampment seemed shorter than he had anticipated. This might be because the night was spent and day was at hand. The lifting of the dark curtain, the re-appearance of verdure, the twitter of birds; all these had a cheering effect. And it was good to have a companion on a long and lonely ride, even if it was but a gipsy lad who was sufficiently understanding not to disturb the privacy of a morose man's reverie.

The morning meal was over when they reached the encampment in the glade. Tempest was obviously expected, for a gipsy was holding a saddled horse at the entrance to the lane. Tempest slid from the saddle of his foam-flecked mount and tossed the reins to the man. With a curt: "You wait here," to Gideon, he cantered down to the road.

There were signs of communal life on every hand. Men were at work in the fields, women in some gardens were spreading clothes on the drying-bushes. Others stood at cottage doors. Tempest rode fast, regardless of curious looks. The nearer he got to his destination the more pronounced was his disquietude. He felt that he fought against time. Why had the black gone lame? The morning was slipping away!

As soon as he entered the hamlet of Upton Magnus intuition assured him that some occurrence of consequence was afoot. The turnpike was deserted. He slowed to a walk as he looked keenly about him. He noticed that there were people in the lane which led to the church. At the lych-gate he could see a small cluster of women peering curiously into the churchyard. Children played in the roadway, or climbed on fences. From a nearby house came a fair-haired girl who had been home to fetch her doll.

He bent from his saddle and spoke to her in a voice which he fought to sound unconcerned. "What is happening here, my dear?" He was sure what the answer would be before the child opened her lips.

"Squire's daughter wed, sir."

"Is the wedding to be this morning?"

"It's all over, sir, by now. They went to church some time since."

"Too late!"

The look in Tempest's eyes must have frightened her. She turned quickly and ran away, hugging her doll to her pinafore.

Tempest stared blankly at the church tower which rose in dumb mockery against the blue sky of heaven. Even as he looked a bell pealed. It gave forth a vigorous, hearty sound. The bell was the fore-runner of a joyous peal.

Wedding bells!

Sadly Tempest turned his head away. He turned his face from the church. He turned his tired steed's head towards the Hall.

At a walking-pace he rode wearily forward, and as he rode thus, he carefully looked to the priming of his pistols.

CHAPTER THIRTY-TWO

THE parish church of Upton Magnus had been built within easy walking distance of Upton Hall for the patronage was vested in the Upton squires. An air of sacred peace clung to the venerable building which stood quietly amid its yews and cypress trees well away from the turnpike from which it was approached by a side road which passed through the hamlet. A lych-gate gave access to the churchyard. From the gate a broad walk led to the porch which was situated at the base of the squat tower which endeavoured to add dignity to the western end. The church consisted of a nave and chancel with a south transept, erected by Uptons when Anne was queen, so that it might accommodate the family pew. This was entered by a small pointed doorway, conveniently placed (rumour had it) so that a somnolent squire might surreptitiously steal out should the sermon prove tedious. A special path led to a gate of wrought iron in the wall of Upton Park connecting the Hall with the church.

The gate in the park wall was open that sunny morning, but the lych-gate was padlocked. Though a cluster of villagers peered through the bars, the sexton was on duty to prevent any unseemly scrambling over the wall. The entire village knew—doubtless by gossip from the servants' hall—that Miss Celia had returned home and was to be wed. Within the Hall the convivial atmosphere usually associated with such occasions was entirely lacking. The household staff performed their duties with due decorum but in subdued silence. The dining-room was set out as if for a banquet. It is true that preparation had not been made for many guests, but there was, nevertheless, a lavish display. Plate, bearing the Upton crest, had been brought out for the occasion.

Mr. Upton wore a suit fresh from his London tailors. He was fastidious in matters of dress, particularly on formal occasions. The Squire ran his finger around his high black stock as though its tightness interfered with his breathing. He rang the bell and sent for his daughter.

Celia, arrayed in bridal attire, entered. Her face was blanched, well nigh the colour of her veil. She moved listlessly, looking broken in spirit.

"Charming, my dear, you look charming," said her father, with simulated heartiness. "But for heaven's sake get some colour put on your cheeks. It is fashionable, I am told, for a bride to appear demure, but I insist on a little more animation."

"Will you please tell me something?"

"Well, what is it? Whether I answer or not all depends."

"Is it true that Harry Standish is in prison? You swear it is true?"

"Oh, it's true enough. Nothing easier than to get a man in prison if you know the way to go about it. Of course, neither Guy nor I could sit on the Bench when he was brought up, but we took good care that the other Justices, being good neighbours, knew what line to take."

"But you knew that he had nothing to do with the affair?"

"How was I to know? He never opened his mouth. When asked if he pleaded guilty or not guilty he merely shrugged his shoulders."

"He would not speak for my sake."

"Could you ask for more damning evidence of his guilt?"

"Could you ask for any greater proof of his loyalty to me?" cried Celia, with the first touch of animation she had displayed. "Poor lad! What treatment. And in a civilized country! He is nothing but an impetuous boy, as honourable as ever lived, and you treat him like a criminal. Is he still in gaol?"

"Of course."

"Pray why? He was charged with kidnapping me, and you have proof that it is not true. Ah, I see! Perhaps you detain him because he has murdered me?"

"He will be released today. In honour of your wedding."

"How magnanimous of you! I trust he sues you for wrongful imprisonment!"

"You forget yourself, girl!"

"I wish I could. I wish I could forget everything; drink some opiate that would dull my senses and obliterate this hideous nightmare. Father, have you no compassion? Are you utterly indifferent to the happiness of your only child?"

"Indifferent? What a thing to say. I am providing for your future, girl. I have arranged an admirable match. It is your wilfulness, your defiance of your father's wishes, which has brought all this about. You have only yourself to blame for your unhappiness. You are a very disobedient girl. You know the text 'Children, obey your parents'? It's in the Bible somewhere. I asked to make sure. Very proper too. Have you been obedient? Caused me days and weeks of worry? Put me to no end of expense?"

"But Father, I cannot marry this man. I cannot. If you only understood how I loathed him. I could not endure his laying a finger on me."

"Now! Now! Don't get talking like that. I call it very sporting of Guy to go through with this business. There are not many men in his position who would take back a girl who has been chasing about the country with some rascal about whom we know nothing. That fellow is the rogue who should be behind bars, not that present young fool. Let me get my hands on him and I'll have him transported to the colonies. I'd have him hanged if I could. To think that he dared lift his eyes to a daughter of mine—an Upton of Upton Magnus."

The Squire blazed with the indignation of outraged pride.

"You shall not say a word against him. He has shown himself more chivalrous than the brute you would tie me to. I could say that he has shown me greater regard than my own father."

"Silence, girl. How dare you speak in that way!" Mr. Upton raised his eyes to the portraits on the wall as if appealing to them to take note of his forebearance in face of such arrant provocation. "I am thankful your dear mother has been spared the sight of her daughter fallen so low!"

"Mother! I wish she were alive. She would not have allowed me to be treated thus." Celia paused, and took a deep breath. "No, I take back what I have said," she continued with forced calm. "I am glad she is not alive. Had she been here you would have been as deaf to her pleadings as you have been to mine. You would break her heart as you break mine."

"Silence, you impudent child. I do not break your heart, but by heaven, I'll break your stubborn will. You shall be married this morning. I am resolved on it. Guy is resolved on it. And put all thoughts of escape from you. I tell you, there shall be no escape. You shall go through with this wedding. You hear?"

Celia was staring out of the window as a condemned criminal might take a last look at the blue of the sky. "I hear," she said. "I am submissive. You will be able to boast to your cronies that you broke your daughter's will—and her heart. I shall not live long and my blood will be upon your head."

"Don't talk like a fool! I know what is best. You're frightened at the thought of marriage. Hysterical. You're not the only girl who has lost her nerve. You'll be all right. But I want your assurance that there'll be no scene in the church. You will go through with the ceremony for the good name of the Uptons."

"The good name!" her lip curled. "I will give you my word on one condition. That is that you swear by all that is sacred that you will release Harry Standish today! By all that is sacred," she laughed bitterly. "Is anything sacred to you? Yes, I believe that you would regard my mother's picture so. Swear on her portrait that Harry Standish shall be released and I will undertake to submit to this mockery without another word of protest."

The Squire looked critically at his daughter as though he scarcely recognized her. He saw a slim young girl in a wedding robe and veil, he saw her bright eyed now, and with a feverish flush on her cheeks. Determination was stamped on her features.

"I believe you mean it," he said with surprise in his tone. "Right! That's easily settled. I swear by the portrait of my dear departed wife, and by her sacred memory, that this young man Standish shall be released from prison instantly if you go through with your wedding."

For a moment Celia looked wistful. "I have done what I could!" she whispered.

Then she turned to her father. "I thank you for sparing me the mockery of bridesmaids," she said with quiet dignity. She opened the door.

Bates, key in hand, was at the threshold.

"Lock her in her room, Bates. There is another half-hour yet before we leave for the church."

The Squire's voice was devoid of emotion.

.   .   .   .

It was a subdued ceremony. Only the bride's father was there to give her away, and the witnesses necessary to make the marriage legal. The bride's voice was almost inaudible. But when the bridegroom and bride left the church the peal in the belfry broke the silence with jocund clangor. Sir Guy had bribed the sexton to pull the bell-rope right lustily. To Goadby it was an occasion for jubilation. Down the private path to the wrought-iron gate in the park wall went the bridal party. Celia, her head bowed, walked as though in a dream, Sir Guy, head held high, moved with a swagger of satisfaction. He had gained the day.

Celia would not take his arm. She kept as far from him as the path between the laurels would permit. When they reached the great doorway of the hall they found the servants respectfully lining the steps. The baronet in his exuberance, drew a handful of coins from his breeches pocket and flung them largess. The coins fell with a musical clatter on the stone steps. A half-witted kitchen maid was the only member of the staff to stoop to retrieve one.

Mr. Upton led the way to the dining-room. Guy snatched a decanter of port and splashed some into a glass.

"Lady Goadby, your health!" he cried in his elation. "I vowed I would wed you, and I have done what I said I would do, in spite of your antics. In spite of your bullies. In spite of threats. When I want a thing I get what I want despite all the devils of hell. I vowed I'd wed you, and I've done it. I've done it."

"There is no occasion for repetition, Sir Guy. To my cost I know what you say is correct. May you never regret the day. Your vow may prove expensive."

It was the first time Celia had spoken since the ceremony. "I shall not live long to be your chattel. You have made my life intolerable and, I warn you, I shall take my life at the first opportunity."

Guy laughed incredulously and helped himself to more port.

The Squire looked annoyed. "Come, girl, this is a festive occasion. It is time you had finished with this silly talk. I know you resent your marriage, but you are too young to know what is good for you. Anyone might think you meant what you said."

Celia turned to her father with amazement in her eyes. "You think I don't mean it? How little you know your only daughter."

"Eat your food," he ordered abruptly. "And talk sense."

"I cannot eat. Food would choke me."

"Then have a glass of wine, and for heaven's sake look more cheerful. This is more like a funeral than a wedding."

"That is as it should be." Celia was cryptic.

"Well, if the bride will not eat, the bridegroom intends to," cried Guy, wolfing. "And he drinks, too!" He called to a servant to fill his glass. The Squire essayed to swallow some food but for once his appetite had deserted him though he was regarded as a good trencherman.

The breakfast, like the wedding, was a mockery. In place of guests were empty seats. Despite the silver and the glitter and the formality, the atmosphere was chilly as the tomb.

The Squire tugged at the bell-rope. "Send the housekeeper here," he ordered the footman. "Also Miss Celia's maid—damnation, I mean Lady Goadby's maid!"

When the women appeared the Squire sent Celia to her room to change from her bridal attire. This instruction Celia obeyed with alacrity. "And see that she does no harm to herself," Mr. Upton shouted.

"Aren't you eating?" inquired Guy, laying down knife and fork, and fumbling for a spoon.

"No, that little fool's tantrums have put me off my fodder!"

"She'll get over it. Don't take her temper too much to heart, Upton. Cheer up, our estates are joined now. For all time."

"Looks to me as if you, by getting the heiress, would have the best of the bargain," muttered the Squire morosely.

"She'll not be an heiress until you are dead, you fool. Then what does it matter provided the estates stay with one of the blood?"

"Ay! I hope we are not driving her too hard."

"Don't be a fool. She'll get over it."

"I think I'll go upstairs and see whether she is all right. I wish she hadn't raved like that. It's upset me."

He walked slowly to the door, which was opened by the

footman. Allen held the door open, watching his master's retreating form until it had disappeared up the stairs. Then he stole a surreptitious glance at Guy. Alone at the deserted table in the well-appointed room, the baronet bent over his plate, satisfying his appetite. The footman crept out.

Sir Guy Goadby ate contentedly. It had been a great day in his life. A day of triumph. A day of success. He had had his own way in defiance of difficulties which would have deterred a man of less stubbornness. As for Celia, she was his! He was satisfied now. If she did not prove a tractable wife, he knew of other sources of consolation. He grinned to himself at the thought.

The heavy door closed softly. At the click of the key turning in the lock Guy reached for his glass.

"More port," he said. There was no response. A flush of anger darkened his face.

"Hurry!" he snapped. "I said 'More——' "

As he wheeled, the words faded from his lips. It was no uniformed footman who stood with his back to the door. In Allen's place was a man in a green coat. A haggard man with intolerant eyes.

"I have not come to give you port!" Tempest chose his words carefully as though he experienced difficulty in speaking.

"You have come to congratulate me on my marriage!" Guy spoke with forced gaiety. His laugh was without conviction. He helped himself to more wine with attempted insouciance.

"I said I would marry the lady, my good man, and despite your threats I have done so. I am not in the habit of allowing anyone to cross my will—let alone a highwayman, as I presume you are—or some masterless vagabond."

"You broke your parole!" said Tempest. "You only gained your freedom by a lie. You vowed you would not pursue her any more."

"You fool!" Guy was scornful. "A promise exacted under duress is not binding. Every man of honour knows that."

He drank deeply and boasted. "I said I would marry her and I have done so. I vowed, and I keep my vow."

"And I," said Tempest, "vowed that rather than let you have her I would kill you. And I am here to keep my vow."

His right hand, which had been in the breast of his coat, came out so swiftly that Guy was barely conscious of the movement until he found himself gazing into the menacing mouth of a double-barrelled pistol. He blanched and made a half-hearted motion to reach for his own breast pocket. Something of this nature had not been unanticipated and he had gone to the church armed, expecting a disturbance on the way. But the very quietude of the ceremony had lulled him into a sense of false security.

"Stop!" cried Tempest. "Put up your hands. And don't shout or I'll fire!" The baronet's face was pale enough now. As he rose to his feet he trembled.

"So you want to murder me, eh?"

Tempest stared at him. "I meant to kill you as one would exterminate vermin. . . . But I can't kill you in cold blood."

There came a laugh of relief from the baronet. "I thought you would lose your nerve!" Guy sneered. His eyes sought the bell-pull.

"Don't move or I'll fire. I saw you reach for your coat-pocket—are you armed?"

Guy did not reply.

"Answer!" Tempest's voice was low and tense.

Guy nodded.

"Then you shall have your chance. Wait. In another two minutes the clock will strike the half-hour. Stand at that end of the table. You shall have your back to the light—that ought to give you a sporting chance. When the clock strikes, we fire."

Guy moistened his lips. "Your pistol is in your hand."

"I will replace it," said Tempest. "The chances shall be equal."

Cautiously Tempest crossed to the table. Sir Guy, knowing that the barrel followed him, walked to the end nearer the window. As the two men stood in silence facing one another, Tempest, with his eyes on his opponent's face, slowly thrust his pistol back into his breast pocket, and dropped his hand to his side.

There was the sound of a heavy step in the hallway outside. The Squire's voice sounded.

"Guy! Celia's changed, and is ready to leave."

The two men stood, hands ready, waiting. Neither looked at the clock.

"Guy!" The Squire thumped on the door. "Guy! What's the matter with you, man?"

There was a whirr. The clock struck.

.   .   .   .

Servants in the outer passage said afterwards that the two shots rang out so close together that they sounded like one.

CHAPTER THIRTY-THREE

THERE was consternation throughout Upton Hall. A pistol shot can echo ominously within four walls. The servants had been hovering discreetly in the passage, torn between curiosity and awe of their master. The Squire himself, tense from the ominous discovery of the locked door, grew excited. His rubicund face went a deeper crimson as he hurled his shoulder against the panel. The butler hurried up, regardless of deportment. The housekeeper and the tiring-maid ran to the landing. Allen, the footman, had kept unobtrusively in the background as though he did not desire to attract undue attention to himself. At his master's command, he pushed his way forward. The men flung their combined weight against the door and the lock burst under the pressure, sending them staggering into the room.

Wisps of smoke still curled faintly. The smell of gunpowder hung pungent on the air.

The body of Sir Guy Goadby lay prone. One hand clutching a pistol, was outstretched across the carpet. In his fall he had struck the table and he lay surrounded by fragments of broken china and shattered glass.

"He's killed himself!" The Squire's shout revealed not merely consternation but amazement. He steadied himself against the table and peered fearfully down upon the motionless form.

The butler crept forward, dropped on his knee and felt the pulse.

"Dead?" asked the Squire.

"Dying, sir, I think."

"He's done himself in!" The Squire spoke in a dazed tone. Then he turned on the butler savagely as though to ease his suppressed feelings.

"Clear those women away! Why are you doing nothing, you fool? Send for a doctor! Clear the hall. Send those gaping idiots about their business."

The butler, glad of an excuse to escape from the horror, hastened to disperse the frightened domestics.

Mr. Upton walked shakily to the door, fumbled with the

lock, and closed the portal. Then he summoned the footman. "Stand here on guard," he ordered. "No one is to enter until I have sent for the constable."

He went unsteadily to the gun-room and poured himself a stiff glass of brandy. He was dazed. What had made Guy act in so unaccountable a manner? His girl had threatened to kill herself—but Guy! Why had Guy shot himself?

As he sat pondering, the footman, standing in the hall, glanced surreptitiously about him. Then he ventured to open the door. A slight movement under the table caused him to bend down. Struggling to his feet on the far side was Tempest, holding a napkin against the side of his head where Goadby's bullet had seared the flesh.

"Here! Tie this for me!" he commanded.

When the man complied, Tempest demanded: "Where is she?"

"Upstairs in her room." Allen spoke softly.

"Tell her to come down," said Tempest. He picked up a carafe and gulped some water. "I'm all right now. We must get away."

The man tiptoed to the door and began to mount the stairs. As a step creaked the Squire came into the hallway and bellowed: "Where the devil are you off to? I told you to stay on guard at the door. Why—it's open, you scoundrel!"

He strode angrily up the passage, grasped the door-knob—and then paused as if petrified. Tempest, with a blood-stained bandage about his head, was standing before him, pistol in hand.

"Ah!" The Squire opened his mouth to shout, but Tempest was in no mood for ceremony. He brought the barrel of his pistol crashing on the man's temple, and stretched him on the floor as he slumped forward.

"Celia! Celia! Here! Quick!"

Tempest ran up the stairs two at a time, calling out to Celia. She heard his voice and ran to meet him. In the confusion the housekeeper had forgotten to relock the door.

"Jack! I knew you would come!" Then she paused, staring at the bandage. "You are hurt!"

"No! Hurry. My horse is outside."

The servants came crowding into the hallway, but at the sight of the pistol they backed away. Perhaps they were not sorry, in their hearts, that matters had taken the course they had done. They cared for their young mistress.

Pistol in hand, Tempest ran out of the front door. His sweat-streaked horse was near the mounting-block. Once in the saddle he pulled Celia before him. Then he trotted down the drive, pausing once to glance back at the group of servants who stood in bewildered silence at the top of the steps. There was no sign of pursuit.

"Gideon is waiting with another horse just beyond the village." They were the only words he spoke.

At the sound of his horse's hoofs trotting down the turnpike a number of villagers looked from their doors. They set up a shout and flocked into the road with one accord.

There was something unusual about this shout which reached the ears of Black Tom, who was taking his ease in the King's Arms. It caused him to set down his tankard and spring towards the open door.

He saw a sight which shook his imperturbability. Tempest, with Celia on his saddle-bow, was trotting past, and his right hand held a levelled pistol. Mr. Thomas Black did not attempt to interfere. He contemplated the retreating horseman quizzically.

"It would seem," said he aloud, though no one was near, "that the worthy Sir Guy has not kept his blushing bride very long. Well, he paid me to bring her back and I did so. If he wants her again he must enter into a new agreement. It all means cash! I make no complaints!"

Black Tom walked back into the parlour of the inn and picked up his tankard. As he squinted out of the window the suspicion of a smile twisted his unlovely features. Raising his mug on high he drank to the man on the horse.

Men admire a daring deed.

"I wonder," said he as he set down his tankard, "what can have happened at the Hall. That bandage suggests there's been some scrapping. I think I'll just stroll over and find out."

CHAPTER THIRTY-FOUR

IT was fortunate for Tempest that there was no immediate pursuit. His horse was weary, and with its double burden the animal could not be persuaded to go faster than a trot. Now that the excitement was over, a reaction swept over Tempest. His head ached and smarted. Blood had caked his cheek. When they came to the lane which led to the place where they had found Jasper's gipsy encampment, he was thankful to turn his horse that way. There was no Jasper now, but Gideon was there with a fresh horse. Tempest got the gipsies to help Celia from the saddle. He, too, slid to the ground, but so unsteady was his gait that he would have fallen if he had not clung to the stirrup-leather.

It was clear that he and Celia must both rest before they could attempt the arduous ride to the coast. The gipsies concealed his horse, and dispatched Gideon to the ford to see whether Jem was there with the fresh mounts. The women of the encampment took Celia under their care. One of the men dressed Tempest's scalp. The bullet had merely grazed the flesh but the wound had bled profusely. Obediently Tempest swallowed some concoction which lessened the pain and then, stretching himself on a bed of boughs in one of the shelters, he fell into a sleep of utter exhaustion.

It was evening when he awakened, stiff but refreshed. The headache had disappeared; only the smarting of the raw flesh troubled him now. As he sat up, the leader of the gipsies came to him. Men, he reported, had ridden post haste along the Shrewsbury Road. It would not be safe to set out before dark.

Now that the pursuit had started the situation was tense, but until Celia was strong enough to sit a horse there was little he could do. So he loaded his pistols afresh and lay resting in a position which enabled him to watch down the lane. He was prepared to fight rather than allow the girl to be recaptured. Yet all the time he was wondering how he could expect to keep her indefinitely now that the police were on his track. Thus he brooded, a prey to his own black thoughts. Almost he felt resentful. The situation seemed to be of his own creating yet he failed to see how he could have acted otherwise.

A slight movement in the encampment caused him to turn his head. Celia was walking slowly towards the fire. As he rose he saw her stretch her hands to the blaze as if they were cold.

She glanced up at the sound of his approach.

"Do you feel rested?" he inquired.

She nodded her head as though speaking would prove an effort.

"We have sent Gideon for Jem and the horses," he resumed. "They should be here by dusk and then we must ride for the coast."

She continued to stare at the flames, hands outstretched. Tempest glanced fondly at the hands—they were white and slender and tapering. Beautiful hands, he decided. Then he started. On the third finger of her left hand a gold band glinted.

"Great heavens!"

At his ejaculation Celia turned quickly.

"What is it?" she demanded.

She saw Tempest pass a hand across his brow as though still dazed.

"Does your wound trouble you?" She was solicitous.

He forced a laugh. "Nothing to speak of. It's not that. It was just that I'd forgotten."

"Forgotten what, Jack?"

"That I had arrived too late!" He pointed to the wedding ring.

"Oh, that?" Celia spoke with studied unconcern. "I'd forgotten, too."

The fingers of her right hand began to twist the ring in a manner which showed that she was more agitated then her tone implied. "You had forgotten, Jack, and I had forgotten. The whole thing is unreal. Shall we go on forgetting?"

She plucked the ring from her finger and raised her hand to fling the offending symbol into the flames. As she glanced into his set face, hesitating, watching his reaction, she felt her wrist caught.

Wheeling she saw a gipsy woman behind her.

"Get rid of it, pretty lady, by all means, but don't fling it into the fire! It is good gold and should not be wasted."

Celia tossed the ring to the woman. "Much good may it bring you," she said. "Do what you will with it but never let me see it again."

"Come away," said Tempest taking her arm in a firm grip. "We must be alone. We must talk." He led her to the trees.

In the shade of a crag he paused and dropped both hands on her shoulders. For a while neither spoke. Tempest never forgot that silence. His eyes took stock of the place automatically, noting the ivy tendrils trailing down the rock face, the tiny ferns in crevices, the dead leaves carpeting the earth, and all the while his mind was groping for words.

"I have shot Goadby," he said.

"I know." Celia's tone was calm.

"You do not shrink from a man who has shed blood?"

"You did it for my sake. From your wounded head I conclude there was a duel. Knowing you I know that it was a fair fight."

"I tried to make it so." He gave a harsh laugh. "I may as well finish my confession. I hit your father over the head with my pistol."

"Why?"

"He tried to stop me. I was mad to get to you."

"My wedding festivities appear to have provided some novel entertainment. Tell me, is Guy dead?"

"I don't know. I dropped to the floor dazed when his bullet grazed my head. I expect he is dead—I aimed to kill."

"If there is any doubt, Jack, it will never do for me to get into his power again. Tell me, Jack—if you thought you'd killed him why did you carry me off?"

"It is hard to explain rationally now that it is all over. I was beside myself with rage and disappointment—wild to think he had broken his parole. I rode in the hope of saving you from the wedding and when I found I was too late I had Allen smuggle me into the house intending to kill Goadby rather than let him take you against your will. He wasn't fit to live."

"You saved my life, Jack, if that is any consolation. I meant to kill myself rather than submit to him."

He crushed her in his arms.

"The possibility makes me shudder," he confessed.

"You haven't told me yet why you carried me away."

"I acted without reason, I suppose. If Goadby was dead the threat to your happiness was removed. There was no need."

"No," she agreed deliberately. "There was no need. So why did you?"

She was very close to him and her face was appealing. Hesitation fled. Self-deception fled.

"Because I love you," he said. "Because I wanted you for myself. Because life without you would not be worth living." He kissed her until his passion had spent its fierceness.

"I suppose," he confessed, "the motive was all wrong. I meant to serve you out of gratitude for your goodness to me. I meant to be chivalrous. So much for good resolutions!"

"Thank heaven for that!" exclaimed Celia with relief. "Too many good resolutions can be very boring, my dear. You've been very chivalrous, Jack, and very noble, but much nicer than all that is for a woman to know that she is loved."

"Well, you are loved. Utterly." He kissed her again and she settled in his arms comfortably as though well content.

"Tell me, Jack, why did you run off with me?" she asked presently.

"Because I loved you and wanted you. I've already told you once."

"Told me once! I want to be told hundreds of times. Thousands of times."

"Until I weary you by the monotonous repetition?"

"Try it and find out. I want you to say it every day for the rest of my life."

He did not reply and glancing into his face she saw the hard, set look return to his eyes.

"Jack!" she exclaimed. "You have changed. What is it? Something is troubling you."

"I love you, but what have I to offer you? I am a fugitive."

"I don't care."

"The police are after me."

"I care not so long as you love me."

"I may be taken. It will mean transportation—or the gallows —if I'm captured."

"It would be worth it—to snatch this short moment of happiness rather than be tortured all our days by the misery of unfulfilment. But you mustn't be captured, Jack. You must out-wit them. If I am a hindrance to you then you must leave me. Your liberty comes first."

"You precious illogical woman. Without you my liberty would be a mockery."

"Then we'll both escape and be happy. I think that's a wonderful idea."

"It will be a hard life, Celia. No fine clothes. No palatial home. No servants. Hardship and risk and privation."

"I don't care. You really want me?"

"Want you! Of course I want you. I want you for ever, woman I love."

"Then I shall be content to be with you wherever you go, man I love. The moors by night. The smugglers' cave. Camp or cottage, I care not provided you are with me. Whatever the venture I will share it. I will not question or quibble."

He took her in his arms and kissed her "Camp or cottage?" he repeated.

"That was what I said, Jack."

"Suppose it is a ship?"

"Well, provided it is the *Rising Gull* I might consider it. What have you in mind?"

"I must leave this country——"

"*We* must leave this country."

"Very well. *We* must. I thought once of Ireland but it is——"

"Too near, dear?"

"Yes, it is too near. We must get far away where no one can interfere with our plans or with our happiness. It is possible to escape. Heilyn, loyal friend, has planned it all. He is standing by to assist us. He has provisioned the *Rising Gull*. All your possessions will be on board. This very minute she is waiting for us off the coast. Heilyn took it for granted I should bring you back."

"How well he knows you, Jack! You could not fail."

"So we must ride hard tonight. It will be worth the effort. Ride hard. Out-distance our enemies—or outwit them. Once we reach the bay a boat will be waiting there for us."

"Jack! We *must* get there. We *must*."

"We shall. Have no fear."

"I'm trembling with excitement. And Jack. I have some money. I hid it in the barn at the farm. We must stop there on our way to the coast to recover it."

He barely heeded her excitement. His face had set stern. "This country has been cruel to us!" he said. "Cruel to you and cruel to me. It has shown us no mercy. I have done with it. We will shake off the dust from our feet. We will seek a clean new world; a place where there are no debtor's prisons. A place where girls are not forced into fashionable marriages. We will go to a country where courage brings its rewards."

"Yes, my dear, we will go. And where you go I will go, and where you stay I will stay. I do not fear hardship. What is it you have in mind?"

"Would you brave the Atlantic?"

"In the *Rising Gull*? With Heilyn in command? Of course."

"Would you settle in the forests of Nova Scotia?"

"Anywhere with you, dear."

Tempest drew a breath of relief and straightened his shoulders. His weariness fell from him. He was renewed, replenished. The fighting look had returned to his eyes. He was resolute again.

"See!" He pointed suddenly to the woodland path. "Look there—under the beech trees. Jem is here with the horses."

CHAPTER THIRTY-FIVE

It was dark beneath the shadow of the trees, so dark that Celia was content to let the reins lie loose and allow her horse to pick its own way along the path. It was very silent too. Just the soft padding of the hoofs, the faint creak of leather, and the heavier breathing of the animals when they came to a slope. At times a cobweb would brush the girl's face. Slight though the thread was it had an eerie feeling in the darkness of the woods. With the gipsies scouting ahead, the horses walked in Indian file. Tempest led and Jem brought up the rear.

When the stealthy cavalcade reached the edge of the forest a pause was made for a whispered consultation. Celia was aware of a dark figure advancing slowly towards them. Her companions peered anxiously towards the newcomer. A low whistle reassured them. It was Gideon. In the faint light of the moon Celia could see the youth's eyes sparkling with excitement. The adventure was entirely to his liking.

When they again moved forward the order varied. It was Gideon who ranged ahead now. Jem followed, this time at a tactful distance. Tempest rode alongside Celia, who forgot her weariness of body in a sudden exaltation of spirit. The troubled days had become a thing of the past and she was conscious only of a great content. Danger lurked on every side but she gave it little heed, so secure did she feel in the midst of friends. Tempest was so close to her that at times he would stretch forth his hand to touch hers as though to reassure himself that she was actually there and not a product of his imagination.

Celia sighed and Tempest glanced towards her solicitously.

"Tired, my dear?" he asked anxiously. "You must be utterly spent."

"I am too happy to be conscious of tiredness, Jack. I think that must have been a sigh of relief."

So they rode on through the night, Gideon leading them by devious ways. Only once was there an alarm. The gipsy lad came stealing back to them when they were close beside a copse which ran at no great distance from a turnpike.

"Horsemen on the road ahead," he said in a low voice. "Hear hoofs. Better remain quiet here until the way is clear."

So they all dismounted and stood close to their horses' heads ready to prevent the animals neighing.

They had not waited long before the rhythmic beat of hoofs approached at a slow trot. Presently, in the dim light, they were aware of horsemen jogging down the road to the west. Silhouetted as they were against the night sky the watchers could discern the shakos of cavalrymen.

"Soldiers!" whispered Celia when they had passed out of range.

"Yeomanry," replied Tempest in a low voice. "Your father must have used his influence as a Deputy Lieutenant to summon the military."

"Is—there—danger?" Her voice was anxious.

"From catching cold if we remain here any longer." Tempest spoke lightly, and glancing into his face, Celia saw that he was smiling to himself as though well content.

"If we cannot outwit blundering soldiers it will be a strange thing," he said. "Don't give them another thought, my dear. Their presence adds excitement to the venture."

Before he lifted Celia to the saddle Tempest kissed her.

"Is that part of the procedure?" she asked.

"The latest regulation," he assured her gravely. "The penalty for non-compliance is serious."

"Very serious?"

"Very. Life-long regret for a wasted opportunity."

"Jack, you ought to be more serious."

"Do you wish me to be?"

"No. You are like the old you I used to know, and I feel more like the old me—not the hunted creature who was for ever looking over her shoulder."

"You are still hunted."

"It's different now. I feel safe."

"You are safe. No harm shall ever befall you. Happiness and freedom lie close ahead. It is written in the stars."

Once over the Welsh border they kept as far as possible from roads. They paused when the light of coming day showed pale in the eastern heavens. Instinctively they reined in their mounts and sat in silence, hand in hand, watching the miracle of the dawn. Both felt that for them it meant the dawn of a new day —the day of freedom.

"I grow careless," observed Tempest, rousing the weary horses. "We ought not to have paused on that rise. Our figures must have shown clearly against the sky."

Celia looked about her.

"There's nobody within sight," she observed complacently.

Tempest kissed her.

"Mr. Tempest, that was not intended for a hint!"

"Madam, I can only express my profound regret!" He bowed in the saddle and they both laughed happily. It was good to be free. They coaxed the horses into a trot but it was obvious that they were tiring.

"There is a farm-house not far away," said Tempest looking about him. "It would be well, I think, if we paused to give the animals a rest and a feed."

When they saw the white walls show palely through the dawn light, they turned aside and rode slowly towards the shelter. Celia, now that a dwelling was at hand, was conscious of her hunger and her weariness. She felt sleepy, too.

A stir ahead aroused her with a suddenness which set her heart palpitating. There was a movement at the farm gate. Two mounted men rode out, men who wore uniforms. A hoarse voice shouted: "Surrender in the name of the law."

It all happened so suddenly that Celia could do nothing but give a gasp of horror. Not so Tempest. His hands reached for his holsters.

The gloom was stabbed by orange spurts of flame, and Celia's ears seemed split by the sudden crash of his heavy horse-pistols.

She saw, as in a dream, one horse rear, flinging its rider, while the second horse pitched forward and rolled on the earth. Her own animal began to plunge. Then Tempest's strong right hand grasped the rein. She felt him lug their mounts around so that they headed for the open moors. She was conscious of the rush of cold wind in her face as they galloped away from the farm. Tempest laughed happily. "The game warms up!" he cried.

"Oh, Jack!"

"Are you all right?"

"Yes—only trembling a little, and—wasn't it exciting! But those poor horses."

"Better kill horses than men."

"Were they constables?"

"I should imagine so. They caught me napping, Celia. I must keep my wits about me. No more love-making, my dear, until you are safe aboard the *Rising Gull*."

They heard a shout behind and presently Jem overtook them, curious to know the result of the shooting. Gideon too, came making inquiries.

Tempest sent the gipsy boy ahead to Jem's farm to order a meal. Now that the excitement of the ambuscade was over, Celia was showing signs of exhaustion.

Jem scouted across the moors in the direction of the road. More than once Tempest looked back, puckering his eyes as he stared intently into the distance.

"What is it, Jack?"

"I don't know. I have a feeling that we are being followed."

"By whom?"

"I could not say. I can see nobody but I have caught a slight movement more than once." He shrugged his shoulders. "It may only be a sheep!" But his tone lacked conviction.

Though Tempest was anxious to reach the coast he felt that it was impossible to get Celia there until she had rested, so risk or no risk, he resolved to linger some hours at Jem's farm.

A warm meal awaited them, but before Celia would relax, she instructed Gideon where to find the money she had hidden in the Evans's barn and sent him off to recover it. After the meal, Celia was prevailed upon to lie upon a bed to snatch some sleep, Tempest assuring her that he and Jem would keep watch from an adjoining knoll which afforded an uninterrupted view over a wide expanse of moor.

*   *   *   *   *   *

When Celia roused it was to find Tempest holding one of her hands.

"Awake! Sleeping Beauty! Let me explain that I am Prince

Charming, in case you don't recognize me!" said Tempest with mock solemnity.

"Great heavens!" ejaculated Celia. "It's nearly dark! You've let me sleep for hours and hours!"

"You slept so long that we decided you might as well finish your slumber while you were about it. It may, after all, be safer to ride by night. By the time we have eaten, night will have fallen. Then we had best be off if we are to reach the coast by dawn. We have fresh mounts."

Celia snatched away her hand. "I must look a fright!" she exclaimed, running her fingers through her untidy curls.

When she descended Celia found not merely a well-spread table, but Gideon seated beside the board, on which were neat piles of golden coins.

"Oh, thank you, Gideon. You have accomplished your mission. But you must let me give you a guinea for yourself."

The boy shook his head. "You will need them all," he said. "Pray do not spoil the pleasure of serving you. But I have something else for you."

"What is it, Gideon?"

"Let me tell you first. When I reached the farm a man was there."

"What sort of man?"

"A young man. One who worked on the new road."

"Not Mr. Standish? Not Harry Standish?" Her tones showed surprise.

"That was his name, Miss Celia."

"But I thought he was—in prison."

"He had only just got out. He told us so. He looked pale."

"But what was he doing at the farm? How did he get there?"

"He came seeking you. He said he hoped that you might have returned there."

"Confound his impudence," interposed Tempest.

"Be quiet, Jack. Harry is a friend of mine. You are not to be discourteous. Now, Gideon, tell me, how do you know this?"

"He was asking everybody if they had seen you."

"The young fool!" ejaculated Tempest.

"He said it was a matter of life and death, so I asked him if I might take a message to you."

Tempest frowned. "You did not reveal where Miss Celia was hiding?"

"As if I would, Cap'n! No, I said that when I was riding the moors seeking cattle, I often saw folks, and if, by chance, I should come across Miss Celia, was there any message I could give her?"

"That's more like it," observed Tempest, nodding approval.

"So he gave me this note." And Gideon held out a soiled slip of paper.

Celia, her eyes wide with curiosity, opened the missive slowly. Without comment she passed it to Tempest.

Dear Miss Celia,

Should this reach you, by any chance, let it assure you of the Gratitude of One who owes so much to your Kindness of Heart. Until I was clapt into Prison I never realized how much Freedom meant or how vile injustice can be. I owe my Liberty to you and I have ridden hard through the night hoping I might overtake you or come across some trace of you, but all in vain. I wanted to thank you but I must be content, it seems, with this note—which I send by a Messenger, and hope for the best. I feel like one who shoots an Arrow into the air nor knows where it may fall. Now, if this reaches you, be on your Guard. The evil man who has wronged us both so cruelly—I name no names—lingers between Life and Death—but the pursuit is taken up by a Certain Person you know well, who raves like a Fiend Incarnate. He vows that a certain person shall be sent to the gallows, and that he will have you back if it break him in the attempt. The Constables and the Yeomanry are out. But worst of all he has paid a great price to the man who brought about my undoing, and he also is out like a bloodhound on your trail. Be on your guard. I can say no more. And do not, if you value Freedom, go back to the place you left.

I fear I shall never set eyes on you again, but I shall carry with me a memory which will live as long as Life shall Last. In haste. And with Affectionate Gratitude. One who signs himself, devotedly

H.S.

Tempest handed the note back. "You will wish to keep that," he said succinctly. "Now, finish your meal while I see to the horses."

"I must get Jem, or his lad, to get through to the cottage and tell Heilyn to cruise off the coast. We'll light a gorse fire to signal where he is to land."

Though Celia felt refreshed by her long rest she was more apprehensive than she had been the night before. The thought that Black Tom was engaged by her father to seek her, hung like a thunder cloud over the peace of her mind. His dogged persistance was more terrifying than the might of the military or the law. More than ever she turned away from her ruthless father; more than ever she clung to the man of her choice.

Tempest rode in silence, too, and he was very watchful. He was a man entrusted with the safe-keeping of something infinitely precious.

When dawn came they had left the moors behind and were looking down from the heights upon the sweep of the sea and curve of the coast.

The sight of the schooner cruising under easy sail a mile off land made Celia's heart bound. Heilyn had proved true to his trust. And farther westward was the little *Gwynedd* with her patched sail. The seaman was evidently making doubly sure that the runaways should not be missed.

Jem had taken his farewell and his departure. The little man had ridden home sad of heart. That he was now in sole charge of the free traders was small consolation for the loss of friends. The boy Gideon had set off to make his way by stealth to the cottage to rejoin Miriam and tell her the news.

Tempest and Celia were alone.

"Safety at last! Jack, it seems almost too good to be true." She sighed.

"We are very nearly safe," he agreed, kissing her. "We're not quite out of the wood yet, beloved. I find it inadvisable to count my chickens until they are fair-sized pullets."

She looked about them. The trees were tranquil in their green serenity. Only the twittering of small birds which fluttered busily among the bushes disturbed the utter stillness.

"We must go," he said. "There is a landing-place east of yonder headland. I think that will be the safest place. I can fire the gorse near the cliff top and Heilyn will send a boat ashore."

They rode slowly, conserving their horses' strength lest they should have to ride hard. But all was quiet.

When they came to the turnpike, Tempest dismounted and crept to the shelter of the hedge. He made sure the highway was deserted before they ventured across it. Not a soul was stirring. Only curls of grey smoke from cottage chimneys indicated that morning fires were being lit by the fisherfolk and quarrymen who dwelt in the vicinity.

When they were near the cliff edge, Tempest dismounted. Taking out his tinder box he went in search of a gorse bush which would be visible from the deck of the *Rising Gull*. Heilyn, he felt sure, would have his glass trained on the shore. Celia could see Jack crouching as his hands deftly struck steel to flint before the tinder caught.

Then the bush flared its signal and Tempest came running towards the horses.

"This way. There's a path to the hollow near the foot of the rock. Long ago, before the road was built, the old track went that way."

They rode quietly down the path, that mild sunny morning. The skies were blue and the sea was blue and the sunshine set the world at peace.

Once Tempest paused and pointed. A boat was rowing briskly from the schooner. He sighed with relief. The rocky promontory rose steep above them. On one side were grass-topped cliffs of clay; on the other, surf-washed rocks glistened in the sunlight. A rocky pathway cut like a ledge along the face of the sea cliff. Tempest dismounted and patted the neck of his favourite black.

"Good luck, old lad," he said.

"What will happen to the horses?" asked Celia with sudden concern.

"Don't worry about them. Jem is sending a man to collect them."

He lifted the girl from the saddle. As her feet touched the grass his arms tightened about her.

"No regrets, darling?" he inquired.

"No, Jack, no regrets."

The boat from the schooner was approaching rapidly. He

could see Heilyn scrutinizing the shore for a safe place to beach.

A movement down the coastline held Tempest's gaze. There were men moving among the gorse, men who hurried in their direction. They were well over a mile away. He said nothing to Celia, who stood at the grassy edge of the low cliff looking thoughtfully down upon the translucent edge of the sea. She saw the tiny pebbles glistening beneath their covering of pellucid water. It was the margin of the land. The place was symbolical. She had reached the parting of the ways. Henceforward the country in which she had dwelt since childhood, the land she had grown to regard as her own, would know her no more. This very spot where the wavelets lapped with melodious ripple against the strand, was the line of demarcation which severed the old land from the new, the past from the future. She was taking a step into the unknown.

For a moment her courage seemed to forsake her. She stretched forth a hand and caught Tempest's strong right arm as though she needed his support. Then she glanced up quickly into his face. She found his countenance as resolute as the rocky headland and calm as the morn. It gave her renewed confidence and fresh hope.

The man seemed to divine her thoughts for he looked down and smiled.

"There is still time to return. Are you still determined to seek freedom?"

Celia nodded and forced a smile. "There's no turning back, Jack, I have burnt my boats. I am resolved to go through with this. Only—I could not face the ocean crossing without you."

"You will never be alone, my dear."

"Then I do not care where we go provided you are at my side."

Her smile was brave—not only brave, but confident. Tempest glanced over her head. The men among the gorse were perceptibly nearer.

"It is time we descended to the shore," he said quietly, and assisted her down the cliff. They stood beside the gentle wavelets in silence for there are times when human emotions are too profound for expression in words.

There was no sound but the wash of the water on the shingle, and the call of the gliding gulls and the rhythmic creaking of the oars in the thole-pins as the boat from the *Rising Gull* drew nearer and nearer.

Celia could see Heilyn, burly and bearded, smiling a welcome as he sat with a brawny hand on the tiller. He, too, looked calm and confident. Celia's fears left her. She knew that she was with those who were dear to her, men who would protect her, and their nearness gave her assurance. Her fears fled and in their place came a surge of excitement. The great adventure was at hand.

As the boat's bow grounded, Tempest swung her off her feet and waded to the stern sheets where he placed her. Then, shoving off, he leaped aboard and the seamen pulled rapidly for the *Rising Gull* hovering gracefully, ready to commence her flight.

Tempest, casting a glance back at the disappointed figure which had halted along the cliff top, smiled grimly to himself. He put his arm protectingly around the girl. They were safe and away!

Celia laughed happily. The thought came to her that life's prizes were for those who dared, and not for the faint of heart.

THE END